D0465142

GAME

of

SECRETS

GAME of SECRETS

KIM FOSTER

Sky Pony Press
New York

Copyright © 2018 by Kim Foster

All rights reserved. No part of this book may be reproduced in any manner without the express written consent of the publisher, except in the case of brief excerpts in critical reviews and articles. All inquiries should be addressed to Sky Pony Press, 307 West 36th Street, 11th Floor, New York, NY 10018.

First Edition

This is a work of fiction. Names, characters, places, and incidents are from the author's imagination, and used fictitiously.

Sky Pony Press books may be purchased in bulk at special discounts for sales promotion, corporate gifts, fund-raising, or educational purposes. Special editions can also be created to specifications. For details, contact the Special Sales Department, Sky Pony Press, 307 West 36th Street, 11th Floor, New York, NY 10018 or info@ skyhorsepublishing.com.

Sky Pony® is a registered trademark of Skyhorse Publishing, Inc.®, a Delaware corporation.

Visit our website at www.skyponypress.com.

www.kimfoster.com

10 9 8 7 6 5 4 3 2 1

LIBRARY OF CONGRESS CATALOGING-IN-PUBLICATION DATA
Names: Foster, Kimberley, 1972- author.
Title: Game of secrets / Kim Foster.
Description: First edition. | New York : Skyhorse Publishing, [2018] |
Summary: In Victorian London, sixteen-year-old Felicity Cole is awaiting execution when she is rescued and taken to a secret spy school for the Tainted—those born with special physical and mental abilities.
Identifiers: LCCN 2018006393 (print) | LCCN 2018014644 (ebook) | ISBN 9781510716469 (eb) | ISBN 9781510716445 (hardcover) | ISBN 9781510716469 (ebook)
Subjects: | CYAC: Ability—Fiction. | Spies—Fiction. | Conspiracies—Fiction. | Schools—Fiction. | Great Britain—History—Victoria, 1837-1901—Fiction. | Fantasy.
Classification: LCC PZ7.1.F673 (ebook) | LCC PZ7.1.F673 Gam 2018 (print) | DDC [Fic]—dc23
LC record available at https://lccn.loc.gov/2018006393

Cover photo: iStock
Jacket design by Sammy Yuen

Hardcover ISBN: 978-1-5107-1644-5
Ebook ISBN: 978-1-5107-1646-9

Printed in the United States of America

Interior design by Joshua Barnaby

For Alice.

CHAPTER ONE

"Death doesn't change us more than life."
—Charles Dickens, *The Old Curiosity Shop*

March 1887
London

It's early on the first day of spring as I hurry to the market, my tattered boots splashing in the muck that lines the cobblestoned lanes of Whitechapel.

I stride briskly, my heart bright and full. The first day of spring brings fresh starts and new beginnings.

I adjust the basket of flowers under my arm and keep moving. The truth is, my little brother and I sorely need a fresh start. Today, at long last, there will be money for new bread. And maybe—if we're lucky and my flowers sell well—a small mutton pie. I can imagine Nate's shining face when I return to our tiny attic room with the pie steaming in its paper wrapper.

So as I walk, I smile like a fool.

I turn a corner, emerging from the darkened lanes into the sun-filled streets of Whitechapel Market. The sound of the hawkers reaches my ears—fishmongers, charcoal peddlers, and every other form of costermonger, calling out their wares from clustered stalls. "Chestnuts, a penny a score!" and "Herring! New herring!" and "Get your turnips!"

My nose fills with the pungent smells of fish and cabbage rotting in the gutters. Others may find it foul, but to me it's the smell of hope.

It was a long, bitter winter. Many of our neighbors suffered horribly. Four of the five Craddock children who live below us died. Two of consumption, two of starvation—including the wee babe, just three weeks old. I caught a glimpse of him when the undertaker came to retrieve his tiny gray body, an icy breeze lifting a corner of the blanket. By then, the sound of Mrs. Craddock's howling and wailing had given way to the chilled silence of acceptance and despair.

But we survived, me and Nate. Somehow, we made it through, when so many others didn't. I figure it was sheer willpower and more than a little luck.

And perhaps because I won't allow anything to happen to my brother. He's only seven, and he has only me. I'm the only thing preventing his secret coming out, and I'll do whatever it takes to protect him.

In the market, my eyes dash to my favorite corner for selling. It's an excellent spot, right near the busy onion cart. Thankfully, it's unoccupied. My heartbeat quickens and I dart to claim the site. Good. Old Lady Beatrice is lazy—she must have slept late. Surely I'll sell all my flowers. And then? *Hello, mutton pie.*

Carriages and omnibuses rumble by on Whitechapel Street, horses' hooves clattering on the cobbles. I watch the ladies shopping in the market in their high-necked dresses and buttoned boots. These are the wives of railway men and cabinet makers, men who earn a decent living. I dip the hem of my skirt in a puddle of rainwater caught between the cobblestone cracks and scrub at some of the dirt on my cheeks. I don't care about the nice clothes or shoes. But I do care if people buy my flowers. And they'll be more likely to buy from a clean-faced girl.

I arrange the daffodils in my basket, the biggest and cheeriest on top, and push it forward a little, beaming my brightest smile. On the other side of the street, the accordion boy plays a jolly tune, further lifting my mood.

I spot a woman who looks like the housekeeper of a grand house. I smile and show her my basket. "Flowers for sale! Bow pots! Two a penny!" She frowns and hustles by. My smile falters only slightly.

No matter. It is a beautiful day. There will be plenty of customers.

Boys race by me, mud larks on their way to the riverfront to search for bits of coal, old rope, bones, and copper nails. Anything they can sell. My throat tightens. Nate would do that, if I let him. But we can't take the risk.

After selling a few blooms, I have two pennies and a farthing. I tuck them away eagerly. During a lull, I pull out the knob of bread I've saved for my breakfast. A dog comes around the corner—the scrawny creature I've seen skulking about for the past few days. It sniffs the ground then stops, looking up at me with big, melting eyes.

I glance down at my meager bread and try to tuck it away, but the dog locks his eyes on it. I turn my back, trying to ignore him.

I take a large bite. A faint whimper sounds behind me. I chew vigorously and swallow, pushing it down. There's quiet. I glance over my shoulder and see the dog, still sitting there with his matted fur and visible ribs, as pathetic as can be. The bread feels like a hard lump in my chest.

"Oh, here you go, you mangy thing." I break off a piece and toss it to the dog. The creature darts forward to snatch up the pitiful offering, gobbling it down. My mouth crooks into a grin.

Then a feeling of being watched prickles over my skin. I glance around—perhaps there's a customer interested in buying a flower—and catch a glimpse of a man watching me from across the street. He wears a pale gray suit and a matching silk top hat. He blends in with the smoke rising from the chestnut roasters' carts. Above an ivory silk cravat, his salt-and-pepper beard is neatly trimmed. Our eyes meet only for a second, but there's something familiar in that glance. I take a closer look at the gentleman and a sudden twist of recognition takes hold.

An omnibus rumbles by. It passes, and the man is gone. A chill washes over me.

I crouch down to give the dog's ears a scratch. "Did you see that?" I shake my head. Could I have imagined it?

As a shadow falls over me, I look up from where I crouch and my heart sinks. Beatrice Fowler glowers at me. "Felicity, you're in my spot again. Move off or I'll break your arms." Old Lady Beatrice is as large as a chapel, with a square, fleshy face and a temper to match her size. She likes to brag about her age—fifty-four—knowing it's older than most will survive. Beatrice's moth-eaten shawl trails over her skirts. She wears an enormous straw bonnet with ragged feathers and grimy silk flowers—a prize she stole from a neighbor last year and that she now wears with great pride.

"There's plenty of room, Beatrice," I say, my voice even and strong.

She takes a step closer. Two other women come to stand behind her. "I don't want your scrawny arse scaring away my customers. There's room enough for *one*."

You're right, there's only room for one . . . when that person is the size of an ox. But I hold my tongue. Scrapping will not serve me. Getting into trouble, drawing the attention of the Peelers—it's the last thing I need.

"Beatrice, be reasonable," I say, holding my ground. "It's not us against each other. It's us against *them*." I gesture around us at the ladies shopping and the carriages trundling by. "You and me, we're not adversaries."

"Oh ho! *Adversaries*, is it?" Beatrice moves in closer, her flinty eyes fixing on me. "Listen, little miss hoity-toity. You think you're better than us, with your fancy words and your big brown eyes." She pokes a stubby finger into my chest. "But down here, in the gutter, we're all the same."

She looms over me, her sour breath hot on my face. I refuse to cower. I jut my chin forward. I will not back down this time.

The other women laugh. "Have you received your invitation to the Golden Jubilee yet, Miss Felicity Cole?" one says in a mocking voice. "Your presence is required at Buckingham Palace . . ."

More squawking laughter.

I say nothing.

"Nobody is impressed by your la-di-da words here," Beatrice snarls. "Shove off." She turns away, settling herself into the spot.

"Come on, Beatrice. I'm just asking you to *think* for a second—"

She spins around, eyes ablaze. "Are you saying I'm stupid? You're smarter than me, is that it? Your pa may have taught you to read and write." Her mouth curls. "But your pa is *dead*."

My face goes hot. Anger boils up inside me. Then I spot the blue uniform and peaked hat of a Peeler strolling through the market, nightstick at his side.

Fighting with Beatrice could mean a night in the clink. And who would take care of Nate then? Both our parents are gone—our father died last year in an accident at the factory; our mother was killed years ago. If the Peelers took me away, even for one night, they might investigate, ransack our little attic flat. They'd find Nate, and send him—or us both—to the workhouse. Or, worse, discover Nate's secret.

I shudder. It's something I can never let happen. I promised my father.

My eyes dart around the busy market, across the gathering crowd. I'll have to walk away now or risk everything I've worked so hard to keep. Gritting my teeth, I seize my basket. "I would never call you stupid, Beatrice. That would be an insult." I pause and lower my voice. "To stupid people."

Before her face can even register outrage, I swivel on my heel and race away, breathing deeply, trying to calm down.

I settle into a new, much less desirable spot in the shadows on the other side of the street. People like to shop in the sunshine. But it's no good feeling sorry for myself. I can still do decent business here, and I will. I lift my head. "Flowers for sale!"

I gaze west, toward the posh side of town. Not that I can see anything other than our crowded slum. But I can imagine it. *Buckingham Palace*, Beatrice's cronies said. For a moment I envision what that would be like. The Golden Jubilee . . .

I immediately stop myself. It's ridiculous. The poet Thomas Gray said, "Ignorance is bliss."

And I believe it. In fact, it's practically a requirement for survival here.

Although I take a slight exception to the use of the word *bliss*.

I glance down at my basket and spot a flower that's completely wilted. Nobody will buy it, but it'll do as a wish flower.

I pluck it out and close my eyes. The wish I make is not for the fancy life of palaces and balls and jubilees. It's the same one I always make: keep Nate safe.

And, although I hardly dare think it . . . someday may he be cured.

"I'm not sure which looks more beautiful—the flowers, or the seller," says a familiar voice, just behind me.

My heart skips a beat as I turn. Kit stands beaming down at me through his grime-covered face. "Morning, gorgeous," he says.

Kit is several inches taller than me, with sandy hair that perpetually flops over his forehead. As a blacksmith's apprentice, he has developed wonderfully broad shoulders in the past year.

My stomach does a small flip as his arm goes around my waist.

A few ladies look on disapprovingly. I turn away from their judging eyes. Who would chaperone us, anyway? My parents are both gone. Kit has never known his father, and his mother works far away in a factory up north.

"Don't worry about them, Flick," Kit says, gazing at me with his stunning blue eyes, flashing me a dimpled smile. "Besides, you're sixteen now. Most of them were married by your age."

The mention of marriage makes my pulse flutter. We dance around the subject, but I have a feeling Kit is going to ask me soon, once his apprenticeship is over.

"Shouldn't you be at work?" I ask, chewing my lip. The blacksmith works him hard for a pittance, but jobs aren't easy to come by. He can't lose this one.

"Sent me down here to get more coal."

Kit glances toward the other side of the market. Beatrice is watching us both, glaring. She spits in my direction. But as soon as a customer approaches, she quickly regains her composure, all sweetness and gentle smiles.

"Beatrice giving you a hard time again?" Kit asks, frowning.

I shrug. "She's become nastier than a one-eared cat."

Kit laughs.

"She has it in for me. I've no idea why."

"Ah, she's just getting grumpy in her old age."

I smile, and then an unpleasant thought occurs to me. With a sudden intake of breath, I turn back to Kit. "You don't think she . . . suspects the truth about Nate, do you?"

Kit is the only person who knows about Nate besides me. The only one I trust. "No, I don't think she suspects," Kit says. "If she did, well, she'd probably do a lot worse than glare and spit at you."

He's right. Not that it gives me much comfort.

People like my brother are called the Tainted. And when someone is discovered to be Tainted . . . bad things happen.

"Have you heard anything more about Mr. Clegg?" I ask Kit hesitantly.

He frowns and shakes his head. "Nobody has."

One day in the market last month, a turnip cart overturned and landed on one of the mud larks—a scrawny young boy of six. Within seconds, Mr. Clegg, the old milkman, had hauled the entire cart upright with his bare hands and helped the poor lad out. Saved his life.

But those who witnessed the incident couldn't help noticing. It was an awful lot of strength for a man of his years. *Unnatural,* people whispered behind their hands.

Three nights later, the Peelers turned up, as Beatrice gleefully reported the next morning. She said they carted Mr. Clegg away, tossed him in the back of a wagon.

Nobody has heard from him since.

Usually when someone displays . . . similarly unnatural abilities, they're taken, never seen again. Occasionally, an angry mob takes matters into their own hands, stoning a victim, or ripping them limb from limb.

And then there are the rumors of the Huntsmen.

I look up at Kit uncertainly. "Yesterday, I heard some of the ladies in the market telling a tale of a Huntsman raid over in Spitalfields."

He hesitates, then nods. "The boys in the smithy were nattering about something similar." Concern clouds his eyes, but he quickly clears it. "Don't worry, Flick. It's just another story mothers tell their little ones at night to make them behave."

The Huntsmen. Every child has heard tales of the shadowy gentlemen who make it their mission to root out the Tainted among us. Stories of people disappearing . . . or worse. But what if there's truth to them?

I bite my lip and wonder how much longer I'll be able to keep Nate's secret hidden.

Kit looks down at the wish flower resting limply in my hand. "What did you wish for, Flick?"

"Same thing I always do," I say, shrugging.

He remains quiet. I look into his eyes, exasperated. "Nate never asked for this. It's not his fault."

If only whatever made my brother Tainted would go away as quickly as it came. If someone found a cure, somehow, he'd be safe. He could live a normal life, be happy.

Kit puts his arm around me once more and pulls me back into the shadows of an alley. He puts his hands up to my face, tilts my chin up, and kisses me tenderly. His warmth envelops me, the scent of his skin, the smoky smell of soot in his hair, his clothes . . .

"If anyone can keep him safe, Flick, it's you. Plus, you've got me, remember? We'll do it together."

I nod. "It's just . . . it seems to be getting stronger. His . . . *affliction*. It's getting harder to hide—"

"What do you mean, stronger?"

"He used to know what I was going to say before I said it. Now . . . he can tell how I'm feeling, what I'm thinking. And he's started talking to me. *With his mind*. Eventually, he's going to slip, and people will know he's—"

"Tainted," Kit finishes.

"Shh . . ." I glance around. "Someone will hear you."

Kit lowers his voice. "Has he been able to do anything . . . more?"

The Tainted have skills that manifest in different ways. I've heard rumors of incredible strength, like Mr. Clegg, or speed. The ability to see in the dark. The power to charm and move objects without so much as a brush of the fingers.

Nobody knows why it happens—this affliction. This curse. But there are enough theories: it's an illness or demonic possession or an experiment gone wrong. The tongue-waggers like that explanation most of all. I've heard wild whisperings about Atlantis, about Darwin, about good old-fashioned witchcraft. I don't know the truth, and I imagine I'll never know.

"Flick, it'll be fine. He knows you'll do whatever it takes. And I know it, too. It's one of the things I love best about you."

A warm surge of gratitude flows through me. What would I do without Kit? For so long I've had to keep people at arm's length, afraid of them learning the truth about Nate. But not Kit.

He kisses me again, lightly, then lifts his head from mine. His eyes darken as he looks over my shoulder back toward the market.

I turn and take in a sight that makes my stomach twist.

CHAPTER TWO

"Nothing is so painful to the human mind as a great and sudden change."

—Mary Shelley, *Frankenstein*

A coach has stopped in the street, polished, lustrous black, with enormous, brass-trimmed wheels, led by a glossy thoroughbred. Its presence makes everything around it look even shabbier.

Out steps a gentleman with a luxuriant black mustache. He wears a black hat and the whitest gloves I've ever seen. As soon as the gentleman's feet touch the ground, he raises a kerchief to his face, blocking out the smell, no doubt. Behind him follows a huge footman carrying a small square box, one side opening like an accordion and a small brass cylinder attached to the other. I've only seen something like it once before—but I'm quite sure it's called a camera. The gentleman and his footman begin across the market.

"Slumming," Kit says with a growl. I watch, nodding. It's become a fashionable new pastime for the upper classes.

Kit stands stock still, his arms folded over his broad chest, watching the strangers warily.

Behind me I hear a faint scratching sound. "Felicity?" says a tiny voice.

I turn to see my brother. Nate has the fine bones of a bird. His cheeks are pale beneath the grime, and his grubby clothes hang off his skinny frame, but a smile illuminates his face when I crouch down to him, setting his apple cheeks shining.

"Nate, what are you doing out here?" I scold, smoothing the hair that falls across his forehead. I don't like the idea of his walking even the short distance from our little attic to the market, alone. I always feel more comfortable when he is safely at home, stirring the soup pot or reading a book. Our father taught us both to read, and it's a love we share.

"I had a bad feeling," he says. His hands go to the edge of his jacket and fiddle with frayed threads there. "I needed to find you. To make sure you were okay."

I look at him sharply. "A bad feeling?" We both know what that could mean.

Then his face seems to grow smaller, more scared, as he gazes past me. "Who is that?" he asks, a small trembling finger pointing over my shoulder, toward the stranger. As I stand and turn, I can feel Nate tucking in close to me, holding on to my leg for comfort as he often does.

The gentleman in the black hat moves through the crowd, narrowing his eyes at people with a mixture of curiosity and disdain. His footman walks a step behind, a predator of a man with enormous hands and a cold glare; people cower as they move past.

The men move closer and an uncomfortable feeling stirs deep in my gut.

"I don't know who he is," I say to Nate. "I'm sure he'll leave soon, though."

I look uneasily back at the strangers who are coming ever nearer. The gentleman is not purchasing any of the items for sale. In fact, people are barely attempting to draw him to their wares.

He pauses and gestures to his footman, who promptly unfolds a spindly stand and positions the camera on top of it. He stands behind the contraption, maneuvering himself in front of Sam the fishmonger's stall. A gentler man you'll never meet than Sam. He tries to ignore the strangers and continue his business, but his ears have gone pink and he squirms with discomfort.

Kit grunts. The muscles in his jaw flex. "Who does that toff think he is, prancing around like he's viewing animals in a zoo?"

My stomach tightens. Kit's right, but it worries me how angry he's getting. "Just calm down. They'll be gone soon."

"It's not right. You know it's not." His blue eyes are even darker now, deep pools filled with all his powerless rage.

I look back to see the gentleman taking photographs of Sam. A bright light flashes and sparks fly. "That's perfect,

Cobbs," says the gentleman to his servant. "If only the poor man didn't have such a dreadfully dour expression . . ."

I tuck Nate behind me, and call out boldly to the stranger. "Flowers for your lady, my lord? The first day of spring is auspicious—St. Archibald's Day. It's bad luck to go without a daffodil, something an educated gentleman such as yourself knows well, I'm sure."

It's a lie. There's no such saint as Archibald.

The stranger's head whips in our direction. "I say. A flower seller! How fascinating. Here, get some photographs of *these* specimens, would you, Cobbs?" The gentleman eyes us with delight.

Kit grunts. "If you're not going to buy anything," Kit says forcing the words through his teeth, "then it's time for you to leave. Go back where you came from. You don't belong here."

My eyes dart to Kit. He's being too bold.

But the stranger barely pays Kit a passing glance. He makes no move to leave.

"M'lord?" says the footman from behind the camera. "Is this the angle you'd prefer?"

The gentleman narrows his eyes, lining up the image before he fiddles with a knob on the camera.

"Do *not* take a photograph with that contraption," Kit says. His voice is low and tight. A warning. "We are no curiosity."

The stranger ignores Kit and continues fiddling with the camera. Kit's muscles are coiled, ready.

I push Nate even further behind me. "Go stand behind the onion cart," I whisper to him. "Stay hidden, and do not come out."

A crowd's gathered now. Restless unease washes among them along with muttered words.

"Leave it be, Kit," says John the turnip man, in a low voice. "Let the man take his photographs and be gone."

But Kit remains tense beside me. I need to do something.

"Oh, you don't want to take our photograph, my lord," I call out to the stranger. "There are more pleasing subjects to be found in Trafalgar Square, surely. The morning sun rising on Nelson's Column, perhaps? Undoubtedly a much finer view . . ."

The gentleman takes no notice me.

"Besides," I continue, "you may find folk demand payment for such a thing." I look pointedly at his waistcoat. "And I must say, your purse looks quite heavy there. I would hate to think of a pickpocket taking advantage of your distracted state . . ."

This, at least, causes a flicker of hesitation. The stranger inspects me more closely this time. Something in his expression changes. Some sort of . . . recognition.

"Ah. *Interesting*," he says slowly. "My dear, after I am finished with my photograph, I believe we may have matters to discuss."

I frown and take a step backward. What is he talking about?

Kit moves in front of me. "You have no business with her," he says, tucking me protectively behind himself. "Now, I'll give you one more warning."

The stranger pauses, eyes Kit. "Or what?" he says in a tone that has lost its edge of humor. His face, too, has transformed into something dark. But either Kit doesn't notice the change or doesn't care.

"Or I'll *make* you leave," Kit says, drawing up to his full height, chest spread wide. "This is my home, and these are my people you're insulting. We want you to go."

In spite of my fear, a spark of pride warms my chest. Kit has many fine qualities, not the least of which is bravery and honor. He knows exactly who he is.

The stranger's nostrils flare. "If you know what's good for you, boy, you had best stand down."

"Do not call me *boy*," Kit says with a snarl.

The gentleman pauses and his mouth forms a tight line. He turns his head slightly, to address his footman, though his eyes remain fixed on Kit. "Cobbs? Take a picture of this . . . *boy* first. He is a most interesting subject. A great deal of talk for one so powerless and pathetic. See if you can capture that angry glint in his eye—"

With a great roar, Kit lunges at the stranger, fists raised. And then, an impossibly loud sound cracks through the square, silencing everything.

Kit falls like a hammer. Muffled screams surround me as the air thickens with the smell of gunpowder.

Deep red blooms on Kit's chest. I'm at his side in an instant. A spasm of pain tears across his face, eyes widened. He takes one last shuddering breath, and then the light of Kit's brilliant eyes is gone from them forever.

I look around me in disbelief. The stranger glances down at us indifferently. A faint wisp of smoke escapes the pistol in his hand. The footman also holds a gun and he swings his eyes around the crowd, eager for any new challenge.

"I believe it's time for us to have that talk, Felicity," says the stranger. I barely register his words.

My gaze is pulled back down to Kit. All around us, people are cowering, huddled behind their carts. I want to scream, to howl, to cry . . .

Instead, a deep burn kindles in my gut, a tingle crawls over my scalp. Then, something inside me breaks loose.

CHAPTER THREE

"I can't go back to yesterday—because I was a different person then."
—Lewis Carroll, *Alice's Adventures in Wonderland*

Movement around me slows. The mist from the horses' nostrils hangs suspended in the air. Carriage wheels on cobbles and the bells from St. Paul's Cathedral sound stifled—dampened and low.

I see everything at once. Time bends, curving around me.

Locals and customers cower in the market, screams frozen on their faces. They crouch behind carts. A surge goes to my muscles and somehow I know—I just know—I can do impossible things. I am not thinking. I am pure rage. A deep burning takes hold of my bones.

I reach Kit's murderer in a heartbeat. Impossibly fast. Before he can fire his pistol again, I punch forward, catching him square in the throat. His eyes pop wide. I chop the hand that holds the gun and it skitters away on the ground. He staggers. I punch him again, smashing his nose, and blood spurts everywhere. I kick at his knees, sending him to the ground. I don't know what I'm doing, or how I'm doing it, only that it's coming from somewhere deep inside.

Everything around me is slow, like it's moving through water. Sliding like molasses. But I am a spark. Fire. Lightning.

I hear the report of a gun—a dull, low rumble, not the sharp crack it should be—and I have time to spin. The bullet tears from the footman's weapon in a plume of smoke. But I don't feel the sharp agony of the shot. Instead, I see the bullet as it comes toward me. It moves through the air trailing a spiraling smoke wisp behind it like a comet. I slide out of the way, ducking easily underneath it.

With a slow, deep thud it slams harmlessly into a vegetable cart behind me, smashing into the cabbages and sending a fountain of dusty hay into the air.

And now the footman is mine.

He struggles to reload his pistol. The gentleman is still on the ground. Still unconscious. Breathing, but not an immediate threat. Cold fury surges through me. A lifetime of oppression and bad treatment condenses to a single moment.

Sounds swirl around me, a fugue. The crowd, the market, everything has faded to a blurry distance. All I feel is the pinpoint focus of my hatred, bent on my target.

There is murder in the footman's eyes. He means to stop me. To kill me.

That's not going to happen.

As the footman pulls his gun and points it in my direction, I cross the short distance in two quick strides. I crouch down before he even realizes I'm upon him and rise up under his arm, grasping and twisting it, forcing his shoulder around and sending the pistol skittering away. He is much larger than me but I feel impossibly strong. Impossibly agile. I don't stop to think about it. I just move.

I lever the man's arm and push him down with tremendous force and then he's kneeling in front of me. Before he can stand or turn around, in one quick, vigorous motion, I wrap my arms around his head and twist. *Snap.*

I feel his large body go slack beneath my hands. He drops to the cobblestones, dead.

"Felicity!" a child screams. "Stop!"

At the sound of my brother's small voice, I abruptly come back to myself. The world snaps back to normal speed. Screams ring sharply in my ears.

I take in the scene: Kit, dead in a pool of blood; the footman, dead, neck at an unnatural angle; the stranger, conscious now, on his hands and knees, blood dripping down his face.

A wave a fatigue and nausea passes over me and I stumble forward. I know my hair is wild, my dress torn; blood spatters my knuckles.

Everyone in the market is looking at me with horror.
A clarion realization slams into me: I am Tainted.

CHAPTER FOUR

"I have my own matches and sulphur, and I'll make my own hell."
—Rudyard Kipling, *The Light That Failed*

The world crashes down. I'm falling into an abyss, arms pinwheeling as I tumble through the rabbit hole.

I glance around me. Do they all know now? Surely everyone saw what I did, what I am capable of. I did nothing to hide it. Didn't even know there was anything to hide.

Bitterness floods my veins. All those years of hiding Nate's secret, and now mine has been laid bare for all to see.

Felicity, we have to go. Run. Now. Nate's voice inside my head is desperate and urgent. I vaguely contemplate my ability—not mental, not like Nate. Physical, obviously . . .

There is a tight grip on my arm. "Oh no, you're not going anywhere. You're coming with us." Two policemen in their blue uniforms and brass buttons flank me. *Peelers.* Where did they come from?

On the other side of the crowd, another policeman is helping the gentleman up, handing him a handkerchief to stanch his bleeding nose.

I have nowhere to go. I reach out, hoping to touch the ability again—but I feel nothing. I have no clue how to summon it back.

Nate stands in the crowd, giant eyes staring out from his small, pale face, and I realize the horrible mistake I've made.

"No, wait. I can explain." I can't let the police take me away. I can't leave Nate alone.

Last year, a woman killed her husband in our neighborhood. Shot him right in the eye, when she learned he'd been messing about with the washerwoman down the street.

Even with her three babes at home, the police carted her away to Newgate Prison. Less than a week later, she was swinging from the gallows.

My eyes swivel wildly as I scan the crowd for someone, anyone, who will help me, help us. But I've always been so careful to keep the world at arm's length.

My gaze lands on a man—the one I saw in the market earlier wearing a smoke-gray suit. He is very still, watching me. Then the crowd shifts, and he disappears from view.

The Peelers push me with rough hands toward the police carriage. Movement catches my eye—Nate, running toward us.

Panic blisters my mind as I'm shoved ever closer to the yawning doors of the carriage. Nate's hollering, fighting through the crowd, but he's not strong enough. Fat tears make tracks down his thin, grimy face.

I struggle against the policemen but it's futile. "Nate," I scream, "find the seamstress—the old lady in Plough Street!" But the crowd is too loud. He can't hear me.

With one final shove, they push me down inside the wagon, my palms skidding on the rough floor. I twist around with desperation and open my mouth to shout to Nate again. But the doors are already halfway shut.

I shout repeatedly, my throat burning, screaming out in vain.

Nate's tiny face in the midst of chaos is the last thing I see before the cruel doors seal me inside the blackness. My own hoarse voice is the only sound echoing in my ears as the carriage lurches forward, tearing me away.

CHAPTER FIVE

"Night, the mother of fear and mystery, was coming upon me."

—H. G. Wells, *The War of the Worlds*

Two guards drag me from the carriage. My wrists are bound in heavy iron handcuffs, and I stumble, blinking in the morning's cold light.

Stone walls loom over me, reaching into the sky. The smell makes my eyes water—human waste, filth, and desperation. I don't have to ask the guards where they've brought me.

Newgate Prison.

They push me forward through the gate and as the door slams behind me, I turn to catch the last sliver of brightness.

I wonder if I will ever see daylight again.

Pushing that thought away, I focus on breathing. Though the guards prod me through a bewildering series of doors and gates, I'm trying to keep my wits about me. And all the while I have one burning thought: I must find a way out.

I cannot leave my brother alone on the streets. I spent the entire terrifying ride trying to open my mind to Nate, but it hasn't been working and I don't know why.

Perhaps it's the terror of what's happening to me now. Or the horror of what I did in the market. Or maybe—and I can barely stand to think it—something has already happened to him.

No.

There must be a way out of here. An escape. I just need to find the right person—someone understanding and sympathetic. Someone who will know that I do not belong here. Except . . .

Perhaps I do belong here. I killed a man.

Hopelessness pushes at my consciousness like flames licking the edges of paper.

The guards march me down a long corridor, saying nothing. We enter the area for female prisoners. Some of the bedraggled women slink to the front of their cells to see the new arrival, squinting at me through the bars as I pass. I hold my chin high, and try not shake too much.

At last, we stop in front of an empty cell. One of the guards opens it with a large key. The sound of grinding metal echoes down the corridor.

This is my last chance to escape before they lock me inside. If only I knew how to harness my Tainted ability. But I have no idea how to even begin. Perhaps it is not even possible to control.

The cell door swings wide and a guard shoves me inside. I fall to my knees as the door clangs back in place. In the cell directly across the corridor, an old woman with wild hair is staring at me with a crazed expression. She grips the bars with gnarled fingers, and makes chomping, smacking sounds with her gums.

I back into a corner, shivering in the cold and damp. The air reeks of urine, vomit, and feces. I didn't think anything could smell as bad as the slums. I was wrong.

Somehow, I have to stay calm, even as the pieces of my mind threaten to fly apart. There must be a way out of here. Nate can't afford for me to crumble.

Scratchy, witchy voices creep out of the darkness. The voices of nightmares.

"You'll never get out of 'ere."

"Nothin' but death coming for the likes of ye now."

"We'll see you in hell, dearie."

I try to block out the voices and focus on Nate.

Images flash in my mind of him on the street, terrified, huddled against the cold. Not knowing where to go or how to get help. He is so young. He must be hungry.

Will he go home to our attic flat, or will he be too scared, worried that the police will come for him?

Somehow, I have to get word to him.

A guard comes by soon after, patrolling the corridor. "Sir, could I please have paper and a writing instrument?

It's terribly important. My little brother—he's all alone. I must send him a message."

The guard blinks at me—a blank look—and then walks away, leaving me staring helplessly at the bars of my cell.

My stomach roils. How did this happen? I am overcome by a desperate, irrational wish to go back in time and change that moment. Have everything be normal again.

There is a thin, stained straw pallet in one corner. My mind goes to the soft bed my brother and I shared in our cozy attic. I stop the thought quickly when it threatens to pull me under. Crawling to the pallet, I slip in and out of dreamless sleep.

When I wake, some time later, my stomach cramps with hunger. A small tray rests in front of the bars—water in a tin cup and a chunk of stale bread. As I chew, my mind spools back to the market.

The man in the smoke-gray suit, who had looked at me like he knew me, who was he? Why was he there? And then I recall something else: the man who killed Kit, he said, *It's time for us to have that talk, Felicity.* He used my name. I frown and try to concentrate, but suddenly nothing in the world makes any sense.

A vision of Kit enters my head. *Oh, God, Kit.* Lying dead on the ground, a black pool of blood beneath him. . . .

I squeeze my eyes shut, willing the image from my mind. The bread sticks in my throat, and I take a sip of the cool water to force it down. And breathe. The prison is quiet now, allowing me to organize my thoughts.

One pushes ahead of the others: *I am Tainted.*

How did I not know?

I recall a story going around last year about a Tainted who could do incredible things. *Terrible things.* They say he could plant thoughts in a person's mind. Make a mother think she wanted to murder her own baby.

Sam, the fishmonger, once told me about a Tainted who could tear down walls with her mind. Control fire. Cause untold destruction just by willing it to be so.

I want no part of any of it.

I think of all the theories about the curse, the causes people have guessed at over the years. There must be someone out there who knows why it happens.

I shake my head, trying to rattle the pieces into place, but it's impossible. There's something I'm missing. Something I could make sense of, if only I could clear my thoughts.

Use your head, Felicity. That's what my father always said. What he would say if he were here now. *It's all up there.* He would tap a finger to his temple. I can see him now, a ghostlike remembrance. . . .

My father came to England as a young man from Greece. He and my mother were newlyweds, on the adventure of a lifetime, seeking new opportunities. He was an educated man and a stonemason, a respected craftsman in his mother country. But in England, he had no status. On

British soil, he had no choice but to work as a laborer, building roads and digging ditches. The lowliest jobs.

By the time they considered returning home, my mother was pregnant and unable to travel. They settled into a meager, but content, life. And then, after a while, came another baby.

After our mother was killed, it was up to our father to raise us. Which he did in the best way he knew how.

My heart aches thinking of my father now. He gave me all he could.

And now, I have let him down.

"You must keep your brother's secret, Felicity," he told me over and over again when I was little. A cold pain twists my gut as I think of why he was so firm on this, so desperate.

My mother's death was no accident. She was killed because a neighbor discovered she was Tainted. It doesn't take much for the fearful to turn into a mob, evil and murderous.

Three Tainted in one family. It's like the plague. Or that cholera discovery in London a few years ago. I remember my father showing me the newspaper stories about a scientist who proposed a "germ theory" about an outbreak, the Broad Street cholera outbreak they called it, not far from where we lived. He claimed it spread on the handle of a public water pump.

A tiny glimmer of hope sparks in my brain. If being Tainted is an illness like the plague, like cholera . . . perhaps there is a cure.

But I quickly push that thought aside. All I can afford to think about is getting out of here.

The guard returns to collect the tray. When he bends to scoop them up, he shoves a piece of paper, a quill, and ink through the bars.

I stare at the items and almost weep. It's the first niceness I've received since entering these walls.

I hesitate, then fill the page, reassuring Nate that I'll be all right—although it is a lie—telling him exactly where he needs to go and what he needs to do. *Whatever you do, don't let them take you to the orphanage or the workhouse. Find a way to get to the old seamstress in Plough Street. She will help you. She will know what to do.*

I can only hope it's true. It's the best plan I can come up with.

I dig into my skirts and find the two coins I earned this morning in the market. They feel cold and smooth in my hand. Finishing the letter, I carefully fold it with one of the coins inside, and then wait for the guard to return.

One of the other prisoners begins speaking to me. Her voice creeps out of the darkness like a spider. "Hey, girlie. What's yer name?"

I say nothing.

"It's Felicity, innit?" the voice hisses.

I take in a sharp breath. Were the guards talking about me while I slept?

"Ooh, it *is*," says the voice, gleefully. "Perhaps you might like to know what they're sayin' about you."

Still, I remain quiet, but hold my breath in anticipation. Maybe the authorities have realized they've made a terrible mistake. I don't belong here.

"Tell me," I whisper.

There's a pause. And then a raucous laugh. "They say you're going to hang. That right proper gentleman? 'E says you and yer friend attacked him, tried to rob 'im."

"No! That's not true!"

"Yer friend in the market who got shot—who was that? Yer sweetheart? Cousin? They're calling that self-defense. Gentleman who shot 'im will walk. But you, dearie, you are going to *swing*, my sweet."

The room spins. I retch, right there on the prison floor. The pathetic serving of bread and water—the whole thing—comes up, burning my throat with bile. My stomach and sides ache from the heaving.

I lie there on the ground, losing grip on my resolve. I am breaking apart in a hundred pieces.

Then I hear footsteps. The guard. He's back.

I scrabble forward, clutching my letter. "Please, sir. I'm not asking for anything for myself. Just my brother. If you could arrange to get this to him. It won't be much trouble—if someone might give it to the first Whitechapel fishmonger or flower seller they see, they'll know how to get it to him."

The guard tilts his head.

I swallow hard. "Please, sir, if there's any humanity in you—" My voice breaks. "There are two coins. One for him—he has nothing, you see—and one is for you."

My hand stretches forward, holding the letter and the coin out. I hate that the paper trembles. I'm begging. But I have no farther to fall.

At last, he reaches forward and takes the letter.

"Thank you, sir," I say, tears welling up in my eyes. "Oh, thank you so . . ."

The words die in my mouth as the guard tilts my folded letter, dropping the coin out of it. He holds both coins in his hand and smiles wide.

"Deliver the letter, you say? Sure thing."

He turns to look at the woman in the stall across from me, the mad old bat, and tosses the paper through the bars.

'Ere you go, sweetheart. Want a letter?"

She scrabbles after the folded paper, picking it up, and with lunatic eyes wide, shredding and tearing at the sheet before stuffing the pieces in her mouth and chewing.

My gaze swings back to the guard as he pockets the coins and strolls away, whistling.

CHAPTER SIX

"A lie that is half-truth is the darkest of all lies."
—Alfred, Lord Tennyson, *Harold: A Drama*

I barely sleep that night. Or the next.

Over the next few days I hear more rumors about my fate and they all say the same thing: I am going to hang.

The authorities are speeding up my trial. They say the public is in need of a good execution. The system has become soft of late and it's good for morale to have an evil girl from a depraved neighborhood meet her maker for her crimes, a good lesson for everyone. And entertainment, to boot.

I do not speak to the other prisoners. I avoid the gazes of the guards. To pass the time, I eat the meager food they supply and find what little comfort I can in the straw pallet, in my cold, dirty cell. And I worry about Nate ceaselessly.

The voice in my head remains silent.

And then one night everything changes.

I must have been sleeping because I'm startled by a faint scratching outside my cell. *A rat*, I think drowsily. No shortage of those. I turn over, ignoring the sound.

But the rat continues its scraping. And then the rat clears its throat.

I sit bolt upright. Standing outside my cell is a man. In the gloom, I can just make out his silhouette. Including a dark top hat.

My heart seizes with terror, and I scramble toward the back wall of my cell. *The stranger who killed Kit.*

"Quiet," whispers the man. "I'm not going to hurt you."

He steps forward and his face is illuminated by the dim moonlight filtering in from a lone window. It's not the gentleman who murdered Kit. It's the man with the trim beard and light eyes, the one in the smoke-gray suit who was watching me in the market.

I feel relief, but only a little. "Who are you?"

"Your last chance," he says calmly.

I say nothing. Glancing past him, I wonder where the guards are.

"I'm here to free you," he says. "You must come with me now."

I don't move.

He stares at me levelly. "While I commend your skepticism, the truth is if you want to live, you'll have to come now. I am the only one who can help you."

I frown. "Why would you do that?"

"Because you are one of us," he states flatly. His cold eyes flick around, like a wolf's.

"You're Tainted," I say, not really a question. "Who is 'us'?"

He is dangerous, that much I can tell. And though I'm desperate to be free of these walls, I'm not keen to go from the frying pan into the fire.

"My name is Nigel Hawksmoor. It is my life's work to find people like you, people who are Tainted—although we don't call ourselves that." He waves a hand, dismissively. "I will explain everything later, but it's imperative that you come with me now. We must not wait one minute longer."

I narrow my eyes. "What do you . . . *do* with the Tainted you find?"

"We give you a chance. And a life. An opportunity to contribute to something important." I wait expectantly. He looks at me with great intensity. "*Queen and Country* important."

This is a trap. A trick. I'm not going anywhere.

Nigel Hawksmoor exhales impatiently and tightens his jaw. He moves one step closer to my cell and crouches down low so that he's on my level now, staring at me through the bars.

"Miss Cole, you will hang," he says in a low, even voice. "And perhaps you don't care about yourself anymore. But what about your brother? How well do you think he will fare without you?"

I keep my face impassive, but my ears are ringing. How much does he know about Nate?

"Has he been able to reach you?" he asks. "Do you know what's happening to him, even now?"

How does he know so much about us? Who *is* this man?

"Take my hand. I can help you . . . see him." Hawksmoor stretches a hand through the bars.

I hesitate. But if he's telling the truth, and he really can help me contact Nate . . .

The instant my fingers touch his, the prison grows foggy and my mind is whisked away. There's a voice. The fogginess clears, and I see an image of Nate cowering in an alley, scared, alone, and shivering. Dark shadows smudge the hollows beneath his eyes.

I choke, screaming out to him. He must get to Plough Street . . . or find the fishmonger . . . anyone who might help. But Nate can't hear me. I sob, shouting his name.

And then a hand clamps tightly over my mouth.

I feel myself pulled away from the alley as if by a wire. I'm back in the prison cell. Nigel Hawksmoor's hand is tight over my mouth. "Hush," he hisses in my ear.

His gaze pierces mine, shocking me into silence. Eyes widened, I nod, and he removes his hand.

"How can I trust you?" I whisper.

"What choice do you have?"

I struggle to form a response.

"I guarantee you this, Miss Cole: if you don't come with me now, they *will* find you again. And then you'll wish the executioner had had his chance with you."

"Who will find me?"

"The Huntsmen."

"How do you know that?" My voice is a hoarse whisper. "And what do you mean 'find me *again*'?"

"You've already encountered them. One of them killed your friend."

My mouth goes dry.

"And although I can't be certain, I'm reasonably sure he was there for you, Miss Cole."

My stomach twists as I remember the moment in the market. *We have business to discuss*, the stranger had said.

"I have to get to Nate."

Hawksmoor shakes his head once. "I have sent a man. On my word, he will collect your brother. You will both be brought to safety. Come with me now and I will take you to the Academy."

Academy? My brain is muddled, a blistered mess of fear and exhaustion. So little of what Hawksmoor is saying makes sense, and I'm not about to abandon Nate to go off with this stranger.

"Miss Cole," Hawksmoor says, as though reading my thoughts, "you cannot go back to Whitechapel. An escaped prisoner? Your face can never be seen there again."

I lick my lips, trying to think through all he has said. I've heard the stories. Escaped prisoners suffer the worst fate of all, once caught. Could I make it on my own? And if this man is being truthful, if he really can help us . . .

"There comes a time when you have no choice but to trust someone," he says.

I stand and draw nearer, searching his face, hunting for the truth behind those wolf-like eyes.

There are no answers there. I don't know with any certainty what will happen if I go with him, but the trouble is, I do know exactly what will happen if I *don't*.

"All right, Mr. Hawksmoor. Let us go."

CHAPTER SEVEN

"The game is afoot."
—Sir Arthur Conan Doyle, *The Return of*
Sherlock Holmes

I hardly see how he does it. One minute, the bars of my cell are shut fast. Hawksmoor places his hands on the iron lock. And suddenly, the door is swinging freely. How did he pick the lock so quickly? And with what? I saw nothing in his hands.

"Follow me," he says before turning and moving swiftly down the corridor.

I swallow. Last chance to change my mind.

After a second's hesitation, I step out of the cell, following Hawksmoor as we hurry away from the guard's station, deeper into the hushed prison. I wonder where we're going but Hawksmoor is moving too quickly.

The prisoners in the cells we pass by are all asleep. Any minute, one of them will wake at the sound of our footsteps, hollering bloody murder at the sight of us.

The smell of the prison—the acrid scent of urine and rot—make my eyes water as we pass through the shadows. Only faint slivers of moonlight guide us. But Hawksmoor seems to have no trouble knowing where we are going.

At the end of a long corridor, after a sharp bend, we stop before a door. It looks like it hasn't been opened in a hundred years. But, once more, under Hawksmoor's hands, the door swings open with a low creak. A long, dark corridor lies ahead of us, lined with bare stone walls.

"Where are we going?" I whisper as we travel the length of the hallway.

"Shhh. Almost there."

"Almost where?"

Then, Hawksmoor freezes. My eyes jerk to his. Has he heard something? He pushes me into a tiny gap in the wall, although I barely fit. "Stay here," he commands. "Do not move. If you can manage it, don't breathe."

"What—" I begin to ask, but his piercing glare silences me.

He quickly glances around, then clambers up a wall—all the more impressive given his fine suit—and I gape as he effortlessly swings up into the beams that crisscross the roof of the tunnels. He tucks himself small and goes still, just as three figures turn the corner ahead of us. I can see them through a small crack in the stone. My heart thunders and I push myself deeper into the shadows. They stalk in our direction, heading toward the prison.

They are dressed like gentlemen, and are carrying weapons. But as they pass, talking among themselves, they don't sound like gentlemen.

"Warwick says 'e wants her taken alive," says one.

"Got plans for her, does 'e?"

The others laugh. I bite my tongue so hard the coppery taste of blood blooms in my mouth.

"Kill the guards if you 'ave to," says the first man. "Kill whoever gets in your way. But take her alive. She's a feisty one, so 'ave a care."

A chill slides down my spine. Are they talking about me? I hold my breath, praying they don't see or hear us.

Mercifully, they pass us by without detecting our presence. When they are gone and we can no longer hear their voices, Hawksmoor detaches himself from the ceiling beams and clambers down. He beckons me to come out. "It's safe now."

"Huntsmen?" I whisper.

He nods.

"Who is Warwick?"

"The Duke of Warwick. The man you encountered in Whitechapel Market. The one who shot your friend."

That man was a duke? I swallow. Dukes are powerful. The have money, power, influence . . .

"Come now, Miss Cole. We must hurry. It will be a matter of minutes before they discover you've escaped and then they will return this way. We need to be gone."

My heart beats a galloping rhythm as we fly down the tunnel. I'm gasping for air, ears pricked, sure I hear footsteps pounding behind us.

At last, Hawksmoor pauses, then points straight ahead. There's a trapdoor in the floor, just past the next crossing of tunnels. He levers it open and sends me through first. I clamber down and find myself in an even darker tunnel. Dripping water echoes through the damp space. The smell is even worse than the prison.

Hawksmoor closes the hatch firmly above us, then lights a lantern that had been hooked on the wall.

We walk quickly, sloshing through inches of cold muck that swirls around our feet. After several minutes, hope begins to flutter in my chest. Surely we must be near the exit by now.

A crash sounds behind us.

Hawksmoor grabs my hand. "Run!"

We race, splashing through the tunnels, no longer concerned about making noise. Terror claws at my throat at the idea of being captured by those men. The walls of the tunnel feel like they're closing in.

At last, the tunnel ends at an old iron gate, and we emerge into a small London square. Though both exhausted, we don't so much as pause. Hugging closely to building fronts and shadows, we walk briskly through the streets, leaving the prison far behind.

There is no sign that the Huntsmen have followed.

The sky is pink with daybreak. I glance sideways at Hawksmoor. The set of his jaw is firm with determination as he leads us forward, but the fire of panic in his eyes has been extinguished. Have we eluded the Huntsmen?

The streets here are alive with uproar and motion: newspaper boys hawking headlines, carriages rattling over cobbles, the earliest risers making their way to work. It must be early morning, though I have no idea how many days I was trapped within the prison's walls. We turn a corner and the enormous gleaming dome of St. Paul's rises up ahead of us.

Hawksmoor pauses and pulls me into an alley. He draws a small waterskin from his cloak. "Here, drink this," he says, pushing it at me. My mouth is dry as tinder. Without hesitation, I take a deep pull, savoring the cool, fresh liquid as it trickles down my throat.

But as I swallow, a sudden thought crosses my mind. Could that water have been poisoned? I wave away the worry, but a more troubling feeling replaces it, settling in my belly: I am beginning to trust Hawksmoor. This scares me almost as much as my recent ordeal.

I watch him as he, too, takes a drink from the waterskin.

Hawksmoor is helping me, it's true. And he has plans for me.

But I have plans of my own.

I will go along with him for now. I'll escape to wherever he is taking me. But I have no intention of staying at this Academy, whatever it is. Once I am reunited with Nate, we'll run away. Head north, perhaps. We can make a go of it on our own, just the two of us.

Hawksmoor finishes drinking and tucks the waterskin away, before he motions us forward again.

I am going to find a way to get my life back—the one I had with Nate. I am going to find out why we're Tainted. And then I am going to find a way to cure us of this curse.

CHAPTER EIGHT

"The past is but the beginning of a beginning, and all that is or has been is but the twilight of the dawn."

—H. G. Wells, "The Discovery of the Future"

I know I'm meant to be blending in, but I can hardly contain my amazement as we walk into Paddington Station. My eyes swing skyward. The ceilings are impossibly high, soaring above us. Trains hiss and squeal on the tracks, their gleaming black engines emitting great plumes of steam.

People bustle to and fro on the platforms, carrying carpet bags and parasols. Uniformed porters lug trunks under the close scrutiny of ladies in the finest fashions. Conductors' shouts and whistles echo upward to the vaulted ceilings. The air is heavy with the smells of axle grease and roasting chestnuts. This will be my first experience traveling on an actual steam train.

I tug self-consciously at the plain linen, high-necked blouse and skirt I'm wearing, and try not to trip on the boots that are two sizes too big. Hawksmoor had the disguise stashed in an alcove within St. Paul's, complete with a traveling cloak and bonnet that covers much of my face.

As we travel, we are an Oxford haberdasher and his daughter.

"Should anyone ask," Hawksmoor says, "we do business in buttons, lace, and notions. You are learning lacemaking, and I—who never had any sons—am grooming you to take over the shop. We come into London to do trade—our trunks are making their way to Oxford."

Hawksmoor's smoke-gray suit has been replaced by one of plain brown wool, paired with a tweed waistcoat and a bowler hat. He's also applied a fuller, fake beard and gold-rimmed spectacles to complete the disguise.

To reach the train station, we took an omnibus—my first ride on one of those, too. After the crowded stuffiness of the omnibus, with its mildewed blue velvet seats and straw lining the floor, the airy train station is like a different world.

The air clangs with the sound of metal. The smell of soot and forge overwhelms me with a sudden memory of Kit.

Apprenticed to the blacksmith, he was forever walking around in a cloud of char. How I loved that smell; it meant he was nearby. A ghostlike remembrance of his touch suddenly comes to me and I can almost feel has hands going around my waist. Warm hands. No matter how frosty the air, his hands were always warm, like the coals of the smithy's fires.

We climb onto a long black steam train and Hawksmoor leads the way down a narrow corridor to our compartment. We speak very little, which is fine with me.

As we settle into the plush seats of our train compartment, I allow myself to exhale. It's a breath I've been holding since escaping the prison.

We're one step closer to safety, although I know the danger is not gone. Perhaps it never will be.

I reach up to move the curtain aside and realize my hand is shaking. Peering out the window through clouds of steam, I expect to see a Peeler come striding toward us any minute, whistle screeching.

"It was a narrow escape," Hawksmoor says. "Here. Take this." He thrusts a flask in my hand. I start to protest, but he insists. "You need it." The brandy burns as it goes down my throat, but it also softens my limbs.

My thoughts return to Nate. "I need to know where my brother is. If he is all right."

"Of course," says Hawksmoor. "Your brother is just fine."

"I need to know more than that."

"Here. Why don't I show you?" he says at last. I let Hawksmoor hold my arm, as he did in the prison, and I am instantly whisked far away.

I see Nate traveling in an enclosed carriage. He must be journeying a different route to our destination. He jostles in the seat as the carriage travels swiftly. He appears . . . content. Safe, and cared for. He looks eagerly out the window, as though he's on an adventure, and he eats a small treacle tart with delight. A matronly woman sits beside him ramrod straight, looking directly ahead. Although her eyes are not on him, there's something decidedly . . . protective about her bearing.

I feel a pang. It should be me watching over him, not a stranger. But I know it's not possible. Not yet.

"Satisfied?" Hawksmoor asks, when he releases my arm, returning me to the train car.

I nod. Although the ache in my chest is still there, I know I will see Nate soon, and that gives me some comfort.

"Thank you," I say, my voice little more than a whisper. Nate is everything now; he is all I have left. Especially now that Kit is gone. . . .

A black curtain of despair threatens to pull me under again. I dig my nails into my palm, forcing myself upright. Nothing can bring Kit back now. I have to stay focused on moving forward. On reuniting with Nate.

A conductor knocks at our compartment to inquire if everything is suitable. Hawksmoor stands and fusses with his valise, speaking to the conductor in a low voice. The man nods and I can just make out the words, "Very good, Delta," before he moves on to the next compartment.

"What was that about?" I ask.

"You don't miss much, do you, Miss Cole?" Hawksmoor's mouth twitches into a half smile. "That's good."

I keep my face neutral, waiting.

"You will soon learn we have something of a network. Eyes and ears throughout the country. It helps us in our work."

He offers me nothing more. The train starts up with a great squeal of wheels on the track and a hiss of steam. I watch the city of London slide by. Great plumes of smoke rise out of the factories we pass, and I gaze at leagues of red-bricked row houses interspersed with hospitals, church spires, and workhouses.

The city soon gives way to countryside, with rolling hills and hedgerows, and stone villages tucked into green valleys.

"You've never seen the countryside before?" Hawksmoor asks.

I can't peel my eyes from the window. "It's wonderful." My whole life has been people, streets, commotion, smog, and soot.

"'Come forth into the light of things, let Nature be your teacher,'" Hawksmoor recites.

I nod. "Wordsworth. I've always preferred Coleridge."

He inclines his head and a smile plays upon his lips.

In my father's homeland, women were respected. Which is why he taught both me and Nate to read and write. To play chess. We spent long hours discussing philosophy, politics, science. Nate and I never went to school, but still we learned.

Tea sandwiches and scones are soon served in our compartment. I try not to gobble them down, but I'm so famished I can hardly help myself. Hawksmoor disappears into the train, and returns, carrying a folded newspaper.

"Here. You might be interested in this," he says. "The morning *Times.*"

I stare at the outstretched bundle.

"Come now, Miss Cole, I am well aware you can read."

The front page is emblazoned with headlines about the financial markets and a story about the Tower Bridge that's being built over the Thames, with a spectacular illustration of its ongoing construction. A piece about the Queen's Golden Jubilee decorates much of the lower front page. It's a few months away still, but I read about the preparations that are well under way. There's to be a banquet, a parade, and a ceremony in Westminster Abbey. I wonder what that would be like. . . .

Hawksmoor turns the page, and points to a small piece at the very bottom of page three: *Dangerous Murderess Executed Early This Morning at Newgate Prison.*

I scan the words below. *Miss Felicity Cole, a criminal of the most vicious sort, was this morning hanged* . . .

I stare at the page, then look up at Hawksmoor. "This is . . . your doing?" He nods.

I hand the paper back to him, and turn back to the window and lose myself in the farmland rushing by, hardly hearing the clattering of the train on the tracks. My eyes slide over a small white chapel, and then a stone wall and a tiny cottage. Sheep dot the pastures.

Dead. I am officially dead.

I feel strangely . . . *free*. Nobody will come hunting for me. I am not an escaped convict. The story is over, and society is satisfied with the outcome.

I frown, thinking of the Huntsmen. Will I be safe from them wherever we're headed? Will they be fooled by the fabricated execution? A few years ago, this plan wouldn't have gone off, but the government abolished public hangings. Perhaps there's a chance.

"I suppose you'd like to know something about where we're going," Hawksmoor says, raising a china teacup to his lips.

"Very much."

He settles back into his seat and takes a thoughtful sip. Returning the cup to its saucer, he steeples his fingers. "Have you ever heard of a man named Christopher Marlowe? He was a playwright in the sixteenth century."

I nod. A rival to Shakespeare. "He was murdered."

Hawksmoor gives me a small smile. "Well, that's what the world believes. But he wasn't killed. His death, like yours, was faked."

As the train flies past farms and villages, Hawksmoor explains. "Christopher Marlowe was, indeed, an Elizabethan playwright. He was also Tainted, making him perfectly qualified for his work. His more important role was spy and assassin, in service of Queen Elizabeth herself. At the age of twenty-nine, when his secrets were in danger of being compromised by a great treachery, his death was counterfeited. This allowed him to go deep underground where he was able to continue his work."

"As a secret agent for the crown?"

"Indeed. Being officially dead allowed Marlowe the freedom to create a large, secret network that has grown ever more sophisticated in the three hundred years since."

Hawksmoor sips his tea again and continues. "The Queen granted Marlowe use of a large country house, Greybourne Abbey in Oxfordshire, from which he ran his operations. He kept the name, but turned it into Greybourne Academy, an institution to recruit people with . . . rather special talents."

"Tainted?" I whisper, although I know we can't be heard. Hawksmoor nods over the rim of his teacup.

My brows knit together. "I'm to believe that there have been Tainted throughout England for over three hundred years? That there's a secret underground network of people . . . just like me?"

"We don't call ourselves Tainted. That's the slur of those who misunderstand and fear us. We use the ancient name—we have long been known as the Morgana."

The Morgana. I let the name roll around in my mind. There is something deeply familiar about the word, though I can't quite put my finger on why it seems so.

"It was a stroke of luck that I happened in Whitechapel Market when I did," Hawksmoor says.

"When you saw me?"

"Just before the Huntsmen found you." He watches me intently. "It was fortuitous timing, to say the least. Shall we call it serendipity? I believe these things happen for a reason."

I'm not sure I believe in fate, but I remain quiet.

"I do apologize for leaving you in the prison as long as I did. I needed to be sure everything was set for our escape; I needed to select the correct moment."

I sip my tea.

"At any rate, it is for Greybourne Academy that I have recruited you, as you have probably surmised." He watches me carefully. "Being among the Morgana is a gift, Felicity."

Being Tainted is a curse. It has always meant danger for my brother. It meant death to my mother.

"At Greybourne, you will embark on a very special path. Your gifts make you perfect for this role. You will become a sharp instrument to do the necessary work of shaping the country and the Empire."

I frown. "What does that mean, exactly?"

"It means you will be trained to be a secret agent and assassin."

I almost drop my teacup. "I'll be trained to be . . . a what?"

CHAPTER NINE

"The wicked are wicked, no doubt, and they go astray and they fall, and they come by their deserts; but who can tell the mischief which the very virtuous do?"
—William Makepeace Thackeray, *Vanity Fair*

A n assassin. And a spy." Hawksmoor looks at me carefully. "There are evil men in this world, Miss Cole. Men who would do great harm. You will eliminate those men. It is a great honor to protect Queen and Country."

My mouth works, but no words come out.

"I can see you are not pleased," Hawksmoor says drily.

How could I be pleased? I have no interest in being a secret agent. And as for being an assassin . . .

I have a sudden flash—a memory of killing the footman in Whitechapel Market. How could I possibly do that again, and . . . intentionally?

I look at Hawksmoor, sitting across from me. Is refusal an option? I'm conscious of how much I am at his mercy. I shift with discomfort. I still need his help—for this escape, and to be reunited with Nate.

"I think you've overestimated my abilities," I say. "I couldn't possibly become what you say."

"On the contrary, Miss Cole."

"But I know nothing of such things," I object, my voice growing firmer. "Being stealthy enough to . . . kill someone? It's the last thing I'm capable of. You saw me back in Whitechapel. Was I stealthy then?"

"You will learn," he says mildly, plucking a piece of lint from his trousers.

I cross my arms over my chest. "And if I don't wish to learn? If I refuse?"

His hand stills. He gazes back up at me and any trace of humor has left his eyes. "Need I remind you that you—and your brother—remain in great danger? Without the protection of the Academy, you would not last a week."

I bite the inside of my cheek. Is that a threat?

"You will see, in time, that the world needs you, Miss Cole, and your skills. This really is a great honor."

At that moment, a steward comes by to refresh our tea.

We travel on in silence for several minutes. I nibble at a scone. "How long until we get there?"

"The train ride to Oxford will take us another hour. Then we'll go by carriage the rest of the way. Perhaps another hour after that."

Two hours. Two hours to come to terms with everything this stranger has told me, to figure out what my own plan is going to be. I know a few things already: I am going to survive this; I am going to keep my wits about me, find a way of getting back to normal, and find a way to save Nate.

"And when will Nate arrive at the Academy?" I ask.

Hawksmoor watches me without expression for several moments. "Unfortunately, your brother won't be coming to Greybourne."

I blink. "What did you say?"

Outside, a small village flashes by. Hawksmoor remains quiet. My vision narrows and I can hear blood pulsing in my ears. "You *said* he was coming, too. You had sent someone to retrieve him. I saw him on the journey." My voice becomes increasingly shrill as I press the words through clenched teeth. "That was the only reason I left London with you."

"Miss Cole, I said he would be brought to safety. And that is true. I did not specifically state that place would be Greybourne. That was your assumption, I'm afraid—"

"You bloody bastard." I say in a low voice. "Where is he? What have you done with him?"

"As I said, he is safe." Hawksmoor checks his pocket watch. "In fact, they should be there soon."

I stand, one thought driving me: I must get off this train. My eyes move around the compartment. There is no door to the outside, and the window won't open wide enough. I ride a wave of nausea.

"Miss Cole, do sit down."

I ignore Hawksmoor. The liar.

I fling open the compartment door and stalk out into the corridor. There has to be a way off this train. An emergency stop, perhaps.

I'm halfway down the corridor when I feel a strong grip on my arm. Hawksmoor pulls me aside. "Miss Cole, I know you're upset, but risking yourself will do you no good. You cannot get off this train. I will explain everything. Do return to the compartment now."

I want to tear into his face with my nails. "What have you done with my brother? Where is he?"

I can think of nothing except this. I will force the answer out of this snake.

Hawksmoor glances up and down the corridor; it remains empty. He exhales with resignation and grips my arms tighter, and I am abruptly flooded with a vision.

Nate is sleeping in a soft feather bed heaped with pillows. The room is in a small, cozy cottage by the sea. Downstairs, in a tiny country kitchen, a round woman is cooking breakfast—I can almost smell the freshly baked bread, soup, sausages . . .

In spite of myself, the searing heat in my blood tempers a little. With simple furnishing and the lemony sunlight filtering in, warmth and safety pervades every freshly swept corner of the cottage. Just beyond the garden a pathway leads to the sea.

Hawksmoor releases my arm and I am back in the empty train corridor, breathing heavily. I glare at him, fire still curling through my veins.

"He's safe in a far better place than where we're headed," Hawksmoor explains. "He is too young for Morgana training. It won't happen for him for a few years yet. This is what we do when we rescue a young Morgana who is not yet ready for training at the Academy."

I continue to scowl, but Hawksmoor is making some sense. If Greybourne is filled with assassins and spies in training, I certainly don't want Nate exposed to that. And even if I were to leave this train now, somehow, I still would have no idea how to find him.

I take a step away from Hawksmoor. He still lied.

"You knew I believed I was to be reunited with Nate. You deceived me."

"The fact is, Miss Cole, there's no way you would have come along otherwise. And then you would either be in the hangman's noose, or at the mercy of the Huntsmen."

I feel my teeth grinding together. Though what he says is, perhaps, true, I'm not about to admit it to Hawksmoor.

I think again of the seaside cottage with its white beach where Nate could run, play, breathe fresh sea air . . .

He will be safe there.

I want to ask Hawksmoor where the cottage is, but I'm certain he wouldn't tell me. Besides, I'd be showing my hand, revealing too much about my future plans.

I will find out on my own. Soon enough, once I'm recovered and able to communicate directly with Nate again, I will find out where they're keeping him.

Nate will be safe there for now. But I won't leave him there long.

CHAPTER TEN

"Daydreams are delusions of the demon."
—Charlotte Brontë, *Villette*

The carriage wheels bump on the uneven ground as we drive along the country road. We've been in the carriage for over an hour, journeying, for the most part, in silence, which has suited me. The carriage thuds over a large hole and I suppress a yelp as my bruised behind bounces on the seat for the hundredth time.

When we pass through a set of gates and begin up a long drive, I peek out the window and suddenly all of my aches are forgotten. At the end of the drive sprawls a large house. Actually, "house" isn't quite the right word.

The grand manor built of honey-colored stone with its endless rows of windows is much more of a *palace* than a house. Lush green gardens surround the manor and parkland spreads beyond that, as far as the eye can see. No fewer than three similarly styled outbuildings rest nearby—including a carriage house, perhaps. And maybe stables, and a guest cottage? It's difficult to tell, and my experience with estates like this is limited to stories and books.

I have never seen anything like it. I have never even dreamed of anything like it.

"Welcome to Greybourne Academy," announces Hawksmoor.

I swallow. *I do not belong here.*

Within these lovely walls is an academy that trains its students to become spies. To sneak, to lie . . . to kill. I wonder about those within. Are they watching, even now?

Curiosity prickles my neck. Could it possibly be true that everyone here is Tainted? Questions tumble in my mind as I gaze at the magnificence of Greybourne.

As the carriage approaches the house, Hawksmoor leans forward to speak to the driver. "Go directly to the carriage house, would you, Tucker? Let's give Miss Cole a moment before we go inside."

I look at the man and narrow my eyes. Is he being kind? Or does he have other motives?

I don't much care. Between my muddy boots and disheveled hair, I am grateful not to have to meet anyone at the present moment.

The carriage rolls into the carriage house and Tucker leaps off to unhitch the horses. Hawksmoor turns to me. "Tucker will take the horses to the stable and I need to see to something. You'll be fine here for a few minutes, won't you? I'll be back shortly to bring you into the house." And then he's alighting from the carriage.

I settle in to wait. Soon, the yard becomes very quiet. I crane my neck to look out the window, but there's not much to see. The air inside the carriage grows stuffy, and I grow restless. A minute later, I climb down, stepping gingerly onto the flagstone.

I run my hand along the other smooth, gleaming sides of the carriages. Dust motes dance within the slanting light of late afternoon. The air smells of wax and leather and horses. I realize my neck muscles are tensed, and I try to relax them, but it's no good. Everything about this place is incredibly posh, and highly unfamiliar.

Not for the first time, I wish Kit were here. He always knew how to handle himself, in any situation. He had a way of appearing confident, even when he wasn't. *They'd be lucky to have you, Flick,* he'd say if he were here now. *Don't let them make you feel bad. They're no better than you.*

He was always my champion, my steadfast supporter.

My throat tightens.

Through a high, open window, the scent of lilies wafts in from the garden. I tiptoe toward the window, wondering if I can get another glimpse of Greybourne. Scraping a stack of boxes across the floor, I step up onto them. Peering over the windowsill, I can just make out one of the wings, the view as grand as my first glimpse of the house.

Another carriage approaches up the drive. I go up on tiptoe to get a better look—

"Who are ye?" snaps an unfamiliar voice behind me. "What are ye doing 'ere?"

I spin quickly, throwing off my balance. If I weren't on a stack of boxes, it wouldn't be a problem. But I am.

The boxes topple from under me and I fall most ungracefully on top of them. Sprawled on the floor, I look up as a young man strides across the floor. He stops, looming over me, arms folded over his chest. "I asked you a question."

The boy is dressed in threadbare trousers, suspenders, and a cap; his hands and face are grime-streaked. But even the thick layer of dirt can't conceal a pair of stunning blue eyes framed by dark lashes.

He has a strong jaw, but his face is youthful. He can't be much older than me. His height and broad shoulders suggest manual labor. He must be a stable hand of some sort.

I soon realize he's made no effort to help me up. Scowling, I scramble to my feet.

"Who sent ye?" he demands.

"Do you mind?" I say, finding my voice at last. "I am a guest of Mr. Nigel Hawksmoor. Who I am is none of your concern. And who exactly are you?"

The boy looks taken aback, and doesn't answer. Then he narrows his eyes again. "Why were ye spying on the house?"

I instantly go red, casting about for a reasonable explanation. Before I can say a word, he takes another step toward me.

"And what 'ave ye done with *Hawksmoor?*" The boy's eyes flash with suspicion. "Where is he?"

"What—what are you implying?"

He takes another step nearer. He is so close, I can smell the grass and dirt on his skin and his clothes. His face is full of accusation.

Heat rises behind my ears and I tighten my hands into fists. I was invited here, and this is how I am to be treated? I received better in the slums. "I could be asking you all the same questions," I fire back. "How do I even know *you* belong at this house? Perhaps you are the enemy and I should be interrogating you." A familiar prickle begins to creep up my scalp. "I've had a very bad past few days. We've traveled all the way from London, and the last thing I need is *you* making unfounded accusations over perfectly innocent behavior."

Something possibly changes in his expression but I take little notice.

"Now, *if you don't mind.* Back. Off."

He reaches forward. "Now just wait—"

Without planning it, I block his hand. A rushing sensation fills me with power and I know I have—somehow—grasped my ability again. Dust motes freeze in midair and a housefly hovers by my face; I can see its wings beating a slow rhythm. The stranger reaches for me again. My brain registers attack.

I grasp his arm and sweep my foot under his—in a heartbeat—flipping him over. Without a thought, I lunge after him and pin him down so he can do me no harm. He lands hard on his back on the ground. Shock washes over his face.

And then, he bursts into a wide grin. "Well done!"

I abruptly return to myself and, realizing my incredibly inappropriate position, scramble off him. He attempts to stand but a jab of pain flashes over his face. He settles for sitting.

"I'm sorry—what did you say?" I manage.

"My commendations," he says, with a nod. "That was very good." The smile brightens his already handsome face. A sweet ache shoots through my chest.

Then I feel immediately guilty. How can I even look at another boy when Kit was murdered only a few days ago?

At that precise moment, Hawksmoor returns.

"Now, Miss Cole, I—" He stops, surveying the tableau before him—me facing off with a stable hand. He raises an eyebrow at the boy sprawled on the dusty ground. "Entertaining our guest, are we?" Hawksmoor waves a dismissive hand at the young man. "Go on. Get out of here."

"Yes, sir," says the young man, disappearing in an instant.

Hawksmoor turns to me. "Listen, Miss Cole. We are already quite behind schedule. Let's go up to the house. We've not much time to dress for dinner. And, believe me, you do not want to be around Mrs. Dempster when people are late. . . ."

He gathers his overcoat from the carriage.

"Who was that, anyway?" I ask, frowning at the carriage house doorway through which the young man has disappeared.

"Not to worry, Miss Cole. I'll introduce you to everyone later."

I nod. "Wait—did you say *dress* for dinner?" My stomach tightens. A formal dinner, inside the manor house? I don't have the vaguest idea how to behave at a formal dinner.

I bite my lip and follow Hawksmoor as he strides toward Greybourne Academy.

CHAPTER ELEVEN

'"But I don't want to go among mad people,"
Alice remarked.

"Oh, you can't help that," said the Cat: "we're all
mad here. I'm mad. You're mad."

"How do you know I'm mad?" said Alice.

"You must be," said the Cat, "or you wouldn't
have come here."'

—Lewis Carroll, *Alice's Adventures in
Wonderland*

We enter the house through giant oak doors that open
into a large foyer, my boots clicking on the marble
floor. I gape at the sight that greets me. A grand staircase
rises up through the entrance hall and a crystal chandelier
sparkles high above our heads, sending slivers of light over
the richly papered walls. The air smells of wood polish and
flowers from the enormous arrangement of white and yel-
low roses on a side table.

A woman wearing a black housekeeper's uniform strides into the foyer to meet us. She is shortish with a brisk walk and graying hair piled neatly onto the crown of her head.

"Ah, Mrs. Dempster," says Hawksmoor, removing his gloves. "Would you show Miss Cole to her room? It's been a long journey."

"Certainly, Mr. Hawksmoor." As he strides off in the opposite direction, Mrs. Dempster turns her gray eyes on me. "Would you come with me, miss?" Her face is impassive. She shows no sign of having noted my shabby appearance, though I know she must have. At the first opportunity, I must brush my hair and see what I can do about cleaning some of the stains from this dress.

I have no bags to carry, so I simply nod and follow her up the staircase and along a long corridor lined with plush silk rugs. I try not to gape at the luxury surrounding me. My feet sink into the thick carpets as I struggle to keep pace. I am so self-conscious in this grand house I barely remember how to walk properly.

Passing tapestries and oil paintings and seemingly endless doors that open into yet more rooms, I think of Nate, and how he would love to see all of this. And Kit . . . These are sights he will never see. My stomach tightens.

I catch a glimpse of a room that appears to be some kind of parlor. In a corner of the gleaming parquet floor sits grand piano. *A grand piano.* I've never seen one in real life.

My only experience with this world has been in books, and the overblown rumors that circulate in the slums.

"They don't actually do any . . . work," reported my friend Jack, once, fresh from one of his deliveries to Mayfair.

"*No work?*" demanded one of the younger Craddock twins. "What do they do all day, then?"

Jack relished his role as that of spy to the upper-crust world. "They have fancy dinners," he said in a hushed tone. "And parties. And afternoon tea. And go a-visiting. And to dances."

There was silence as we digested this new information. "Sounds dreadfully boring," sniffed Charlotte. We all murmured our assent, but secretly, I thought it sounded lovely.

I remember standing beside Kit. How we looked at each other, laughing, as Jack related the bizarre dining rituals. How they break their bread into tiny morsels before eating it. How the servants use a little silver knife to remove crumbs from the tablecloth.

My heart twists at the memory. *Kit.* I will never see him again. Never look into his eyes . . .

I push the thought away, shove it deep down.

Ahead of me, Mrs. Dempster stops. She pushes open a door and stands waiting beside the threshold. "Your room, Miss Cole."

My breath catches as I step inside the grandest bedroom I've ever seen. A four-poster bed with a blue silk canopy sits in the middle of an enormous room. A dressing table and mirror adorn one corner; a plush settee, the other. Velvet curtains frame two large windows that reach right up to the coffered ceiling.

"This . . . is my room?" I ask, unable to stop myself. This can't possibly be where I will sleep.

She nods briskly. "Jane, one of the maids, will be here shortly to help you dress. In the meantime, a bath has been drawn. You will wish to bathe." It's not an inquiry.

A second door opens onto a separate room. I glimpse a claw-footed tub inside and the most heavenly scents drift out. I can't stop myself from gaping. An entire bathroom just for me? There must be some mistake. At that moment, someone clears her throat behind us.

"You must be Felicity," says a girl, standing just inside the bedroom door, watching me carefully. She is beautiful. Golden blonde hair frames a heart-shaped face and a tiny, upturned nose. I would guess she's about my age.

"That will be all, Mrs. Dempster," she says in a plummy, posh accent. "I can help Miss Cole from here."

Mrs. Dempster's hesitation is so brief, I wonder if I've imagined it. Yet she nods stiffly and strides from the room.

The girl takes another few steps toward me. "May I be one of the first to welcome you to Greybourne?" She extends a graceful hand. "My name is Rose."

Haltingly, I wipe my dirty hand on my filthy traveling dress before shaking hers, and then immediately wonder if that was the wrong thing to do. Rose's lavender dress is made of the finest fabric—silk, perhaps?—with lace at the sleeves and throat. Although nowhere near as nice as Rose's dress, I am glad of the linen ensemble Hawksmoor provided me. Glad I'm not standing here in my own filthy clothes. This outfit only needs a quick wash and a brush out.

Rose is obviously the daughter of a fine family. But I wonder—who is she here at Greybourne?

"My name is Felicity," I say. And then I feel like an idiot. Of course she already knew that.

"I am very excited to learn everything about you, Felicity," she says, watching me carefully through clear blue eyes. And then those eyes flit down, taking in my outfit. "But—I imagine you need to freshen up from your journey."

Her words are friendly enough, but the warmth in her voice does not exist in her face. "I'm sure you'll want to be out of that . . . *thing* you're wearing"—she casts a meaningful glance at my traveling dress—"and into your own clothing soon enough."

I remain silent.

She looks past me. "Where is your trunk? I'd love to see your clothes. It'll be such fun; perhaps we can share. You're about my size. Well, maybe a little wider in the waist . . . but we can make do I'm sure. . . ."

"I don't have a trunk."

She frowns, confused. It's too much. Like she's playacting. "Oh, you mean it's to follow later."

"No, I mean it's not coming at all. I—I don't have anything more."

She pauses. "Oh well, what a pity." Her eyes gleam, almost triumphantly.

She knew already, of course, even before she asked. She wanted to make me squirm, make me admit it out loud.

I command myself to keep my chin high, even as a hot flush burns my ears.

"Oh! You're here already," says a voice from the doorway. A young woman in a pinafore bustles in. Her chestnut hair is tied back in a neat bun. Her face is freshly scrubbed, a little older than mine. "I'm Jane and I'll be your maid here at Greybourne, Miss Cole. To tell you the truth, I didn't expect you up here so soon." She glances at Rose. "Begging your pardon, Miss Pritchard, but . . . Miss Cole needs her bath now. I'm under strict orders—"

Rose waves a dismissive hand. "Of course she does. I shall see you at *dinner*, Felicity." She emphasizes the word like she knows the very idea of it makes me uncomfortable.

Somehow, Rose has learned all about me. Who else knows I'm here? And then I remember—this is a house full of spies.

Jane takes hold of my arm and gently guides me toward the bathing room. "Come now, Miss Cole. Never you mind about her. Some of the other Candidates won't take kindly to you, of course, but they're not all as bad as Rose."

"Candidates?"

"Yes. You know, those of you who are trainees. The ones who are competing to be Morgana agents. Hawksmoor has told you about all that, surely?"

I shake my head.

"Oh," she says, and continues ushering me to the bathing room, without another word.

"Jane?"

"It's not my place to speak about those matters, Miss Cole. You will learn it all eventually. For now, into the bath with you. Do you a world of good. You'll be right as rain after."

Jane leaves me alone in the bathroom and closes the door behind her. I put Rose out of my mind and turn my attention to the large claw-footed tub in the center of the room, filled to the top with steaming, perfumed water. My skin tingles at the sight. I've only ever experienced cold baths in a tin washing tub in the corner of our room back home—and that was rare enough.

I undress quickly and slip into the silky water. It is so delicious I might cry.

My skin shivers with goose bumps. I sink lower into the water and breathe deeply. All the exhaustion of the day melts away.

I reach for the fresh cake of soap and fluffy white washcloth that rest on the shelf straddling the tub. Never have I experienced such luxury. I wash away all the dirt and grime—layers of it from the market, from the prison . . .

Then I turn my attention to my fingernails, cleaning the grime out from under them. My breathing stops as I realize it's not grime. It's dried blood. Kit's blood.

I bite my lip and tears slip down into the water. I close my eyes and focus on breathing, on washing. It's time for me to put the horrors of the past several days behind me and turn my attention to the unfamiliar trials that surely lay ahead. I hope I'm strong enough to cope with whatever is coming next.

After a long while, I reluctantly leave the bath. I wrap myself in the fluffy towel I retrieve from a stack next to the bath and step back into the bedroom.

"Right," says Jane, looking me up and down. "Let's get you ready for dinner, shall we?"

I hesitate. "I'm afraid I don't have anything near fine enough to wear—"

Jane waves a hand, quieting me. "That's all been taken care of."

She strides across the room to yet another interior door. Inside is a dressing room, with a gown of deep amethyst resting on a dress mannequin. I blink. A shelf of shoes occupies one side wall, stacks of scarves and gloves and hat-boxes, another. A large jewelry box is propped open, filled with necklaces and bracelets and earbobs.

"Now, let's see what would go nicely with those eyes . . ." Jane says, thumbing through the baubles.

"This is—this is all for me?"

Jane pauses to look at me, suppressing a grin. "While you were journeying from London, Hawksmoor sent word ahead, informing us of your coloring and your dress size. He's very good at estimating these things. Our seamstress has been working all day on this gown. Your daywear and a few more frocks will be ready later."

She continues rifling as I stand there dumbfounded. "Ah, here we are," she says, selecting a few items. She then helps me into the gown. I've never worn such a shade before, but she assures me it's perfect for my coloring. Jane dries my hair with heated irons. She brushes it until it's silky, then curls and fastens it in what she says is the latest style. She chooses a pair of jeweled slippers and long satin gloves. When she's done, she finally allows me to look in the mirror.

I gasp, hardly recognizing myself. My hair is glossy, piled on top of my head in perfect ringlets. And I can see what she meant about the color of the gown. My eyes take on a much more intense hue.

"All right," Jane says. "Let's get you downstairs. We're only a little late at this point."

My stomach gives a flutter. I wonder what will be waiting for me in the dining room. At least I'll blend in now. Maybe nobody will take notice. I can quietly sip my soup. Or whatever it is they eat at these meals.

Jane turns back when I don't immediately follow. "Miss, are you quite all right?"

I swallow. "I—"

"They say you come from Whitechapel. Is that true?"

"It's true."

She nods, knowingly. "Start on the outside."

"Pardon?"

"The outside. You know, the outside fork. Start with that one. You'll be just fine."

I have no idea what she's talking about.

She starts to turn away, then hesitates. "And . . . be sure to break the bread into little morsels. Don't just bite into the entire roll."

"Oh. I shall . . . keep that in mind."

CHAPTER TWELVE

"Since Eve ate apples, much depends on dinner."
—Lord Byron, *Don Juan*

On the way to the dining room, Jane tells me about my dining companions. "All the senior Candidates will be there. About twelve in total, including yourself, miss. Plus a few of the instructors, and the headmaster, Hawksmoor."

I cling to the idea that I can slip in and remain unnoticed.

After many twists and turns, at last she leads me through to the dining hall. It's a vast room, largely occupied by the longest dining table I have ever seen, and it's filled with people in formal dress. Sconces flicker on the walls, and the table is laden with crystal goblets, candles, and the finest china. My heart is beating a quick rhythm. I want to hold on to Jane's hand for support but I resist.

As I enter, Hawksmoor stands. He strides over and Jane melts away. "Ah, Miss Cole! Allow me to announce you." He holds out his arm and I grasp it as he walks me to the table.

"I would like to introduce Miss Felicity Cole, our newest pupil here at Greybourne."

I somehow find the courage to hold my head high, in spite of my thumping heart.

There must be almost twenty people seated at the table. They all stand and begin welcoming me.

"How was the journey?" someone inquires.

"Are you settling in?" asks another.

Hawksmoor holds up a hand to quiet them. "All in due time," he says. "First, let's be seated. Dinner is served."

He shows me to an empty seat at the far end of the table, close to the other pupils, young men and women around my age. He returns to his end of the table. I am served champagne—the very first time I have ever tasted it. I hesitate briefly, but then take a sip. Sweet bubbles tingle my tongue; the taste is like heaven.

While I sip the champagne, I steal surreptitious glances at the others. I recognize Rose, seated directly across from me, but the other boys and girls are strangers. Hawksmoor had told me on our journey, "Greybourne is unlike most institutions in many ways, not the least of which is segregation of the sexes. Or the lack thereof, I should say."

"You mean boys and girls are mixed? In classes, too?" I asked, unable to hide my surprise. This is not how I assumed the upper classes operated.

"We find our purposes are best met by early and regular integration. We cannot afford to be squeamish or coy. All our trainees must be comfortable with the opposite sex. We are dealing with life and death, after all."

I understood what he had said. It mattered little to me—where I came from, men and women mixed much more freely than they did in Society.

Those seated nearest me introduce themselves. On my left is Lucy Rutherford, a younger girl with strawberry blonde hair who watches me carefully. To my right is Hugh Torrington, a broad-shouldered, older boy with frown lines between his heavy eyebrows. Charlie Spooner sits beside Rose, across from me—all ginger hair and wide smiles.

Dinner is soon served. Footmen enter with salad and rolls, and move around the table deftly helping everyone, and ensuring our goblets are properly topped up. I stare down at my place setting; a bewildering array of silverware meets my gaze. Three forks? Two different spoons? And then I remember what Jane told me—*Start with the outside fork*—and I give silent thanks.

I tentatively pick it up. And then I wonder the best way to approach the salad. I'm not sure I've ever been given so many fresh, plentiful vegetables at one meal.

I notice nobody else seems to be having the same struggles. They're all eating and chatting comfortably. I take a mouthful and it sticks in my throat.

As I attempt my next forkful, Lucy asks me a question. "Have you met Julian yet, Felicity?"

"Julian?"

A few other girls titter behind gloved hands, including Rose, who wears a smug smile.

"Why? Who's Julian?" I ask in a whisper.

Lucy raises an eyebrow, but says nothing more.

"Do I need to be worried? What's wrong with him?"

"Absolutely nothing," say two of the girls dreamily, practically in unison.

Lucy laughs. "Oh, just wait. You'll understand when you meet him," she says knowingly.

I shift in my chair. I am fed up with surprises. A footman offers me a bowl of soup and I look down at it, frowning.

"Please, girls, you're being ridiculous," says Rose in her crystalline voice. "You're making Felicity uncomfortable." She turns her blue eyes on me and smiles sweetly. "Don't worry. *Mr. Blake* is very well-born. And the most eligible bachelor in his circle. You have nothing to worry about—he won't bother you a bit. I'm sure he won't even notice you." She stops abruptly. Someone giggles on her other side. "Oh dear," she adds, opening her eyes theatrically wide and putting a hand over her mouth. "I hope you don't take offense, Felicity. I merely meant to point out the advantages of being common." Another pause. "And there I go again, saying the first thing that pops into my mind. . . ."

I narrow my eyes, then smile sweetly back. The other girls go quiet. Someone coughs. A few faces turn to see how I'll respond.

I adjust the napkin in my lap. "Of course I don't mind," I say to Rose, mildly. "And you're quite right. There are worse things than being common." I brighten my smile and flick a glance at some of the others. "You know, like being so stuck-up that everyone dislikes you. I mean, that would be *awful*, wouldn't it?"

There's a tense silence, during which Rose's face goes an unattractive shade of purple, but she remains silent. I feel a surge of triumph, although I know it will be short-lived. I have made an enemy.

During the soup, Charlie—the ginger boy across the table—asks, "So, Felicity, how does it feel to be with the winning team, finally?"

"I'm sorry, what do you mean?"

"You know. The Morgana. Here at Greybourne."

I look at him blankly. "I'm not sure what you're talking about."

"We're the future. You must realize that," adds Hugh impatiently.

"The . . . future?"

I look to Lucy, hoping she'll clarify.

"He's talking about the idea that the Morgana are destined to be in power."

I stare at her.

"Well, perhaps some of us more than others," says Hugh. He smirks unpleasantly at me and lifts his soup spoon. "Which is perhaps why we are not *all* going to make it here."

Rose's self-satisfied smile returns.

I bite the inside of my cheek. I'm still utterly confused about how things work here, how they will select from among the so-called Candidates. But I'm not about to ask now.

Hugh swallows his mouthful and continues. "At some future period, not very distant as measured by centuries," he begins in an affected voice, reciting a memorized passage, "the civilized races of man will almost certainly exterminate and replace throughout the world the savage races."

I recognize the quote instantly.

"Yes," I begin carefully. "But when Mr. Darwin said that, it was within a larger statement. People often make the mistake of pulling those words out of context. It's not that Darwin *wanted* that outcome, specifically—he simply believed it would someday occur."

Hugh's mouth opens slightly and his ears go pink.

I turn my attention to my own bowl, and sip at the most delicious soup I've ever tasted.

"This mock turtle soup is wonderful," I say, hoping to change the subject. I've only had mock turtle soup once before and it was such a treat. The kind old lady in Plough Street shared a little with us two Christmases ago.

Someone at the table sniggers and I look up.

"It's real turtle, Felicity," Lucy says, quietly. "Not mock."

I flush furiously.

A sudden sound at the dining hall doorway brings a merciful interruption.

"Good evening, everyone. Sincerest apologies for my intolerable lateness." It's a young man's voice, deep and smooth, but the tone carries a hint of mischief.

All eyes go to the doorway and heads swivel as the newcomer strides in.

I recognize him—but just barely. The face is the same, only much cleaner. And his eyes, those intense blue eyes. It's the stable hand I met in the carriage house. The one who challenged me. The one I . . . *fought*. I cringe at the memory.

But what is a stable boy doing here? He's cleaned up, and dressed like an aristocrat in a black dress coat and white tie. He still wears the same cocky expression, only now it completely matches his appearance. With a tingle of nerves, I am suddenly aware just how handsome he is.

Hawksmoor stands and indicates an empty seat near him. "I was beginning to think you weren't going to join us, Mr. Blake. Thank you for deigning to honor us with your presence."

I watch the young man with growing understanding as he strolls toward the dining table. The stable hand clothes, the dirt . . . it was all a disguise. Stupid. Of course. I remember where I am.

A small sigh emanates from one of the girls on my side of the table.

"Ladies," he says to us, half bowing. And then his eyes flick in my direction. And he winks.

Right at me.

Before I can react, he sits down at the far end of the table where I can no longer see him. My heart is skipping double time. Rose's head whips toward me.

I dare a glance at the other girls. Lucy is beaming with surprised delight, but Rose is looking at me with barely contained rage.

Mr. Blake. So this is Julian.

At that moment Hawksmoor makes a toast. "Welcome to Greybourne Academy, Miss Felicity Cole." He raises his glass. "I always like to toast with the immortal words of our founder, Christopher Marlowe: *You must be proud, bold, pleasant, resolute . . . and now and then stab, as occasion serves.*"

CHAPTER THIRTEEN

"Fear had long since taken root
In every breast, and now these crushed its fruit,
The ripe hate, like a wine."

—Robert Browning, *Sordello*

The next day, my training begins. Jane wakes me at dawn, startling me by bringing me breakfast: eggs, toast, juice, and tea. I'm not sure I could ever grow accustomed to the idea of people actually serving me.

Still, the food smells wonderful and looks nourishing, so I dig in. Jane leaves me alone to eat and dress in the clothing she has laid out—a simple shift and hose, and flat, soft-soled slippers. The garments are completely different from what I wore last night. I can move in these clothes.

It's a good start.

I lift my teacup, hoping the hot, sweet tea will soothe me. I don't know what to expect from this training, and my nerves are on edge. I wonder if being around these people will help me figure out what has happened to me—and, more importantly, how I might rid myself of these Tainted abilities.

As I sip my tea my thoughts turn to Nate. Last night after dinner, I tried to communicate with him, but failed. I chew my lip. Perhaps now that I am rested and fed . . . maybe I will be more successful?

I walk to the window seat and tentatively reach out. I calm myself, quieting my mind, focusing all thought on my brother.

A glimmer of something pulses toward me—just a tiny, flickering slice. An idea of Nate, safe and warm in a soft bed in the cottage. He is just waking up—

Nate. Can you hear me? It's Felicity . . .

An urgent knocking sounds at my door. "Miss Cole, may I come in?" calls Jane. "We must hurry. It's almost time to go down to your training session."

My connection to Nate instantly dissolves.

I sigh, and rise from the window seat. As I do, I feel a sharp pain at the loss, but I tell myself I will be able to try again. Without Hawksmoor's help, or anyone else for that matter.

"Yes, Jane, come in."

Jane sits me at the dressing table and begins working on my hair, tying it off my face in a simple style.

"What did you mean yesterday, when you said we were 'Candidates'?" I ask, watching her in the mirror.

She hesitates, clearly unsure how openly she may speak.

I press my lips together. "Please. There are too many secrets here. I don't have anyone I can truly trust. Hawksmoor won't tell me—and I'm not sure I'd believe it was the truth anyway."

Her hands twist at her sides. "All right. Everyone knows, anyway. I don't see why you shouldn't know. In the Morgana, there are only ever a few spaces at the top. And, at the moment, there is only one available place."

"One?"

She nods. "Only one of the senior Candidates will be selected."

"How do they choose?"

"There will be a series of tests and eliminations. To even be considered, you must prove yourself to the Elders by demonstrating a mastery of your gift. If you can't, you will be removed from the running."

"What if you're 'out' but you're still Tainted?" I can't believe the Morgana would just throw their own out on the street. Hawksmoor was careful to tell me how dangerous the world is for the Tainted on their own, though I know it from Nate . . . from my mother.

"In that case," explains Jane, "unless your family will take you back and promise safety and secrecy, you're assigned an auxiliary role in the organization. A supportive role, within the Academy."

"Such as?"

"Well . . ." Jane's cheeks go slightly pink.

I still her hand. "Jane? Are you Tainted, too?"

She is quiet for several moments. "I am, miss. And I was a Candidate. I did not pass the trials. But I want you to know that I am not ashamed of what I do. I consider it a great honor to prepare the Candidates. To serve the Academy in the best ways I can. I know I do good work, even if I am not a full-fledged Morgana agent . . ."

I don't know quite what to say. I want to tell her that I have no interest in becoming a Morgana agent, either. That it holds no appeal for me, and I certainly don't think any less of her because she didn't succeed.

But as true as that is, I'm not sure it would strike the right tone with her at the moment. So I say nothing.

"Miss Cole, I have every confidence you can make it," she says brightly. "There's something about you. I can feel it. Maybe it's because you're not like them. You're the first Morgana to come from Whitechapel. You had to grow up tough, fending for yourself." She blushes again. "If you don't mind me saying so, of course."

"I don't mind, Jane. And please—would you call me Felicity?"

She nods shyly, then puts the finishing touches on my hair. For a moment, my mind wanders away to what it would be like—this achievement she, and everyone else here, seems to covet. To be a Morgana agent. To be a highly trained spy. An assassin. Be involved in affairs that can mold the future of the country . . .

No. That's not what I want. The only things that matter to me are reaching Nate and finding a way back to our old life.

"There," says Jane. "All finished. You're ready."

I glance at myself in the mirror. My cheeks have color now and the hollows under my eyes are less pronounced. Although it has only been a day, I already look like a different person.

Jane leads me to an entirely separate wing. I still my nerves as we travel through sumptuous hallways decorated with silk carpets and wall hangings. At last, we reach a ballroom.

Lustrous parquet floor stretches across the enormous space; chandeliers glint off the mirrored, coffered ceiling. A wall of windows, each hung with silk curtains, spans the length of the ballroom. It's a gorgeous hall, meant for parties and dances and formal events . . . but the members of the Academy are using it for a rather different purpose.

Everyone else is already here, which makes my stomach drop. All the senior Candidates, about a dozen of them, are in gymnasium clothes, like me. They are paired off, sparring, practicing the use of swords. Leaping, tumbling, climbing, and doing incredible things.

I realize I neglected to ask Jane what we would be doing in our training session today. I look at her with alarm. "Combat," she mouths with an apologetic wince. Then, with an encouraging smile, she pushes me forward.

I wonder at the sight of them—Tainted, every one. My eyes stop on a cluster of people fighting in the center of the room. One of the fighters is taking on three opponents. He's incredibly fast and strong. Sweat glistens on the back of his neck. He turns and I see his face: Julian Blake.

His opponents come at him all at once. He deftly crouches under one attacker's punch, sweeping another's leg away. His movements are so fast, I can barely make them out. I would probably need to be in my own Tainted state, grasping my own ability, in order to see it all properly.

The third opponent catches him and wraps him up, but Julian quickly flips the attacker away.

There's a small gasp behind me. "My goodness, he's spectacular, isn't he?" says Jane. I glance at her over my shoulder and she looks rather flushed.

She's right, of course. He's incredible. It's like watching a beautifully choreographed dance. My heart gives a slight flutter, and then an immediate pang of guilt shoots through me. Kit was killed before my eyes not even a week ago.

And, as Rose made quite clear over dinner, Julian has no reason to pay me any attention. A young man like him would never be a match for me, not in a thousand years. After he winked at me last night, I heard one of the girls whisper, "Julian Blake is a shameless flirt. Everyone knows that."

Julian quickly dispatches the last of his three opponents, who I now recognize as Charlie Spooner. As the two others lie at Julian's feet in crumpled heaps, Charlie comes up grin-ning. "You're in fine form today, Blake," he says, breathing heavily. Julian grins back at him. They're obviously friends.

And then, Julian turns his head and spots me. His eyes go to mine as though he already knows I am there. My cheeks burn. I look away quickly, but not quickly enough.

"Ah, Miss Cole," shrills a woman's voice from across the ballroom, the sound echoing up to the high ceiling. A lady emerges from the group and beckons me to stand in front of her. "Come over here so I can see you properly. I am Agatha Isherwood, the instructor of this class."

I move forward as Jane ducks back, closing the enor-mous double doors behind me.

Agatha Isherwood is tall—no, not tall. She is of aver-age height, but she holds herself so upright, you have the impression of height. Silvery blonde hair sweeps back from her face, making it all the easier to be watched by her pene-trating, wide-set eyes.

I attempt a curtsy, but since I have no idea what I'm doing, I'm not sure I pull it off.

There is a long silence. "Well, that's the worst thing I've ever seen," Mrs. Isherwood says dispassionately. "I imagine your *gift* is not for curtsying."

A few titters circulate through the group.

"Mrs. Isherwood?" a familiar voice rings out. Rose. "I daresay Miss Cole has us at a disadvantage. She's seen what we can do, but we have no idea where her abilities lie. Being the newest addition to our class, should we not see the current level of her skills?"

My eyes dart around in alarm. Mrs. Isherwood considers this and nods. "Yes, a brief demonstration won't be too much difficulty, I'm sure."

My mouth opens. Demonstration?

Mrs. Isherwood leads me into the center of the ballroom. "Hawksmoor tells me you are one of the best raw Aristos he has ever seen. I, for one, would like to see *that* for myself." Her tone brooks no argument, but her words make no sense to me—*raw Aristos?* I dig my nails into my palm. Why didn't Hawksmoor better prepare me for today?

I glance at Rose, whose mouth twists in a self-satisfied smile, like she's just swallowed a mouthful of stolen sweets. Like she knows, somehow, that I have no capability for channeling my ability at will.

My stomach tightens.

Mrs. Isherwood plants her hands on her hips, looking at me expectantly. I have no idea what she intends me to do. I stare at her dumbly, fidgeting under everyone's gaze. The lights from the ballroom's chandeliers beam down on my head. A drip of sweat rolls down my neck.

"Ah, how silly of me," Isherwood says, after an interminable stretch of time. "To properly show us your skills, you will require a sparring partner."

She turns to the group and selects a boy, though the term is little more than a formality. This particular individual made the transition from boy to man long ago—Hugh Torrington. The posh, snobby one who quoted Darwin at dinner last night. Standing, his height and broadness is all the more obvious. His jaw is heavy, his whiskers fully formed, and a bulk of muscle rounds his shoulders and upper back.

She must be joking.

CHAPTER FOURTEEN

"Be near me when my light is low,
When the blood creeps, and the nerves prick."
—Alfred, Lord Tennyson, "In Memoriam"

Isherwood barely blinks. She watches with clear eyes as Hugh comes forward, approaching me. Am I meant to *fight* him? A spasm of panic grips my stomach.

"I'm not sure I can—"

Isherwood waves a dismissive hand. "Please. We have no time for modesty here."

My eyes lock on Julian's. He saw what I can do in the carriage house. But he doesn't realize I can't control my abilities at will. He gives me an encouraging smile.

I look around for help and spot Charlie Spooner, the friendly ginger-haired boy, standing next to Julian.

"Come on, Felicity," says Charlie, trying to be helpful. "You can do it." But he takes note of my panicked expression and clears his throat. "Although, Mrs. Isherwood, perhaps we should let Miss Cole warm up a bit first?"

"Don't be stupid," says Rose. "A *gift* has nothing to do with warming up."

Isherwood claps her hands once. "All right, Hugh. Don't hold back. Hawksmoor tells me that's when her skills best manifest."

It's now or never. If I'm going to grasp my ability—

At once, Hugh is on top of me impossibly fast. It feels like being hit by a speeding steam engine . . . and the next minute I am flat on my back.

Must get up, I think. Hugh issues two swift kicks to my midsection, and a punch square to my right cheekbone, clearing my brain of all such ambition. Stars explode across my vision.

I lay there curled like an insect, moaning. Praying it's over.

There is profound silence. I'm not sure if it's real or if I have been deafened by the blow to my head.

"Right," says Isherwood drily. "Well, that's quite enough of that."

My eyes, squeezed shut during the attack, crack open.

Pale faces swim in my vision. A few are horrified, but most look on with disgust and disdain. "Pathetic," I hear someone sneer.

I can't see Julian.

"Oh my," titters Rose. "That was really . . . awful."

Now that it's over, the pain flashes through me full force. I want to sob, but instead I grit my teeth. Isherwood stares down at me, mouth pursed with disappointment, arms crossed.

"It is a dangerous thing," she begins, looking away from me to address the rest of the class, "to have the potential of Morgana, without being able to use the one advantage you've been given."

There are murmurs of agreement. Have I just been used as an example? A cautionary tale?

"Somebody get her out of my classroom," Isherwood snaps.

Rose's face appears before mine. Her eyes glitter; she is not even bothering to hide her triumph. "I'll take her to the infirmary," she says in a singsong.

I squeeze my eyes shut again.

With Rose's help I hobble from the room. Just before the doors close behind us, I hear Isherwood address the class. "A Morgana who is incapable of mastering his or her gift is headed for a great deal of trouble, indeed," she says. "Now let's get on with the proper business of training . . ."

The doors close with an echoing boom as Rose and I continue down the corridor.

"It's a pity," she says with a smug smile, now that we're alone. "Although, I suppose it shouldn't come as a surprise. You've learned too many bad habits out in the wild and your gift has been suppressed for too long." She sighs. "But it was worth a try, wasn't it?" Her tone drips with condescension.

"What do you mean—*that's it*? No more training for me?"

Rose shrugs. "Oh, I imagine they'll try to teach you a thing or two. But you can't expect to be a *Candidate* anymore. I'm afraid you're just not Morgana agent material."

It occurs to me now that if I am not accepted into the inner circle, perhaps information will be withheld from me. Panic rises as I consider the grave misstep I have made. But what could I have done?

"Not to worry, Felicity. I'm sure Hawksmoor will find a position for you somewhere in the Academy. A servant or a cook, perhaps. Maybe a maid to one of the other female agents, if you're lucky." Then she gives a little gasp, as though a brilliant idea just occurred to her. "If you like, I could put in a word for you to be mine. Would you like that?"

I'd rather eat glass.

When we arrive at the infirmary, Rose leaves me in the hands of the nurse before turning on her heel and striding back to the combat training. The matron, a stout woman with a large nose and warm hands, clucks and inspects my injuries. When she bustles from the room to retrieve some supplies, I am left alone, staring up at the ceiling.

I spend the rest of the day licking my wounds and avoiding the other Candidates—it's one advantage to being in a house this large. Jane tells me the other Candidates have training sessions in intelligence, code-breaking, and foreign affairs.

But I'm excused from all of that today, given my injuries. My right eye has swollen shut and my left ankle is so bruised I am walking with a limp.

While I lie in bed, resting in the darkness and the quiet, it's impossible not to think of Nate and Kit. Hot tears slide down my cheeks. I would give anything to be back at the market on that fateful day before everything changed. I swallow. Have I spoiled everything? Have I lost my opportunity to learn the secrets of this place and return to some semblance of my old life?

My presence is required at dinner that evening. Which proves to be a painful affair of a different sort. Jane does an admirable job dressing me and disguising the swelling on my face with cosmetics and powders. But it doesn't matter—everyone knows of my humiliation. Nobody speaks about it at dinner, but that only makes the whole affair more awkward.

I still have only the scantest understanding of the silverware and the manner in which I am meant eat. I don't even properly know what I am supposed to do with my napkin.

"Isn't this roast lamb and mint sauce delicious, Felicity?" says Lucy, chattering away. "I bet you've never had anything like it."

In fact, I have had roast lamb and mint before.

A sudden memory flickers before my eyes. Down by the river, a beautiful moonlit spot where Kit and I had sneaked once, to share a stolen bottle of wine and a packet of leftover food given him by the blacksmith in a rare display of generosity. It was a secret spot we'd discovered, and though the gate was locked against trespassers, Kit had known a trick of opening the hinges. As he'd done it, he'd winked at me. "One of the few advantages to being a blacksmith's girl," he'd said. How I had loved the sound of those words.

I was his girl. And now I will never see him again.

I stand abruptly from the dinner table and ask Hawksmoor to excuse me, mumbling about a headache. It's not exactly a lie.

As I turn to leave, I stumble into the sideboard that holds a sumptuous display of marzipan fruits and pastries, balanced on a silver tower. The delicate confections tumble everywhere with a clatter and I let out a sob before I can stop myself. Everyone stares as I do the only thing I can—I race straight for the exit and hurry away without turning.

On my way back to my room, I get lost. It's not a surprise—this house is unreasonably large. And it doesn't help that I'm hobbling along with my injuries and fighting back tears.

Just when I think I've figured out which way to go, I find myself in some kind of drawing room. "Oh, bugger," I mutter.

Only then do I realize I'm not alone.

CHAPTER FIFTEEN

"If the misery of the poor be caused not by the laws of nature, but by our institutions, great is our sin."

—Charles Darwin, *The Voyage of the Beagle*

A gentleman stands by the crackling hearth, a glass of brandy in his hand.

"Oh!" I exclaim. I wipe at my eyes, embarrassed by my tears, and then realize I have probably wiped away all of Jane's carefully applied makeup. "I'm terribly sorry, sir. I didn't know anyone was here."

He is short and balding, with eyes as warm as caramels and a round belly under his waistcoat, like he's hiding a Christmas goose there. I've never met him before.

"I must admit it's a habit of mine," the man says. "Sneaking up on people. Although I think, to be fair, in this situation it really must be regarded as you sneaking up on me."

I flush and shift between my feet, not sure what to say.

The gentleman's warm smile immediately puts me at ease. "I'm only teasing. How very unkind of me. You've been through a great deal in the past few days, haven't you? You must be our newest recruit, Miss Felicity Cole. I'm Mr. Humphrey Neville. I am the Intelligence Master here at Greybourne."

I try not to show my surprise. *The Intelligence Master.* At dinner, I overheard mention of him; from what I could gather he's in charge of running all of the various spy networks. Hawksmoor's second-in-command. Who would suspect such an ordinary, friendly, and unassuming man to be a spy, much less the Intelligence Master?

And then I realize—that's likely the point. An individual with such an unmemorable appearance could easily slip through crowds, into buildings—wherever he pleased. Nobody would pay him any attention.

"Why don't you join me?" he says. "You'll have just enough time for a glass of brandy before Jane comes looking for you."

I hesitate.

He leans forward and lowers his voice. "I know in proper society, gentlemen and ladies do not share brandy together after dinner, but I think you'll notice at Greybourne we do many things . . . differently." A warm smile lights his eyes.

The truth is, I hadn't even known that was a rule.

I sit awkwardly on a smooth leather club chair and a footman is immediately at my side offering me a glass. I don't know whether I'm meant to grasp the glass by the stem or the bowl and fumble between the two.

"It's the bowl in this case," Neville says in a confiding whisper, "to warm the liquor. The stem for dinner wine. You know, I sometimes get that wrong, too."

I raise my eyebrows, then sip my drink in silence. The brandy, sweet and strong, warms my chest. It occurs to me that this Mr. Neville must be full of information. I take my measure of the man as I sip, the liquor creating a pleasant fuzziness in my head.

"You must be utterly bewildered by all that has happened," he says.

"I am!" I blurt out. "I have so many questions, and I don't even know where to begin."

"But Hawksmoor has explained matters to you?"

"Some, but not nearly enough. He said he didn't wish to overwhelm me."

Neville sips his brandy thoughtfully, the amber liquid swirling in his glass. "Well, what would you like to know?"

I hesitate. Can I trust this man? But I'm so desperate to ask, to understand. . . . The more I know, the closer I will be to reclaiming my old life, I'm sure of it. "I want to know why I am Tainted. I mean—Morgana. How could I have gone so long without knowing? What made me this way? What made any of us this way?"

He smiles wryly. "Ah, the mysteries of the Morgana. You don't want to start with something a bit simpler? For instance . . . which way to the conservatory?"

I laugh. "In this house, I'm not sure that *is* the simpler question."

He inclines his head. "True enough."

"There has to be an answer."

"And perhaps there is. But, unfortunately we don't know it. Surely you have heard the various tales and theories?"

"Only when I was little. Tales of horror, mostly. Cautionary stories to frighten children."

He nods. "The cause of the Morgana abilities was a field of inquiry for natural scientists for a while, although it soon became frowned upon—much like the study of mesmerism and alchemy. Even so, I don't believe any firm conclusions were ever reached about the *why* of the Morgana."

I bite my lip.

"Don't despair, Miss Cole. There is a great deal I can teach you about our group."

I sit up straighter. "Such as?"

"Do you know about the nature of Morgana gifts? You have, no doubt, noticed that some of us possess different strengths." He rises and crosses to a bookshelf and runs a hand along the spines of old volumes, finally selecting the one he seeks. The spine creaks as he opens it and shows me. The pages are filled with classical drawings captioned in Greek and Latin.

"Aristos," I say, gazing at an illustration with the word inscribed beneath, breathing in the musty scent of old paper. "That's what Isherwood called me . . ."

"Yes. That's because your gifts lie in the physical realm. Aristos refers to supreme agility and physical prowess." His eyes catch mine. "This, Miss Cole, is you."

I shiver.

"Now, most Morgana either have a physical gift, Aristos, a mental one, Sophos, or a gift with physical matter and objects—that's called Mitos. Rarely, a Morgana is gifted with more than one of these sets of skills. Have you heard of Sir Isaac Newton? Leonardo da Vinci?"

I nod, and Neville continues. "We don't know for sure, but it is generally believed that these men were Morgana, and that they possessed gifts in multiple spheres."

I recall Hawksmoor's actions during my rescue from the prison, his ability to help me see Nate and to get us out of the prison. "Mr. Hawksmoor, does he have more than one gift?"

"Indeed," says Neville. "It is uncommon, but the phenomenon is, of course, not only limited to those of historical note."

"Are those the only three realms of gifts?" I ask.

Neville gives me an appraising look. "Why, what a perceptive question. As a matter of fact, there is one more realm that we know of. It's hard to describe . . . It's of the metaphysical sort. An ability to manipulate time and mortality, in a sense, but not like what you do when you grasp Aristos. It's more . . . an imperviousness to mortality. Rebirth, if you like. Immortality."

I frown. *Immortality?*

"I can see you're struggling with this, Miss Cole. I understand. Many new initiates come from families of Morgana, and grow up being taught the abilities. For you it's all new."

I nod, reclaiming my glass of brandy and staring into its swirling depths.

"It must be bewildering," he continues. "Especially given that you come from Whitechapel. To be frank, we have never had a Candidate from that . . . part of town."

I look up to see his eyes soften, but we say nothing more on the subject.

"Can you explain about the Candidates? Jane told me there are a limited number of openings. Why?"

"Ah yes," he says, pouring more brandy into his glass. "Have you have heard anyone call Hawksmoor by the name Delta? Or Isherwood by the name Epsilon?"

Delta. That was the name the conductor on the train had used. I lean forward as the meaning clicks into place. "They're mathematical terms. Greek letters."

"They are, indeed," Neville says, grinning. They are also code names. The upper echelon of Morgana agents—the elder executives—are each given a code name. For many reasons—secrecy, chiefly, but also effectiveness and security—we keep a tight limit on the number of people within that inner circle. When there is an opening due to death or a retirement from active service, we bring forward a senior trainee, a Candidate. Promote them to full status, give them a code name . . . and allow them to learn all our secrets." He winks. "It's a system that goes back to the Academy's origins with Christopher Marlowe. He, of course, was Alpha."

"Your code name?"

"Lambda."

I take another burning sip of my brandy and mull over all I've been told. The hush in the room sinks into my bones. "Thank you for this, Mr. Neville. There are so many things I don't yet understand and I . . . I suppose I need all the help I can get."

He nods. "We have enough enemies out there," he says, waving his brandy glass. "We are not a well-regarded group, Miss Cole—or well-understood, for that matter. Not unlike your own people, the inhabitants of neighborhoods such as Whitechapel. If you don't mind me saying."

It's the last thing I expect to hear. I never look for any sort of sympathy—least of all from the upper crust.

"Don't look so surprised. I happen to believe it's an abomination what the nobility has done to the lower classes."

"You don't think we deserve it?" I ask. Most of the newspapers blame the poor for their own poverty and squalor.

"Quite the opposite."

It occurs to me that I know nothing about Neville's background. "Are you—"

"No, child. I'm not from the streets," he says gently. "My father was a doctor. But I can see what's happening. And it's not right."

I swallow and nod.

Neville clears his throat. "I've kept you too long. You must be quite tired."

A sudden wave of fatigue passes over me. I thank him again for his kindness, then rise to leave. "Good night, Mr. Neville."

"Just one more thing," he adds, stopping me. "Many new arrivals have these same questions. There is someone I usually suggest they might speak with. A professor by the name of Garrick. He has spent much time studying the Morgana and has written a great deal about it, as I understand. I'm not terribly familiar with his work—most recently he was investigating a cure of all things—but he may have more answers than the rest of us have."

A cure. "Where is he?"

"At Oxford, I believe. Not that I recommend you leaving the Greybourne grounds unsupervised. Far too dangerous, and Hawksmoor would definitely not approve. But . . . should you find yourself at the university at some point, it might be worth your while." Neville sips his brandy innocently.

"Good night to you, Mr. Neville."

I turn to leave, head full of budding plans. I may not be a Morgana agent, but in a house full of spies and assassins, surely there are ways of getting oneself covertly to Oxford. . . .

CHAPTER SIXTEEN

"I shut my eyes and turned them on my heart."
—Robert Browning, "Childe Roland to the
Dark Tower Came"

Finally back in my room, I curl up in the window seat and open my mind to my brother.

Nate, can you hear me?

Nothing. No response. I stare out the window into the darkness beyond.

And then, *Yes, Felicity, I'm here.*

I jump, sitting up straight on the seat. Finally.

Nate, I'm so glad to hear your voice.

Are you all right, Felicity? You sound worried.

Yes, yes. I'm fine. And I'm so sorry about everything. Are you safe? Are you all right?

Oh, it's lovely here. There's more than enough food to eat, and it's always hot. Porridge, toast, eggs, soup . . . So many delicious things. And sticky buns! Oh, you'd love the sticky buns. Do you have them where you are?

A lump forms in my throat. *Yes, Nate, we have sticky buns here, too.*

I put my hand to the cool glass of the windowpane. I wish I could see him, the way Hawksmoor helped me to. But I refuse to depend on the spymaster for anything. I can never trust him again.

Do you like it there? I ask.

I love it. He pauses. *Although, I do wish you were here, too. But Nanny tells me you're training to do very important work. She tells me . . . you're helping to make Britain a better place. Is that true?*

Is it? I have no idea. There is still so much I don't know about this place, the Morgana, and our purpose. But Nate sounds so hopeful. So . . . proud.

That's exactly what we're doing, I say.

I knew it.

Nate, do you know where you are, exactly?

There's hesitation. *Not exactly. We're by the sea somewhere. It's quite far from London. The journey to get here was so long.*

Do you think you could . . . find out somehow? Like a game. Discover the clues. Can you do that?

Yes, I think I can.

I want to tell him I am going to fetch him and we'll run away together, very soon. But I won't get his hopes up. There are so many things I don't yet know. Where would we go? How could I provide everything that is being provided for him? I need to form a better plan first.

Nate is happy and safe wherever he is. I ache to be there, to watch over him. But I know he is better off where he is.

For now.

It is early morning a few days later when I make my way to Hawksmoor's office, passing swiftly through marbled corridors and long, windowed galleries. My breath comes quickly—though not due to my hurried pace. What does he want? Why has he asked to see me so suddenly?

At daybreak, I received a message that had Jane scurrying to dress me. And now, as I rush toward his office, I try to appear unconcerned, forcing a neutral expression onto my face. I'm worried he somehow knows what I'm planning. I need him to believe I am dedicated to the demands of this academy, that I wish to become a spy and an assassin, like everyone else here. I need him to trust me.

I have seen little of Hawksmoor since arriving at Greybourne. He's a busy man, of course, and my time has also been heavily occupied.

Since my arrival, my days have been filled with lessons: intelligence, languages, code-breaking, covert affairs . . . and I have returned to combat training. Of course, Agatha Isherwood—who makes no secret of her complete disdain for me—has determined that I have no skills whatsoever. She's been matching me with mostly junior trainees and those who have no Aristos. Her goal is for me to learn the most basic defensive maneuvers. In spite of the humiliation, I try to hold my head high, although, for the most part, I simply grit my teeth to get through them.

During training sessions, Isherwood watches me with disgust, Rose looks on with barely concealed satisfaction, and Julian regards me with confusion. There have been a few times when he looked as though he would like to say something to me, but then he abruptly turned away. I know why he is confused—I bested him thoroughly in the carriage house, and now I take a beating on a daily basis.

I have no explanation for him, no idea why I can't control my abilities.

My stomach pulls into a knot as I hurry on toward Hawksmoor's office. Has he decided he's made a mistake in bringing me here? Will I be thrown out?

In the east wing, I arrive at Hawksmoor's door—a heavy oak slab with a brass bellpull. I hesitate, then ring the bell.

"Enter," calls a muffled voice from within.

The door squeaks faintly as I push it open. I force myself to breathe calmly before stepping across the threshold. Hawksmoor's office is filled with books, maps, and charts. Two leather club chairs occupy one corner, surrounded by mahogany shelves bearing brass instruments. A stand of newspapers rests by a tray of cut glass brandy decanters. I breathe the faint, sweet smell of tobacco.

Hawksmoor is seated at a leather-topped desk, poring over a newspaper. "Ah, Miss Cole," he says, looking at me over his spectacles with that intense gaze of his. "Yes, come in. Close the door."

I step forward, my palms sweaty. *One of the few with gifts in the mental and physical spheres.* Can he read my mind, even now?

The desk chair creaks as he sits back and steeples his fingertips.

"It seems I have made a mistake," he says.

My heart skips. "You have?"

"I realize, belatedly, that it's impossible to pull someone off the streets and throw them into this odd world of formal dinners and curtsying and calling card etiquette. There's much you'll have to learn. I realize that now."

"Sir?" My face burns.

"Never fear. It's all been arranged. You'll have special tutoring in deportment and etiquette to catch you up. Your first lesson will be out on the south veranda in"—he pulls out his silver pocket watch and glances at it—"*Ah.* Five minutes."

I don't move. Is that all? He wanted to speak with me about comportment lessons?

"Off you go, Miss Cole. South veranda. Your tutor will be waiting for you there." He picks up the newspaper once more and flips a rustling page. "Quickly now. It's impolite to be late."

I curtsy—poorly as ever—and leave the room.

As I make my way to the south veranda, my mind tumbles with rapid calculations. If I can be taught the proper way to curtsy, the proper way to eat a boiled egg without causing grievous offense, I might have a chance of fitting in here. Something I must do if I'm ever to gain a coveted spot on the team.

Turning a corner, I catch sight of movement. I quicken my pace, curiosity piqued. Hugh Torrington is up ahead. He looks over his left shoulder—there is something decidedly shifty about his bearing—but thankfully he doesn't see me. I tuck back out of view to watch him. He goes toward a panel on the wall, and then he pulls a small lever I hadn't noticed before. A doorway swings open like a yawning mouth.

He glances around again before quickly slipping inside. The door closes behind him, leaving no trace of the entranceway.

I wonder where the doorway leads. But I can't follow him. I'm already late for my deportment and etiquette training.

When I reach the south veranda and push open the tall leaded glass doors, all thoughts of secret passages are swept from my mind as I take in the tutor waiting for me.

Agatha Isherwood.

CHAPTER SEVENTEEN

She had an evil face, smoothed by hypocrisy; but her manners were excellent.

—Robert Louis Stevenson, *The Strange Case of Dr. Jekyll and Mr. Hyde*

Isherwood stands drumming her fingers on a table set for dinner with china plates and crystal goblets and linen napkins. Her face looks carved from stone, her chin lifted, her eyes fixed on me.

She doesn't look any more pleased to be here than I am.

"Good day, Mrs. Isherwood," I say.

"And there is your first error, Miss Cole," she says through a pursed mouth. "You do not say 'good day' to your superiors. Your blessings are of no interest to them. You ask, 'How do you do?' because that is all that should concern you."

I dig my nails into my palms.

"Now, let's begin. We have much work to do, and only an hour in which to do it."

Only an hour? How am I going to make it through even ten minutes of this?

"I can see, Miss Cole, from the sour look on your face that you would rather be elsewhere. However, it is my duty to inform you that your failure in this endeavor will result in your cancellation as a Candidate. Now, come and sit down."

I hesitate briefly, then walk stiffly to the table. Her words have caught me off guard, but not in the way she imagines. I assumed I had already been canceled as a Candidate. Does this mean . . . Am I still in the running, somehow?

"Miss Cole!" Isherwood's sharp voice slices into my thoughts. "That is not how a lady takes a seat. You do not *plunk* yourself onto the chair. You alight."

She demonstrates. I try three times to replicate her movements. None of my attempts prove satisfactory. This will be a long hour. On my fourth attempt, Isherwood emits a grunt that I'm not sure is quite ladylike. "Let's move on to silverware," she declares.

She instructs me on the finer points of table manners and decorum, before we move on to visiting and the protocol of calling cards. I sit there, brows knitted, as I try to muddle through the obscure rules. "But—why do we call them *morning calls* if they happen in the afternoon?" I ask. "It doesn't make any sense."

"It doesn't *have* to make sense. If you must know, we use the term *morning*, because they are calls made while wearing morning attire. Now, no more questions."

More than halfway through our session, Isherwood's face looks increasingly flushed and the lines around her mouth are deepening. I'm no model student, but how can I help it? These restrictions and rules are bewildering.

As I struggle my way through a lesson in curtsying, I hear her mutter, "I'm sure Hawksmoor hadn't the faintest idea what he was getting himself into when he pulled you from the Whitechapel gutters."

I pretend I haven't heard and attempt another curtsy, though I'm confident it is even more awkward than the last.

Isherwood hardly notices. "Mark my words," she grumbles, "he would have been better off staying here at Greybourne that day, instead of rushing off to London. *Ridiculous visions,* indeed . . . He should have waved them away and taken another cup of tea."

I readjust and fold into yet another curtsy. But as I do so, the back of my neck prickles. It takes a moment before I can identify what's wrong.

The way Isherwood tells it, Hawksmoor came to London with the intention of tracking me down. But he told me, after rescuing me in the prison, that it was a lucky coincidence that he'd stumbled upon me in the market that day just as I was using my gift to battle the Huntsmen.

Serendipity, he'd called it.

So did he lie to Isherwood? Or to me?

I tighten my mouth. Once again, I see that this place is a viper's nest of half-truths and duplicity. Everyone has an agenda. I resolve, for the hundredth time, to not trust anyone. Least of all Hawksmoor.

I consider asking Isherwood for the full truth and then decide against it. If Hawksmoor meant to keep it a secret that finding me was no accident, I will let him think he has that secret still. It's a small advantage I might be able to play later.

I have spent this whole time feeling at a loss, lowly and unsure. For the first time, I have something with which to bargain.

Isherwood claps her hands, drawing my attention back. "Right. Enough curtsying for now. Let's see your posture. If nothing else, a lady must have proper carriage. Go stand by the doorway and walk toward that urn in the corner."

I walk across the veranda, trying my best.

"Good heavens," she says. "If you cross a room slouching like that, you will be spotted immediately for the street urchin you are."

I try to stand as tall as possible, but after several minutes an ache develops behind my shoulders. Muscles I've never used before begin to complain.

After Isherwood's fourth attempt to teach me how to stand straight and walk like a lady, she throws up her hands, exasperated. "Hopeless! Utterly hopeless." She turns away, unable to bear to look at me any longer. "How Hawksmoor expects me to complete this task is entirely beyond me. There's simply not enough time."

I frown. "What do you mean, *not enough time?*"

Isherwood sneers at me. "You are to join a select number of the other Candidates on an undercover training exercise to the opera. Just the local opera at Oxford—it's not Covent Garden, thank heavens. The point is, you'll be among society. Never mind that you are completely incapable of accessing your gift. Society will sniff you out the moment you set foot among them. You are a danger to the other Candidates. I can't comprehend how Hawksmoor can even consider it."

She pauses, pinching the bridge of her nose. "Close your mouth, Miss Cole. A lady does not stand with her jaw open gaping like a fish. That is exactly the sort of behavior I am referring to."

"I c-can't go to the opera," I manage to stammer. Even I know I will stick out there like a goose among the swans.

"At last, we are in agreement on one thing," she replies frostily.

Later that day, I make yet another turn in the Academy corridors, uttering a curse at the dead end that greets me. Surely the library must be around here somewhere. I glance around—nobody in sight. Isherwood's toes would positively curl if she'd overheard me say such a thing.

Of course, it's because of her that I'm on this wild-goose chase in the first place. Before ending our session, she'd commanded me to obtain a book entitled *Social Etiquette for Young Ladies* by Imogen Brimble, and insisted I read the entire volume before my next lesson. It would be much easier to oblige her if I could locate the library.

I turn down a small corridor. At the end is a double doorway. The plaque above the doorframe reads ACADEMY LIBRARY.

At last.

I push open the heavy door and step inside. The room is dim. When my eyes adjust to the low light, my breath catches.

Several levels of bookshelves rise up around me in the enormous oval of a room. Wooden ladders rest on brass railways that circle the space. A narrow walkway bridges the upper levels, illuminated by a window high above that sends watery light slanting down through the dust motes.

There must be hundreds—no, thousands—of books. More than I could possibly read in a lifetime.

The library is deserted, no attendant in sight. Are Candidates allowed to borrow and read the books at will? The thought—me, a Candidate—feels new, unfamiliar, like a borrowed cloak I've pulled over my shoulders.

I move farther into the library. For the first time since arriving at Greybourne, I feel as though I can breathe.

I glance at the shelves, wondering how to locate Isherwood's book . . . and then something about being in this space tickles my memory. When Neville mentioned the Oxford professor, he'd said he wrote and published a great deal of his Morgana research. And he'd said something about investigating a cure.

I go to the shelves, which are in alphabetical order by author, and find my way to the *G* section in the upper gallery. *Professor Garrick* . . . I run my finger along the spines until I find what I'm seeking.

Tainted in the 18th and 19th Centuries by Reginald Garrick. My heart starts to beat faster. I pull the slim volume from the shelf and flip it open.

On the last page, there is a short note about the author:

> *Professor Garrick teaches and conducts his research*
> *at Balliol College at the University of Oxford.*

Oxford is only an hour's carriage ride away.

I page to the front of the book and scan the table of contents. There's a chapter on the "History of the Tainted," another on "Categorization of Abilities," and a section on "Research Into Blood Type."

Blood type? I don't have the first clue what that could mean.

The library door opens with a loud creak and I jump at the sudden noise.

Julian Blake strides into the library, one level below me.

CHAPTER EIGHTEEN

"The love of learning, the sequestered nooks,
And all the sweet serenity of books."
                    —Henry Wadsworth Longfellow,
                        "Morituri Salutamus"

I quickly tuck the book away, folding it into my cloak, and try to move deeper into the shelves, out of sight from Julian.

But I'm too late. He stops and his eyes go up to the gallery. "Ah, Miss Cole. Fancy seeing you here."

I step out from the shadows. "You're surprised?" I say icily. "You think I cannot read?"

He grins. "I think you could probably do anything you set your mind to, Miss Felicity Cole."

I say nothing, unsure how to respond.

"Right," he says. "Well, I'm going to search for a book. I'm thinking George Eliot. Or perhaps Dumas . . . But please, don't let me interrupt you. Carry on."

I watch him stroll away into the shelves, and then remember why I've come to the library. I need to retrieve Isherwood's book. I realize, with irritation, that my heart is thumping rather hard.

I move toward the *B*'s for Brimble—then run my finger along the shelf.

The small, dark slice meant to contain the book is empty. "No," I utter in exasperation, pushing against the shelf and sending several books tumbling.

Julian comes dashing around the corner.

"What's happened? I heard something fall—" He looks me up and down, his face flushed, then notices the books scattered around my feet. "You're not hurt."

"How observant."

He folds his arms across his chest. "I'd like to point out, Miss Cole, if you're going to be a secret agent, you really need to learn to hide your emotions a little better."

I smile, in spite of myself.

"What happened?" he asks. "Why the clamor?"

"The book I need isn't here. Isherwood expects me to have read the entire thing—"

"Which book?"

I show him the card on which *Social Etiquette for Young Ladies* is scrawled in Isherwood's hand.

"Oh, that old one. Don't worry, I can fill you in on anything you need to know. I've been forced to learn all of that nonsense from the time I could walk. I can teach you, if you'd like. Dumas can wait. . . ."

I want to refuse. I want to tell him that I can handle it myself just fine, thank you very much. But the truth is I need help. I need to learn so much before tomorrow and I've run out of options.

Over the next hour, Julian teaches me everything he knows about social etiquette. At first, I sit stiffly and say little. After a while, my shoulders begin to soften, like butter on toast.

He instructs me on introductions and the proper modes of address at a fancy dinner party. Then the etiquette of visiting. "When you're waiting in the parlor for the hostess to see you, never touch the piano—even if it's open."

I nod, listening carefully.

"Let's practice your curtsying," he says. "Show me what you can do."

As I rise with a wobble I see him cringe and then quickly mask it. "It's terrible, I know."

"Here, try this."

He executes a flawless curtsy.

I gape at him. "How did you learn—"

"Sisters," he says. "Here, I'll show you again."

As I watch Julian sink to the floor, I realize I know very little about his background, other than the whispered gossip of the other female Candidates. "How long have you been here at Greybourne, Mr. Blake?"

"First, please call me Julian. Since I was old enough that the Academy would allow me admission." He pauses, flashing a mischievous smile. "Actually, the truth is, I lied about my age so they'd let me enroll a year early."

"Weren't you ashamed? When you realized you were . . . different?"

He looks at me, confused. "Why would I be ashamed? My Morgana abilities make me who I am."

His expression shifts. His normally jovial tone disappears. I can tell this place means everything to him.

"You're very devoted to the Academy, aren't you?"

"Fiercely. Being Morgana is an honor, but it's also a responsibility. The world is full of darkness, Miss Cole. It is uniquely within our power to stop it."

A barb of guilt pierces me. My hopes for this place are much more . . . selfish. I simply want the means to survive. For me, and for Nate.

"If I'm to call you Julian, would you kindly call me Felicity? Well—not within Isherwood's hearing, perhaps."

He nods, and curtsies deeply.

I laugh.

Julian's expression grows serious again. "I want to explain my behavior the other day. In the carriage house."

"There's no need."

"All the same, I'd like you to understand. I was in disguise, you see, having just returned from an operation in the village—"

"Julian, it's fine. Although—why didn't you just tell me who you were at the time?"

He raises an eyebrow wickedly. "Now what fun would that be?"

My heart thumps, to my irritation. Then, unbidden, an image of Kit enters my thoughts, followed by a ripple of guilt. Kit, golden and smiling, dusted with soot, standing in the market before everything changed so dreadfully.

There's an awkward moment of silence. "Right," says Julian, brushing his hands together. "Now, where were we?"

"Um—"

"Dinner parties! Of course, all the tedious introductions can be somewhat tricky, but once you're through that, you're laughing. And once the dancing starts, you'll be fine."

I try to conceal the panic that I'm sure is washing over my face. But Julian doesn't appear to miss much. "Wait, you do know how to dance, don't you?"

I wring my hands. "I—"

"Come now, I'll show you."

Without another word, he takes me up in his arms. "You put your arm here. And I place my hand here . . ."

He moves our arms and hands into the correct positions and then he begins spinning me around the marble floor of the library. The heat from his body, close as it is, makes my cheeks burn.

"Relax, Felicity. Don't hold yourself so tense," he says. I take a deep breath.

After a few minutes, I begin to lose myself to the movement. There is no music, but it hardly matters. The shelves of books all around us go blurry, like a kaleidoscope, as he spins me. A bubbly feeling rises up inside my chest, not unlike the champagne I tasted my first night here.

And then, at last, Julian slows and we're standing in the middle of the library beneath the skylight. I realize that I am still clinging to his shoulders, and quickly take a step back.

"Thank you very kindly, Mr. Blake. I mean, Julian," I add, smoothing my skirts. "That was most instructional."

His mouth twitches. "You're most welcome, Miss Cole. I mean Felicity. I daresay you're ready to infiltrate the upper crust now. Nobody would ever suspect you weren't born in Chelsea."

I'd smile at the compliment but I'm too busy trying to breathe.

Instead, I attempt to stand straight and clear my throat. "You have done me a great service. At least Isherwood will be happy and can recommend me for the training exercises with the group now. . . ."

He cocks his head. "Which group are you being sent with?"

"Oh, Isherwood said something about an exercise at the opera but I don't know anything more than that. . . ."

My words die in my mouth. A shadow crosses Julian's face, his jaw tightening.

"What's the matter?" I ask.

"The opera is my exercise," he replies flatly, his face shuttered.

I open my mouth to say something more, but am unsure of my words. Maybe, in spite of his encouragement, he's afraid I will jeopardize the operation.

Or perhaps, although he doesn't mind being friendly in private, he has no desire to associate with me in public.

"Oh, well, that may not have been what she said. I can't be certain." I quickly gather my things. "Thank you again, Mr. Blake, for your time, but I must be going. Good day."

And with that, I turn and walk swiftly from the library, ignoring the twist in my stomach.

CHAPTER NINETEEN

"Why didn't you tell me there was danger? Why
didn't you warn me?"
—Thomas Hardy, *Tess of the D'Urbervilles*

The next several days do not go well.

Aside from my private deportment lessons with
Isherwood, the Candidates have an endless array of classes
and training sessions on topics including weaponry, surveil-
lance, covert communications, and of course combat. I am
terrible at all of it. I continue to be incapable of accessing
my abilities, and spend a great deal of time in the infirmary
for my troubles.

Our instructors work us without mercy. They stress to
us that it won't be long before the Candidates compete for
full agent status, and we must be prepared.

The only bright spot is the classes in foreign languages.
My father tried to teach me as a child, and growing up in
Whitechapel, I was surrounded by immigrants from every
corner of the globe. I learned the basics of French, Italian,

and even a little German under my father's tutelage, and then he arranged for me to practice with my neighbors until I was fluent.

In this area, I am far ahead of the other Greybourne trainees. It doesn't lessen the thrashings I receive in every other class.

Some evenings, after dinner, I have conversations with Professor Neville. He is tutoring me on the philosophies and finer points of intelligence work.

"Know thyself, know thy enemy," he says one evening in the drawing room. "It is Sun Tzu, *The Art of War*," Neville explains. Lamplight dances on the richly papered walls around us.

I nod, taking a slow breath. The air is heavy with sweet, smoky tobacco. The phrase reminds me of something. "The Huntsmen, I hardly know anything about them. Why did the Duke of Warwick come for me? What did he want? And how did the Huntsmen know I was in Whitechapel, anyway?"

Neville frowns. "Yes, that is a puzzle that would be useful to understand."

"Are they going to keep coming after me?"

"We have to assume so. But . . . you will be safe here, at Greybourne."

He says the words, but it feels like there's something unspoken beneath them, like the submerged depths of an iceberg. "Is there more I should know?"

He hesitates a fraction too long. But I'm in no position to demand answers from him. So far, he is one of my few allies. Besides, I'm barely even considered a Candidate.

I tuck the question away, adding it to the growing list of mysteries about this place.

Neville waves a hand, dismissing the subject. "What I really wish to discuss is this: to access your gift, you should try letting go."

"Sir?"

"I have been doing some reading on barriers to abilities like the one you've developed. Most people who have grown up—out there—have found various ways to resist and block their gift. This is, I surmise, what has happened with you. Embrace your gift. Do not fight it."

I don't know how to respond. Let go? I have no notion how to do that.

I arrive late to breakfast one day. All the other Candidates are already around the table, talking animatedly. I take my seat, and while I struggle to remember which is the egg spoon and which is the teaspoon, Charlie turns to me. "It seems you're finally going to get your chance to show off your mettle against the other Candidates, Felicity. We're going on a field training exercise this afternoon and you're coming with us."

My spoon clatters against my plate as I look up at Hawksmoor. Is it true?

He nods. "Indeed, we hope this will assist in unlocking your skills."

My stomach flutters. "What kind of training exercise?"

"You'll see."

I flick a glance at Julian. He's staring at his plate of toast with a stormy expression.

After breakfast, I report to the cellar for equipment fitting. This, at least, I'm excited about. I've heard about the equipment technician, Alistair Fergus—generally known by his code name Sig—but have yet to meet him, and I'm curious.

When the cellar door swings open at my knock, I'm greeted by a small man. His features are too large for his fine-boned face—wide eyes, a pointy nose, and a nest of spiky hair atop it all.

"Aha," he says, finger raised up in the air, "the enigmatic Miss Cole, at last." He has a heavy Scottish brogue.

Enigmatic? Me?

"Come in, come in," he urges, dragging me inside. The cellar, his workshop, is filled with brass gadgets and clockwork contraptions. Steam is coming from a piece of machinery I can't identify.

"Now, what are we going to need?" He scurries and darts around, gathering bits and pieces.

"Do you have any idea what this session involves? What we're to be doing?" I ask as he measures my waist.

"Hmm?" he says, looking up. "No, not the slightest. Could be almost anything, really. Of course, I don't believe they're down to the *elimination* stage yet. That'll come later. As I understand it, they're still just testing and training you Candidates."

"What do you mean, 'elimination stage'?"

"Why, when they begin trimming down the field of Candidates, one by one, until the single best qualified person emerges to be raised to full agent status."

He hums as he resumes his work, and I try to still the butterflies in my stomach.

An hour later, garbed in training gear, I'm waiting to settle into one of three carriages along with the other Candidates, before we set off for the countryside.

Just before I climb in, Rose pulls me aside.

"Are you quite certain you're up for this, Felicity?" she asks sweetly, her voice laced with false concern. "Are you perhaps . . . worried you'll be putting everyone at risk?" Her eyes widen, as though we're friends, even as her grasp tightens around my upper arm. "Maybe you should decline to come."

I shake her off me. "Hawksmoor insisted I be included. I'm sure he knows what he's doing."

I'm not about to share with Rose that I, too, have my doubts.

"Hawksmoor may know what he's doing," she says unpleasantly, her breath hot on my face, "but do *you*?"

Her haughty tone makes me bristle. I've already grown tired of her attempts to make me feel less than worthy.

"This isn't a game, Felicity," she sneers. "People can get hurt."

I wait a beat and cock my head. "Oh, I understand. But, dear Rose," I say lowering my voice to a stage whisper, "if you're frightened, I'm sure Hawksmoor won't force you—"

"I am not frightened," she says through clenched teeth. She turns her back to me and abruptly climbs into the carriage.

I catch Charlie's eye. He's grinning ear to ear. Julian's expression remains flat, but there is tension around his eyes. Is he worried about something?

I climb into the carriage I'm to share with Rose, Julian, Charlie, Hugh, and Hawksmoor. The rest of the Candidates are in their own coaches, heading to other locations for different training exercises. Another empty carriage follows our party. Charlie whispers to me that it's merely a precaution should the exercise go wrong. I try to ignore the ominous sound of that.

In spite of my brave words to Rose, my pulse thumps in my ears as we lurch forward.

As we leave the grounds, the carriage pauses and Hawksmoor leaps out, touching the standing stone that marks Graybourne's borders. He utters a word, and through the open door I hear him say, "*Pantos. Raphe. Ergon.*"

The words are Greek, but the combination is nonsense. I remember seeing Hawksmoor do the same thing when he first brought me here, although I couldn't hear what he'd uttered at the time.

"What was that?" I ask.

Julian leans over to me and whispers. "He's reactivating the shield that surrounds Greybourne. It's what keeps the Academy concealed from the general public."

"Magic?" I whisper back, but even as I say it I don't believe it.

Julian shakes his head. "It's one of Hawksmoor's gifts. A talent with matter and physical objects. Only he can create the shield. But the words would work for anyone, allowing them to enter or exit the grounds, or so I understand."

I commit the words to memory. They might be useful . . . someday.

As we wait for Hawksmoor to finish, Charlie turns to Julian. "Did you order those new binoculars Hawksmoor needs for the Jubilee operation?"

Julian nods. "Yes, but Sig agrees they're not quite right. We had to send them back."

Charlie frowns. "Is there enough time?"

"I think so. It's not until the twenty-second of June. We still have weeks yet."

Are they discussing the Golden Jubilee? The celebration of the fiftieth year of Queen Victoria's reign. Now that would be something to see. All those people, the festivities and celebration. "I had no idea the Morgana were to be involved in the Jubilee," I say.

Charlie nods. "It's going to be the devil of an event to protect," he says. "All those foreign dignitaries. All the muckety-mucks. But my friend here is prepared." He claps Julian on the back.

Julian scoffs. "I'm just doing a few errands for Hawksmoor. I'm not in charge."

Rose lets out a snort. "Of course you're not in charge. You're not even a full agent." Her voice is acid.

"How does a Candidate become a full agent?" I ask.

Rose gives me a look of disdain. "Oh, no need to worry about that, Felicity. You *won't* be involved." A serpent's smile twitches the corner of her mouth.

"Don't burst your staylace, Rose," I immediately fire back. "I have no interest. I'm merely curious."

Charlie hoots with laughter. "Now *that's* a proper insult."

At the mention of her undergarments, Rose's face has lost all color. I flash a grin at Charlie. Perhaps my uncouth background isn't always a disadvantage.

Julian clears his throat, hushing Charlie, then turns to me. "The final stage of our training will involve a series of field trials, during which the most capable Candidate will be selected." He nods once. "So you know."

I politely return his nod, then look away out the window.

Hawksmoor returns to the carriage and we drive out beyond the gates, traveling through the countryside for half an hour, before stopping near a long snake of track that trails away into the distance. A steam whistle announces a train approaching from far away.

"Pay attention," Hawksmoor barks. "Your training exercise today is this: you will all need to board that train, and then disembark."

There's a confused quiet.

"Right . . ." says Charlie. "Just—on and off?"

"Oh, did I not mention? The train won't be stopping," Hawksmoor adds.

"*What?*" Charlie sputters. "How on earth are we meant to—"

"That is exactly what you'll need to figure out," Hawksmoor says. "Off you go."

The blood drains from my face. The others climb out of the carriage and it's just me and Julian left. I'm about to tell Hawksmoor I can't possibly complete this task, when Julian clears his throat. "A moment, Hawksmoor." The spymaster waits for Julian to continue.

"I wonder if—I think maybe Felicity should stay here, with the carriage. I'm not sure she's ready for this."

Hawksmoor looks between us. Julian's words make my cheeks flush. It doesn't matter that I've been thinking the same thing; it's an entirely different matter when someone else voices it. I clench my fists. "I can do it," I say firmly.

Julian shifts. "It's going to be dangerous."

"Of course it is," I snap. "What point would there be otherwise?"

Hawksmoor has been watching this exchange silently. At last he says, "I think we'll just see for ourselves, shall we, Mr. Blake? Let's give her a chance."

Several minutes later, I regret my bravado. We've climbed up a hill to an overpass, where a tunnel burrows beneath. A great plume of steam rises up from the train in the distance. Green rolling hills and heather-covered pasture surround us, and a warm spring breeze stirs the grasses and rustles the fabric of my training gear.

I follow as the Morgana team moves into position with grace and speed, working together like finely constructed clockwork. I bite the inside of my cheek.

"What's the plan?" Charlie asks, turning to Julian.

Julian raises field glasses to his eyes and twists them into focus. He hands them down the line so we can all look.

"We aim for those three cars there," Julian says pointing, as Charlie hands me the field glasses. "The three black cargo cars. Before you jump, bend your knees. When you hit the car, hang on." I swallow, looking through the sights, my eyelashes brushing the glass. So that's it. We'll be jumping onto the moving train as it passes into the tunnel beneath us.

Julian pairs up Hugh and Charlie, and decides that Rose will go alone. "Felicity, you're with me," he says. Rose's face pinches. "Once we're all onboard, we'll make our way to the hatch in the rear car. Whatever you do, don't fall off."

"Not to state the obvious," Charlie says, with a smirk.

The train is approaching quickly. Within a minute, it's sliding beneath our feet, churning into the tunnel.

Hugh goes first. Then Charlie. They land solidly, though Charlie stumbles slightly. I spin and see them emerge on the other side of the tunnel. Charlie waves. They've made it.

Rose hunches down, preparing to jump. "Watch your footing, Felicity," she shouts over the thundering of the train. "Wouldn't want to fall." She flashes me a smug smile, but before I can respond, she leaps. She lands like a cat. I can tell she used Aristos, like the others. My mouth goes dry. It's my turn.

A strong wind rises up from the speeding train and whips my hair. Now is the time I need to latch on to my ability. I reach out, but I have no idea what I'm reaching for.

"Just try to let go," says Julian, crouching behind me. "It'll come to you. . . ."

I try again, but nothing happens. I tighten my jaw, wanting to scream. "I can't. It's not there."

"If we wait for the coal car—that'll be much easier. Messier, but definitely easier."

"All right. Maybe . . ."

Julian grabs me by the shoulders. "Listen, Felicity. You don't have to do this. We'll just tell Hawksmoor it wasn't safe."

I hate backing down, but it's so tempting. I can't do this. I can't, no matter what Hawksmoor thinks.

And then a movement catches the corner of my vision. I turn. Five men on horseback are galloping across the open countryside, straight toward us, weapons flashing in the sun.

When I turn back, Julian's face has drained of color.

"Huntsmen." I gasp, my heart slamming into my ribs.

"Those aren't Huntsmen."

"Then who are they?"

"I've changed my mind," he says abruptly. "We're getting on this train. Now."

"Julian, who *are* they?"

"No time to explain. Trust me, we do not want to make their acquaintance."

I swallow and take another quick glance at the men galloping closer.

Aristos or no, there's only one option open to me now. Our carriage is gone—far away, by now. Surely making its way to our rendezvous spot.

"I'll be right behind you," Julian says.

I know the coal car is still too far away. We won't have time to wait before the horsemen get here. We'll have to jump on the roof of the regular cars.

"Ready? Go!"

I bend my knees and jump, hurling myself into the air.

143

CHAPTER TWENTY

"No coward soul is mine,
No trembler in the world's storm-troubled sphere . . ."
—Emily Brontë, "No Coward Soul is Mine"

My stomach flips as I fall. The train comes up fast, and then my feet are crashing onto the roof. The momentum keeps moving me forward and I start sliding toward the edge. Breathless, everything is happening so fast. I can't even scream—

And then a hand clamps around my wrist. I stop sliding. *Julian.*

He's there, holding me fast to the roof, steadying me with Aristos strength and his unwavering gaze. The wind whips his hair and his cloak flaps behind him.

"Hang on," he hollers over the train's whistle. "We're all right."

My heart thumps for several reasons. I can't help feeling angry with myself for being so weak, for needing to be rescued.

As we steady ourselves, I look for signs of the horsemen.

They're far behind us—atop the overpass. One of them punches an angry fist in the air.

Julian wrenches open the hatch and we clamber down into what turns out to be a storage car. It's filled with sacks of grain, oats, flour, and sugar. The sweet smell hangs in the air, and the light is dusty—flour-streaked.

The car is quiet apart from the faint clacking coming from outside. I am dimly aware that this is only my second time on a train in my life.

"So," I begin, once I have caught my breath, "who were they, exactly?"

Julian grimaces, his mouth in a tight line. "There was a girl. I was courting her. It was part of a training operation. I was undercover, you see. But . . . she became rather attached. And it turned out her family wasn't all that nice."

"And that was the family?"

He nods grimly. "Her brothers."

We don't have time to linger. We must find the others.

We make our way through the train, passing through more storage cars. Julian and I cross the outside connections between each car as quickly as we can; the wheels thundering over the tracks are deafening. I struggle to hold onto my nerves as I maneuver the narrow, jostling connectors.

At last, we reach a passenger car. A corridor lines the left side, with compartments to the right, similar to the train Hawksmoor and I took from London.

I go first, glancing through each small compartment window we pass. Halfway through the car, I spot Rose in a cabin with a man I don't recognize.

In the very next instant, I watch as Rose slips up behind the man and drags a six-inch blade across his throat. Dark red blood gushes out and the man flops to the seat; he doesn't move.

I freeze, gaping.

Julian is behind me now. He rips open the door to the compartment. "Rose, what the bloody hell have you done?"

She looks at him calmly. "You have your assignment, and I have mine."

I glance in horror at the dead man slumped across the seat. Bile rises in my throat and I turn away.

"Does Hawksmoor know about this?" Julian demands.

"Who do you think gave me the assignment?"

Julian stares at the man. "Who—who was that?"

"A worthless conspirator. On his way from a meeting to plot the assassination of the Archbishop of Canterbury."

Julian stares at the corpse.

"You should be happy, Julian. Two training exercises in one." She flashes a bright smile. "I get to practice my assassination skills . . . and you get to practice leading a team— even when the plan goes a little awry."

"A little—?" Julian stammers. "You just *killed* a man. That was not part of the plan."

"Exactly. Now show some flexibility. A little . . . thinking on your feet. Because I have to tell you—I do believe he has friends on the train . . ."

Julian grabs Rose by the arm. "We'll deal with this later, once we've completed the mission. We're approaching the gorge."

But instead of exiting the compartment, Rose flings open the door to the outside. Wind rushes in.

"What are you doing?" Julian demands.

"Too risky to climb back through the train. I'm going to crawl along the exterior and meet Charlie and Hugh in the caboose. We can get off that way, jump from the back. I suggest you do the same."

My stomach clenches as she disappears from sight.

"I can't do it," I say to Julian, little more than a harsh whisper. The wind from the open door rushes in my ears, deafening, disorienting me. I can't crawl along the side of a moving locomotive.

His expression is grim. "Fine," he says. "We'll go through the train."

As we exit the compartment, Julian takes the lead. No sooner have I set foot in the corridor than three men are flooding into the space from the adjacent car, hats pulled down low, obscuring their faces.

Julian turns and pushes me back into the compartment, slamming the door closed and snapping the latch shut.

"The brothers again?" I say, breathless.

Julian's mouth forms a tight line. "Not this time."

"The dead man's friends?"

A single tight shake of Julian's head. My mouth goes dry. *Huntsmen.*

I back up and my legs bump against the knees of the dead man. The air is thick with the metallic scent of blood. We're trapped.

Within a moment, they are at our compartment door. The flimsy latch doesn't hold, and the door springs open. They stand there, crowbars glinting in their hands. I recognize the lead man immediately—thick mustache, glossy hat, dead eyes.

The Duke of Warwick.

He looks first at Julian, and then at me.

"Just give her to us," Warwick says. "We'll let you go, Mr. Blake. She's no use to you, anyway."

For a heart-stopping second, I wonder if Julian is going to do as they ask. But he tucks me behind his back. "I shouldn't think so."

My skin blazes as I realize that Warwick talks about me like an object to be traded. In a dark corner of my mind, there's a brief flicker of curiosity—such persistence—what on *earth* do they want me for, anyway?

If there was ever a time to channel my ability, it's now. What have I been told? *Let go.*

I try. Nothing happens.

"You have three seconds," Warwick says, his voice a low, warning growl.

There's only one thing to do. I grasp for the handle of the exterior door and fling it open, grabbing Julian's hand. He turns and our eyes connect. He knows what I mean to do.

We launch off the edge together, and fall, straight down toward the gorge far below, stomachs tumbling. . . .

CHAPTER TWENTY-ONE

"Solitude was my only consolation—deep, dark, deathlike solitude."

—Mary Shelley, *Frankenstein*

Far below, I plunge straight in the icy water, feet first. Darkness and bubbles swallow me, the water stealing my breath as I sink, but I right myself and kick hard, swimming back toward the surface.

As it happens, my father taught me how to swim. No self-respecting Greek, having grown up on an island in the Aegean, would allow his daughter to be uncomfortable in water.

My head breaks the surface just before Julian's does.

I take great gulps of air, twisting in the water to catch sight of the Huntsmen. Will they follow us down?

The train is curving along the bridge on the far side of the gorge now. Two men dive from the train. If they're strong swimmers, they'll be upon us in a few minutes.

"Julian! We have to go!" I gasp, between gulps of water.

We swim with all our strength to the side of the gorge and haul ourselves out onto the grassy bank fringing the water. Dripping and soaked through, we look for an escape route. The Huntsmen are swimming a direct line to us.

Which way should we run?

A carriage careens over a hill, horses churning up the dusty road. Hawksmoor.

The carriage slows, but does not stop, as Hawksmoor flings open the door and we leap on. The driver cracks his whip and we're away.

Through the rear window, I see the Huntsmen emerge from the water, dripping. I can just make out the rage that contorts their features. They grow rapidly smaller as we speed across the landscape.

When I am sure we're safe, I turn back in my seat and exhale. Julian tucks a blanket around my shoulders, sitting close beside me and gazing at me with concern. "Are you all right, Felicity? You must be freezing." I look up into his face and note the blue tinge to his own lips.

Hawksmoor, seated opposite, watches us carefully. "A well-executed escape, you two. You should be proud."

Terror that was previously singing through my bones has subsided to a low hum, making me aware of something else. A certain . . . exhilaration?

"What the bloody hell was that?" Julian demands, turning on Hawksmoor. "Giving Rose a secret assignment? An *assassination?* If my team has side operations, I need to know—"

"*Not* your team, Mr. Blake," Hawksmoor says, leaning in close. His voice is quiet, his words pointed. "*My* team. *My* agents. And I do with them as I please. When you are in charge—should that ever come to pass—then these decisions will be yours. Currently, they are mine."

Julian's eyes widen, but he snaps his jaws shut and says nothing more.

"The spare carriage will fetch the others," Hawksmoor says. "We will debrief when we return to Greybourne."

We ride the rest of the way back to the Academy in silence.

⚜

In spite of the disaster that was my field exercise—or perhaps because of it—I am still required to attend combat training classes. And, little by little, I do learn some techniques: rudimentary assassination maneuvers, and how to handle myself in a fight.

I hear nothing more about Rose's assignment on the train—her secret, private assignment that subverted our training exercise—but she is unbearable because of it. Walking around like a peacock, regarding herself as the most important of us all.

And, I have to accept, she may well be. The truth is, she was successful. She did what we are here to do. Hawksmoor must be pleased with her. Surely she's now the lead Candidate.

I wonder what privileges that might mean for her, if Hawksmoor will share with her secrets he keeps hidden from the rest of us. Not for the first time, I consider: what if that were me, instead?

I spend my spare moments poring over Garrick's book on the Tainted, trying to wring clues from it.

I think about Nate all the time. I try to communicate with him, but every evening when I stagger back to my room, I am too exhausted and there is no connection. There are a few times I manage to snatch a brief conversation, a few pleasant words, just enough for me to be satisfied that he is safe, content, and well cared for. Then I flop face-first into my soft feather bed and fall into a deep sleep.

After one particularly grueling day of physical training, during which I managed to narrowly beat my opponent with a rather clever feint, if I do say so myself, we settle into our places in the dining room for our evening meal. I sigh with pleasure as I take a seat; I finally feel like I'm becoming comfortable with the routines here.

The first course arrives, and I am delighted to see something I recognize for once: a plate of oysters. Pickled oysters from the fishmonger's stand were a staple of life in Whitechapel. But as I take my first bite, I frown.

I lean over to Charlie, seated on my right, and speak in a low voice. "I'm not certain the cook pickled the oysters correctly. These taste a little odd . . ."

Charlie looks at me, confused for a moment, and then his lips twitch as he struggles to suppress a grin. He opens his mouth to explain when Rose, ears ever pricked for a blunder, laughs. "Honestly, Felicity. We don't eat *pickled* oysters. How horrible. Oysters are most properly served fresh." She lifts a delicate oyster, swallows it with a simpering smile, and turns to Hugh who is seated at her left. "Hopeless," she mutters, although she knows full well I can hear her.

"Well, what did you expect?" Hugh says to Rose, glancing haughtily at me. He adds nothing about me coming from the streets, from Whitechapel. But he doesn't have to.

I can't muster the strength for a decent retort. I attempt to eat another oyster, but it sticks in my throat. Somehow, I make it through the meal, but excuse myself before dessert is served.

It's no easy feat to sneak away—my movements are constantly tracked and monitored—and I have to feign illness to keep from being suspected of something more.

Some time later I sit in my nightgown on the windowsill. Candles illuminate the room with a warm, flickering light. I press my face close to the cool glass and stare out at the shadowy hills that surround Greybourne.

I try to reach out to find my brother . . . and at first, there is nothing.

And then I hear a faint voice. *Felicity?*

Nate, thank goodness, I say, the tension melting from my shoulders. *It's so good to hear your voice.*

You sound strange. What's the matter?

Nothing. I swallow. *Listen, I need to tell you something important. Someday, I'm going to escape this place and come to get you.*

What are you talking about? Why would you want to escape?

I don't belong here. This was a mistake. But it's one I can fix. I'm alive, after all, and so are you. It'll be just you and me, like it should be. A lump forms in my chest as I think of it.

Did something happen?

I bite my lip. It's always been impossible to hide anything from my brother. *Nate, this isn't my world. Not only am I incapable of using my ability, I . . . simply don't fit in here. I never will.*

He is quiet a moment. *What do you mean you can't use your ability?*

I wave a hand, though I know he can't see me. *Never mind. That doesn't matter. The point is, we are going to go home soon—*

Felicity, stop. My brother's voice is gentle and so quiet I almost can't hear it. *You can do this. I know you can.*

I shake my head. *No. I can't.* I tighten my hands, grabbing large fistfuls of my nightgown. Frustrated tears prickle my eyes.

We can't go home yet, Felicity. What if the Huntsmen come after us? How will we get away if you don't finish your training?

I don't tell him about my encounter on the train. There's no need to upset him.

Instead, I set my jaw and stare out the window.

You always tell me to try, he says. *We'll be together again. But can you try . . . one more time?*

I'm quiet for a while. There's a kernel of truth in his words. Learning to control Aristos may be the best way for us to survive. But embracing it would mean taking one more step away from my old life. And that's the last thing I want to do.

A sudden memory tumbles over me. My last morning in Whitechapel Market, the first day of spring, before everything changed. The cold, pale sunlight, the aroma of leek stew bubbling at Mrs. Pennyworth's soup cart as I rounded the corner with my basket full of blooms. The air dense with the chatter of sellers hawking their wares. Even fighting with Beatrice, the rage on her face as I tried to stand my ground . . .

It was not an easy life, but it was mine. And I want it back.

Nothing here at Greybourne makes any sense. The rules, the customs, the dangers—it's all bewildering. In this world, I'm not in control of anything. Least of all my own abilities.

For you, Nate, I say, at last. *I'll try one more time, for you.*

For such a tiny boy, he certainly is a wise little thing.

But there was something else he said that worries me. It takes me a moment to catch it—when he said we'd be together again. A nagging pain gnaws at my stomach. A sudden panic, clawing up my throat.

What if I never see Nate again?

CHAPTER TWENTY-TWO

"Honest people don't hide their deeds."
—Emily Brontë, *Wuthering Heights*

The next night I awaken, with a start, just past midnight. I'm not sure what has awoken me, but I can't get back to sleep. There's too much on my mind. Too many unanswered questions.

I rise and dress in my training gear. And when I'm sure everyone has gone to their rooms and the corridors are quiet, I slip out.

I don't know what I'm looking for, exactly, but I know where I'm going to start: the entrance to that secret passage I saw Hugh Torrington pass through the other day. I want to know where it leads.

I reach the hidden doorway underneath the staircase and, after pulling the lever, slip inside. There's no sign anyone has seen me. Lanterns illuminate the walls of a narrow tunnel, but they are few and spaced far apart. I creep along the dim passageway through the musty-smelling air, carefully watching my footing.

The only sound is the whisper of my own footsteps. A cobweb brushes my face, and I suddenly jump. I pause, swipe the sticky strands away, then gather my nerves and keep pressing forward.

A narrow stone staircase spirals, barely wide enough to descend.

When I reach the end, I can see a sliver of light. Muffled voices grow louder.

I move closer, taking care to be quiet. A tapestry covers a larger gap in the wall, and the voices are clearer now. I recognize some of them and my mouth goes dry.

I crouch to peer through the narrow gap between the wall and the heavy fabric. I can only make out half of the room. A large stone table occupies its center; arranged around it are the Greybourne Elders: Hawksmoor, Neville, Isherwood, and Sig. But there are others there, too, young men and a woman I don't recognize.

". . . and the preparations for the Jubilee," Hawksmoor is saying. "How are they coming along?"

"Not well," says a reed-slim man with sharp cheekbones. I've never seen him before. "To be frank, it's an enormous event, and there are a great number of risks to manage."

I press my lips together. This conversation is not meant for my ears. I should turn away, go back the way I came. I know I'm supposed to be training to be a spy, but eaves-dropping still feels wrong to me. It's also dangerous. If I get caught . . .

"We are terribly shorthanded, sir, and in desperate need of another agent," the slim man says.

Hawksmoor nods solemnly. "Agreed, but it needs to be the right agent. I will not put a man into the position who is not ready for the task. I would rather have five highly skilled and capable field agents than ten who aren't up to snuff."

"I couldn't agree more," Isherwood says.

"If we had one more full-fledged agent, though, that would make all the difference in the operation."

"In that case," Hawksmoor says, "we'll have to acceler-ate the selection process,"

Neville clears his throat. "There are some excellent Candidates among our senior students."

"Yes, but I wonder if we agree about the excellence of the same ones," Hawksmoor muses.

"We'll begin the final stages of testing the moment you give the word, Hawksmoor," Isherwood says, shifting in her seat and giving a sharp nod toward the slim man.

"While we're gathered, do we have any further reports on the recent rumors of the so-called cure?"

There is much shuffling of papers and clearing of throats. Somebody at the far end of the table is saying some-thing, but I can't quite make it out. I press myself even closer to the tapestry.

"I have been hearing talk of a weapon being developed for use against the Morgana—" Isherwood says.

I shift to see her better, and the heel of my shoe catches on the edge of a floorboard. My hands reach out to grab for something, anything, to stop me falling forward into the tapestry. But I clutch at air, tumbling into the fabric, before sprawling out into the room, a dozen of pairs of eyes on me.

I squeeze my own eyes shut. How I wish this were a bad dream.

"Miss Cole," says Hawksmoor in an ominous tone, "were you eavesdropping on the Elders?"

I have nothing to say. As I scramble to stand up, Humphrey Neville barks out a laugh.

"Really, I think she should be punished more because of her failure to eavesdrop properly than the fact that she *was* eavesdropping," he says. The others glare at him. "What? Isn't that the sort of behavior we encourage here at Greybourne?"

Hawksmoor turns away from him with a grunt and fixes me with a fierce glare. "Report to my office first thing in the morning, Miss Cole. We will discuss this privately."

CHAPTER TWENTY-THREE

"It seemed as if my tongue pronounced words without my will consenting to their utterance: something spoke out of me over which I had no control."

—Charlotte Brontë, *Jane Eyre*

A few days later, my hands are raw and chapped and my knees and shoulders ache from the interminable hours I've spent scrubbing the kitchen floors. And cleaning the hearths. And washing the windows.

Hawksmoor has stripped me of my status as Candidate. Neville assured me it will be temporary, but nobody has told me how long my punishment is to last.

I hear the patter of heels across the marble floor I'm polishing. "Right," Isherwood says sternly, stopping at my side, gazing down at me like a falcon surveying prey from a high branch. "That's enough of that."

I stare up at her, confused. "Chop-chop, girl. We haven't all day."

I scrabble to my feet.

She leads me to the war room, where Hawksmoor tells me to ready myself for a journey to Oxford, to the opera. I will be joining the Candidates on a reconnaissance training exercise.

My penance is over.

He hands me a small purse of coins. "You may need this. You must be prepared, no matter what you encounter."

As I reach the door, Hawksmoor stops me. "That was your warning, Miss Cole. One more slip, and it will be your end."

Two hours later, I'm climbing into a carriage. I adjust the scratchy lace at my wrists and smooth the silk bodice of my gown. As I wait for the others to arrive, I fidget in my seat. This will be my first time out in the wider world after Hawksmoor engineered my false execution. My first attempt to pass myself off as a lady. And worse—I have my own mission tonight that no one can know about. A trickle of sweat drips beneath my stiff collar.

I hear Charlie and Julian approach the carriage, their boots crunching over the gravel, as they joke and carry on, taunting each other about who will be more successful at this evening's mission. We are to eavesdrop on a secret meeting between a known conspirator and his mystery accomplice. At the sight of me already seated in the carriage, Julian sucks in a breath, clearly surprised to see me. I flush, remembering his words to me in the library, his warning to Hawksmoor before our last training exercise. I give him my haughtiest look. He opens his mouth to say something, but I am faster.

"I do apologize, Mr. Blake. I know you don't approve of me joining this mission, but it looks as though you and Hawksmoor are to have yet another difference of opinion."

"Miss Cole, I think perhaps you misunderstand—"

"I don't believe I do," I say frostily.

Julian snaps his jaw shut. Charlie snorts. "Felicity, remind me to never get on your bad side."

I turn to face the window and try my best not to smile.

The rest of the journey I focus on what's to come next, because I have a very specific plan. My heart races as I run through the steps over and over in my mind. I won't get a second chance.

After an hour's drive, we enter Oxford. It is a magical city of church bells and dreaming spires, honey-colored buildings and cobbled lanes. The horses' hooves clop over a bridge that arches across the Thames, a gentle silvery ribbon this far away from London. Small boats punt along the river, their occupants savoring the early evening air. Our carriage pulls up to the gracefully curved drive in front of the opera house.

As we promenade up the stairs into the theater, I hear strains of music and laughter coming from inside the impressive building.

Just before the entrance, we rejoin the other Candidates. "Oh dear, Felicity," says Rose, "how uncomfortable you must feel. Is this your first time out in Society?"

I keep my chin up. "It is. And your . . . *concern* is too kind."

She eyes my gown ever so briefly. "Ah, I see Jane isn't terribly experienced with selecting the proper attire for an evening such as—"

"Rose, be quiet," snaps Julian. "She looks perfect."

I blink, but say nothing as we move through the doorway and into a magnificent foyer of glittering chandeliers and sweeping staircases, filled with patrons moving gracefully in jewel-colored gowns and sharp black suits.

We make our way, pausing for polite introductions—which I manage to navigate, somehow—into the theater itself. I'm seated in one of the lower boxes along with Hugh and Charlie. The others, including Julian, are in the gallery, farther back. We've split up for reconnaissance, but it's a formation I will be able to exploit for my own purposes.

As the red velvet curtain rises, my breath catches. Violins and flutes come to life as the orchestra swells. Gaslit footlights paint the stage gold. An enchanted forest, branches twisted with flickering candles, spreads before the audience.

A man on stage opens his mouth and a miraculous sound issues forth. For a moment, I forget all about my plans. I am lost, soaring on a magic carpet of music and costumes and lights.

And then I come back to myself. It's time.

I lean over and whisper to Hugh, not Charlie—he'd likely offer to accompany me, and this is something I must do alone.

"I have a headache," I whisper. "I'm going to join the others in the gallery. A little farther back, I think."

Hugh glances at me, annoyed, nods, then looks away. Perfect.

The usher assists me into the lobby. I fan myself with my hand, doing my best impression of someone about to swoon. "My goodness," I say, "I'm feeling quite overcome." He looks at me uncertainly. "Perhaps I'll take some air . . ."

"Is there anything you require, miss?"

"I'll be fine I'm sure, but, please—how long before the first intermission?"

"First intermission occurs in approximately one hour."

I move toward the front entrance and the usher disappears.

And then Julian steps out from a doorway. "I saw you leave. Are you quite all right?"

I clench a fist but am careful to keep my expression masked. "Actually, I have something of a headache. Do you think—could you find an usher and have him bring me some water? I'm just going to lie down on the divan in the powder room. You should get back to the others."

He looks at me with concern.

"No need to worry, Mr. Blake," I reassure him.

Reluctantly, Julian turns away. As soon as he's out of sight, I dart back down the marble staircase and out into the cool night air.

Under quickly darkening skies, I nimbly climb into one of the hansom cabs that line the curved drive. "To Oxford University, please. Balliol College."

CHAPTER TWENTY-FOUR

"With stammering lips and insufficient sound
I strive and struggle to deliver right
the music of my nature."

—Elizabeth Barrett Browning,
"The Soul's Expression"

Several minutes later, the hansom cab approaches Balliol College and stops in front of the main building, an imposing structure of honey-colored stone.

I climb from the carriage and hurry toward the entrance.

A porter stops me at the front gate. "May I help you, miss?"

"I'm here to meet my uncle," I say, more confidently than I feel, in the poshest accent I can muster.

"Name?"

"Professor Reginald Garrick. But—would you permit me to announce myself?" I flash him my warmest smile. "I'm hoping to surprise him, you see. I've just returned from the continent, a week ahead of schedule, and I have ever so many stories to tell. . . ."

The porter's eyes glaze over as I ramble. I keep going until he ushers me through the gate, eager to be away with me.

Inside the main building, I lift my skirts and rush along the corridor, catching glimpses of the manicured quadrangle lawn around which the old buildings are arranged. I tracked down some maps of Oxford University in our library at Greybourne, the only reason I know where I'm going.

It's a long shot, I know. It's unlikely the professor will be here, after hours. But perhaps there will be a way of getting a message to him.

When I arrive at the laboratory and push open the door, I enter a world apart. Specimens in large glass bottles and apothecary jars adorn the shelves, and a chalkboard fills the front wall, every inch covered with chalk scratchings, formulas, and diagrams. The air is sharp with the smells of wood polish and turpentine. Books and clocks and unidentifiable devices occupy every spare surface.

But the room is empty. My heart sinks. I glance at one of the ticking clocks. I have around thirty minutes.

"May I help you?" I spin around. A man in a brown tweed suit stands in the doorway. He sports a thick gray mustache and muttonchop whiskers, and he has, perhaps, the bushiest eyebrows I have ever seen, like two woolly caterpillars, which sit above a pair of piercing eyes.

"Oh yes, I'm looking for Professor Garrick." I hardly dare hope that this is the man himself.

He looks at me uncertainly. "And what business is it that you have with the professor?"

"I must speak with him about a delicate subject related to his work. The matter is rather . . . confidential."

His eye twitches a little. "You are Morgana, I presume."

I stare. "You can tell?" I blurt out before I can stop myself. I press my lips into a tight line, resolving to say no more.

He gives the faintest of shrugs. "I've seen this too many times before. And I'm afraid you're most unlucky, Miss . . ."

"Cole. Felicity Cole."

". . . and you've wasted your effort in coming here."

I try not to betray my disappointment. "Oh, I see. You're not Professor Garrick."

"No, my dear. I am he. But I have nothing to tell you about the Morgana."

"Professor Garrick, I understand your reluctance—"

"No, you *don't* understand. You must leave. Go back to the Morgana."

"But that's just the problem. I don't belong with them."

His abundant eyebrows rise and his mouth opens slightly. "You don't . . . *wish* to be Morgana? You're speaking of the cure."

"Yes, exactly."

He rubs the side of his face absently as conflicting emotions flicker over his features.

I hesitate, suddenly unsure how forthcoming I should be with this man. Although it's true Humphrey Neville vouched for him, he is a stranger to me. But I've come this far . . .

"I need to get my old life back," I say. "I need everything to be returned to the way it was."

"I'm sorry, Miss Cole. I'd like to help you. But the truth is, I don't study the Morgana any longer. It became too dangerous."

"What do you mean?"

"My lab, it was ransacked. All of my papers stolen. It was a stroke of luck that I wasn't there at the time."

"Who would do such a thing?"

"Who do you think?"

Huntsmen.

"But, Professor Garrick, it's because of that danger that I need to find a cure. I'm sure they won't leave me alone now that they know of my existence, and eventually they'll find my brother. I have to keep him safe. I promised my father."

"Your father, he was Morgana also?"

I shake my head. "But he knew the danger my brother faced. It worried him constantly. I'm only thankful Father died before I found out I was Tainted, too." My voice catches on the word.

Professor Garrick gives me a sympathetic look. "One thing I can tell you, Miss Cole. To find a cure, you must first learn the *why*."

"That's exactly what I've been trying to find out. But nobody seems to have any answers."

His eyes twinkle and the smile lines in his face deepen. "Perhaps not. But some of us did come close. It's possible the answer is just around the corner."

"Yes?"

"My partner and I were very interested in the teachings of Darwin, and how they relate to the Morgana."

He erases a patch on the chalkboard and starts drawing. Chalk dusts his fingers and his jacket. He wipes a hand across his face, and chalk smears the end of his nose.

"One theory is that the Morgana and regular humanity evolved separately long ago, like Darwin's finches. Not an intentional process, but a natural one. My colleague and I were investigating that hypothesis until, as I said, it became too dangerous."

"But . . . that doesn't suggest a cure, does it?" I ask, swallowing my disappointment.

"Well, there was another theory that one of our associates in London was exploring. I believe it centered around an illness, comparable to plague."

I look up sharply. I had a similar idea not long ago.

"But, as I said," Professor Garrick continues, "I haven't done any work in this field for a year or more. I have lost contact with any remaining researchers."

"So . . . you don't know if anyone is still researching the origins of the Morgana?"

"I don't. But I will give it some thought, shall I?"

I like the idea of illness being the source. The effects of an illness could be reversed, perhaps. Which means I could go home. Nate and I could return to our lives, just like before.

I glance at the brass clock on the laboratory wall, and my stomach clenches. "I have to go," I say. "If you think of anything, would you please contact me? I'm at Greybourne Academy. It's protected of course, but"—I pause, chewing my lip—"I know how to get in."

He nods. "Very well."

"You must only use it if it's urgent," I add. "And if you ever have need of it, you must say you're an acquaintance of Humphrey Neville when you arrive."

"Why?"

"They won't trust you otherwise."

I try to convince myself it isn't entirely a lie. After all, Neville had been the one who recommended I speak with Professor Garrick.

Several minutes later, I race out of Balliol College. With a little luck, I'll be back just in time.

Clouds have rolled in and a light drizzle has begun. I squander a few minutes trying to hail a hansom cab, but after wasting time with little success, realize I'll have to go back on foot if I'm ever to make it in time. I can run quickly.

I hurry through the darkened streets of Oxford. Gas lamps create halos in the dark mist. Old stone university buildings soon give way to small shops. The sounds of horse-drawn carriages tromping along the narrow streets keep me company.

A lantern flickers overhead and then wicks out.

I look around and realize I'm in a less than savory part of town. Litter clogs the gutters and old buildings are in various states of disrepair. I glance down at my finery. I look a juicy target, that's for certain. Speeding my step, I cut through an alley to recover the main road.

A faint scrape sounds behind me.

Continuing forward, I glance over my shoulder. Nothing. Just the shadows of the street.

Cold trickles through me and I keep moving, faster now. Up ahead, I spot the bridge that I believe leads to the high street.

My gaze remains fixed ahead. Fingers of mist creep onto the bridge from the river below. I'm almost there. I hear another scrape behind me, but again when I turn, nobody is there.

As I step onto the bridge, I exhale with relief. And then a figure steps into my path, blocking the way.

I gasp at the hulking form of a man, his face masked in shadow. I square my shoulders and speak in a loud, clear voice. "Out of my way. I have somewhere important to be, and I don't need any trouble."

A second figure appears out of the mist. His black top hat gleams in the gaslight.

"We don't need any trouble either, Miss Cole. Which is why you'll find it's best that you come with us."

The men take a step forward and their faces are suddenly illuminated: the Duke of Warwick and one of his fellow Huntsmen from the train.

CHAPTER TWENTY-FIVE

"'We must not look at goblin men,
We must not buy their fruits:
Who knows upon what soil they fed
Their hungry thirsty roots?'"
—Christina Rossetti, "The Goblin Market"

I turn to flee the way I came, but another figure materializes out of the mist, blocking my way. Another Huntsman.

They must have followed me from the opera house or the university. I don't know. But it doesn't matter. I must get away.

The men flash crocodile grins as they close in. Their eyes gleam with certain success. They expect this to be easy.

I reach out for Aristos, desperate for the one thing that might help me. But—as always—I find nothing. Warwick carries a dangling length of rope; the other men hold knives. No pistols. I'm not surprised. Nothing would bring the local authorities quicker than the crack of gunshots.

Still, I'm not going to make it easy for my assailants.

Warwick comes at me first with a nasty smile, holding the rope, ready to bind me. I kick at his legs—I haven't spent my time in training sessions learning nothing. He grunts and falls back, eyes widening with surprise.

A sound behind me gives me a second's warning, and I duck. The man flies past, overshooting his target, and lands sprawled on the pathway with a grunt. Hope bubbles up, briefly—maybe I can fight my way out of this. . . .

And that hope then quickly disappears as I feel my arms jerked violently behind my back and my feet lift off the ground. Warwick's voice murmurs in my ear, "This time you're coming with us." He laughs—a low, chilling sound. "You're not going to like it." Terror claws at my throat.

I am dragged backward. The men close in around me.

Just then shouts cleave the air. The bridge is suddenly filled as people clamber up and over the bridge railings. There must be five or six of them, moving so fast, limbs and weapons flashing. I catch a glimpse of one—Julian.

How did the Morgana team find me?

I scream to be released, and Charlie is there, knocking down my captor with one swift blow. Immediately, I drop and tear the ropes from my wrists. Once more, I try to call for Aristos but there is nothing. I will be no help to the other Candidates, the real Morgana.

I spot a lamppost with a broad base on the other side of the bridge and dart behind it, crouching down, hiding.

As I watch the mayhem, something small flies from one of the Huntsmen's cloaks and falls at my foot. It glimmers with a dull metallic sheen. I quickly grab at it, but it's only a cloak pin.

But on closer examination, it carries a distinctive pattern. Familiarity whispers in my ear, although I can't think why. I tuck the pin away in the folds of my cloak.

As the skirmish continues, I try to discern the identities of the Candidates who've come to my rescue: there's Julian, and Charlie, of course. I also make out Hugh and Rose and two others I don't know well, but who were with us on our mission.

The struggle lasts only moments. Apparently, the Huntsmen weren't looking for a fight. Just an easy capture.

As quickly as they arrived, they retreat, dropping over the side of the bridge.

Warwick is the last to go. Before he drops over the side, he looks straight at me. "Don't worry, Miss Felicity Cole. We will see each other again soon."

I lean over—two small boats bob in the water, and the men rapidly row away. Why were they after me?

"Very dramatic," says Julian, the moment Warwick disappears.

"Do we follow them?" asks Charlie, breathing heavily.

Julian shakes his head. "They may have reinforcements waiting around the curve in the river. No, we head back." He looks at me with concern. "Are you all right?"

I nod. "So . . . you knew all along? You knew I slipped away?"

He nods grimly. "And it's a good thing we did."

I'm thankful for the dim light that hides the furious blush of shame rising to my cheeks. Shame at being useless in a fight. Shame at having to be rescued. Shame at being caught escaping.

I watch the half dozen Morgana as they fan out along the bridge, ensuring the Huntsmen are gone and not coming back. I can't help admiring their coordination. Something tightens in my chest. What would it be like to truly be one of them?

"Are you going to tell Hawksmoor?" I ask.

Julian shrugs. "He has his secrets. And now I have mine."

"What about the others?" I glance toward the other Candidates. Surely one of them will say something.

"Let me take care of that."

Rose stalks over. "How could you be so stupid, you classless trollop. When Hawksmoor learns of this—"

"He shall hear nothing more than what a lovely time we had at the opera," Julian replies calmly.

"And I suppose we'll simply tell him we didn't feel like completing our actual mission?" Her eyes glitter as she glances at me, no doubt thrilled at my glaring mistake.

Julian shrugs. "We'll tell him we were spotted. We couldn't jeopardize our identities."

"How can you do it? How can you protect such . . . incompetence?" She juts her chin in my direction. I can't quite meet her eye. Inside I know she's right. "Fine," she says, folding her arms. "If you won't report this to Hawksmoor, I will."

Julian takes a step toward Rose and stops inches from her face. "If you say so much as one word about this, I will tell Hawksmoor about your own blunder last year." His voice is low, almost a growl. "You know to what I am referring, dear Rose."

Rose's mouth opens in a small circle. Her eyes jerk to mine.

"We all make mistakes, Rose. You know that as well as any of us." he says with finality.

Rose's nostrils flare. She looks like she might spit nails. But she snaps her mouth shut and stomps away.

"Thank you," I mouth to Julian. I don't inquire about the specifics of Rose's blunder. I know he wouldn't tell me.

And while I'm relieved my mistake won't be shared with Hawksmoor, my belly flutters uneasily. Rose now has something she can use against me.

I put my hand inside my cloak as we walk away from the bridge, my fingers meeting the cold smoothness of the pin. I'm not sure why, but I decide not to tell anyone about it. I want to think first, see if I can remember where I've seen it before. I run my thumb over the metal.

There are so many things I don't yet understand. But one thing is clear. No matter what else happens, I am going to learn how to access Aristos. Never again will I cower behind a lamppost.

CHAPTER TWENTY-SIX

"The forceps of our minds are clumsy forceps,
and crush the truth a little in taking hold of it."
—H. G. Wells, *A Modern Utopia*

When we return to the Academy, I tell everyone I'm exhausted from the evening's escapades and wish to retire for the evening. Instead, I slip down to the cellar. I need to talk to Sig.

As I hurry down the stone staircase, I tuck my hand into the folds of my cloak and tightly clutch the strange pin I found on the bridge. I hope Sig has some answers.

I knock on Sig's door, holding my breath as I wait. The door opens and I exhale.

Sig looks startled to see me standing there in the dark hallway. "Miss Cole! What fortuitous timing!"

He pulls me inside before I can utter a word. The lab smells strongly of chemicals. A flask bubbles in one corner, clockwork ticks in another.

"Now, let me show you what I've been developing for you," he says, rubbing his hands together gleefully.

"For the Candidates?"

He nods. "For the Candidates with Aristos."

He shows me a tunic made of some kind of lightweight protective fabric. I finger the shirt—the material is fascinating, strong yet flexible.

"And this," he says, moving quickly to another corner of the workshop. "I'm particularly excited about this one." He produces a frothy green umbrella with a curved handle.

"A . . . parasol?"

"Not just any parasol. Look inside."

When I open it, the lining is chain mail. "The perfect defense for a lady," he says with a grin that overtakes his face. "I'm thinking of making one for Queen Victoria, herself."

He chatters on, showing me various bits of equipment and gadgets. I tighten my hand around the strange pin in my pocket as I wait for an opening in Sig's discourse.

"Listen, this is all wonderful, really. But . . . I did come to see you for a specific reason."

He looks up at me through goggles that magnify the size of his eyes. Withdrawing the pin from my cloak, I hold it out to him. The pattern is odd: geometric with three bars, six dots, and a pair of triangles in a linear formation. It has an ancient look to it, although I can't quite explain why. The pattern feels somehow . . . intentional. Not just decorative.

I'm not sure it's a device, exactly, but I feel like it has some purpose.

Sig steps closer. "May I?" He pushes his goggles up on his head and gingerly takes the metal from my fingers. After studying it for a moment, he asks, "Where did you get this?"

"It fell from the cloak of one of the Huntsmen." I lift my chin slightly. "The Huntsmen in the tunnels when I was escaping Newgate Prison. I scooped it up at the time, and I've been wondering about it ever since." I can't help noticing how smoothly the lie glides off my tongue. My skills are growing.

He nods absently, keeping his attention on the pin. After inspecting it for several moments, peering at it through his goggles, and uttering various grunts, he looks back up at me at last. "Well, Miss Cole. I have come to the conclusion that I have absolutely no idea what this is."

"Oh." I can't hide my disappointment.

"In truth, I've never seen anything like it. That alone fascinates me. Would you mind leaving it with me, so that I might continue to study it?"

"I suppose I don't need it for anything."

He clucks his tongue. "It's a shame. Huntsman paraphernalia isn't exactly my strength. If only Dexter were here."

"Dexter?"

"My partner. Well, my former partner. Until he went"—
he lowers his voice to a whisper—"mad."

"Oh dear."

"He had a particular interest in the Huntsmen. Knew
more about them and their inner workings than any of us.
His research took him to London, where, unfortunately, he
began turning to . . . certain pursuits to soothe his nerves.
Last I heard, he never leaves Tianjin House."

It sounds like an opium den. No shortage of those in London.

"How dreadful."

At that moment, the door flies open and Rose stalks
inside. "Sig? I need a new knife. This one wouldn't be fit
for a scullery maid chopping cabbage . . ." She stops short
when she sees me, narrowing her eyes. "Oh, Felicity. I
thought you'd gone to bed. You must be tired from your
exertions this evening." She pauses theatrically. "Oh wait,
that was me. Me, fighting off our enemies while you rested
behind a lamppost in a faint."

"What are you two on about?" Sig asks. "Weren't you at
the opera this evening?"

"Rose has an active imagination," I say quickly.

"Oh dear, did I say this evening?" Rose frowns with faux
innocence. "I meant this morning. During our training session." A sly smile plays on her lips.

There are so many things I would like to say in retort,
but none of them would be wise at the moment.

"As it happens," I say, "I was just about to retire for the evening." Pressing my lips together, I swiftly take my leave. I'll continue my conversation with Sig later and sort out what to do next, although I'm already formulating a plan.

Returning to my rooms, I fall instantly asleep, but it's a restless slumber filled with nightmares, and I wake very early, before the sun has risen.

As I stare up at the canopy overhead, a determination takes hold in my belly. I rise and quickly dress in my training gear.

It doesn't take me long to creep from my room and make my way to the ballroom where we conduct our combat training. Surely no one will be there at this hour.

But when I arrive, the door is already open. I stop, and peer inside. A lone figure is there, his back to me. His shirt is off; sweat shimmers on his skin as he moves with fluidity and power through a routine of combat exercises.

Julian Blake.

I'm frozen in place, mesmerized. I can't move. I can hardly breathe. I know at any moment he'll turn and see me, so I hurry to slip out of sight. I am too slow.

"Felicity?"

I blush all the way to my toes. "Ah yes, hello, Mr. Blake," I say, stepping out into view, avoiding his eye and his state of undress. "I see you were practicing. I'm sorry to disturb you. Good day." I begin to turn to leave.

"Wait!"

I hesitate.

"You're dressed for combat, too. Were you planning to practice?" he asks.

I turn back and glance down at my outfit. "Oh, ah, yes. I couldn't sleep, and I thought I might as well get an early start. . . ."

He grins. "There's plenty of room. Please, do come in."

I can't think of a plausible excuse. There's nothing for it. I walk into the ballroom. As he re-dresses I let out a small sigh of relief. Relief tinged with . . . something else. It wasn't an unpleasant sight.

I move to the far corner and prepare to start training, doggedly ignoring Julian's gaze. My skin crawls with the awkwardness of it. As I turn, I catch him smirking at me.

"Listen, Felicity. Why don't we practice together?"

"Oh, no need for that. I'm quite content—"

"I'm sure you are. But, even so, there are drills better undertaken with an opponent." He tilts his head. "I'm bored of training on my own."

He holds his hand out quite insistently. I hesitate a moment longer. In truth, it would be better to practice with a partner, but I'm not sure I'll be able to concentrate with him even closer than he already is.

"All right. Just a few minutes, I suppose."

He flashes me one of his dazzling grins. "Now, where shall we start?"

He demonstrates some maneuvers to help limber me up, and then teaches me a self-defense move I've never tried before.

He moves my arms into the correct position, the warmth of his hands seeping through the thin fabric of my training gear.

"Now you try it on your own," he says.

He watches with a patient eye as I do my best. "That's good," he says. "You're a quick study, Felicity."

I struggle to keep my face neutral as my heart speeds up with pleasure.

He glances out the window. "The sunrise is spectacular. Let's continue outside."

We climb up to the rooftop, taking a shortcut through the billiards room. The rooftop here is flat, and the air is cool. A perfect place to practice. We run through combat training drills high above Greybourne, the Oxfordshire countryside spreading out beneath us.

"Now follow me," he says, and sets off at a run across the roof.

He leaps across between two rooftops and lands like a cat. My eyes go wide as I realize what he's done and I stop myself, just in time. He used Aristos for that move. I frown at my feet.

"What's wrong?" he hollers from across the other roof. "Come on, Felicity!"

"I can't."

"Yes, you can." He leaps back across and stands in front of me. "You can if you access your Aristos," he says deliberately.

I am quiet a moment. "Yes, well, that's the trick, isn't it?"

"Come on. I have an idea."

CHAPTER TWENTY-SEVEN

"The golden moments in the stream of life rush past us and we see nothing but sand; the angels come to visit us, and we only know them when they are gone."

—George Eliot, *Janet's Repentance*

Julian leads me over the roofs of Greybourne to a hidden garden overlooking the grounds, and stands me before a large cast-iron urn. The air is lush with the scent of lilacs. A gentle breeze stirs the stray hairs around my face. "I can't believe there's a garden on the roof! I've never seen such a thing."

"Yes, it's peculiar," he murmurs, "but quite pretty." He gives me a pointed look and a blush rises to my cheeks.

Without further comment, he rubs his hands together. "Now, from what I've observed, you only seem to be able to access Aristos when you're angry. True?"

I nod.

"Right. Well, let's see if we can get around that. Now pick up that urn."

I doubtfully eye the enormous vessel. It's far too heavy to lift. Julian waits patiently at my side. There's nothing to be done but to wrap my hands around the rough edges and try to lift it. It doesn't budge a hair.

"Try harder."

"I *am* trying."

"No, you're not."

I scowl at him. Not for the first time, I wonder why he's doing this. Why he's spending time with me. In spite of my bold words to Rose that first night, I know there was a kernel of truth in what she said. Julian Blake is of a different world. And no matter what else I may be, I will always be common. I am from the slums. Nothing can change that.

"Call to Aristos. Try thinking of something that makes you angry," he suggests. "Like . . . Rose, perhaps?"

I let out an inelegant snort, then I try to let anger flow through me. As always, nothing happens.

"Maybe something else, then. Hawksmoor? Or . . . what about the reason you came here? Something happened, didn't it, the day Hawksmoor found you? Something bad. Something that made you angry enough . . ."

As he speaks, I'm thrown back to that day in the Whitechapel Market. The crackle of roasting chestnuts. The rhythmic clopping of horse hooves over the cobblestones.

The familiar smell of rotting cabbage and piss in the streets. Then the face of the Duke of Warwick. The cold look in his eyes as he killed Kit.

"Think back to that moment, Felicity," Julian is saying, though his voice is distant and muffled in my ears. He takes a step closer. His skin smells like soap and pine needles and sweat from our training session. I'm again back on the rooftop.

No. I shake my head and block out the distraction. I think of Kit. *Kit*, in the market . . .

"Cut out all other emotions and grasp the anger. Dig down and find it."

Warwick's face swims into view, his triumphant look as he killed the boy I loved. There's grief, yes, but it's the anger I want. I let the rage pulse through me. There's a prickle in my scalp and a faint buzzing sound in my ears—

The weight shifts a little.

I leap back and Julian's widened eyes meet mine. "That's it. You did it."

I did it.

Immediately, I need more. "I want to try it again."

I grasp the urn and let myself go back to that moment in the market, let the anger flow through me, release the constraints. I grunt and lift the urn a few inches off the ground. The prickling in my scalp spreads over my skin, and movement around me slows. From the corner of my eye I see a hummingbird hovering in the garden and can make out its wingbeats, slow and rhythmic.

The weight of the urn feels even lighter. I am doing it. . . .

The urn suddenly grows impossibly heavy. I drop it and jump back as it crashes down.

Julian looks up at me, grinning. "Now, how did that feel?"

I'm breathing heavily. "It was like letting my mind off its leash, like a dog on the hunt. I just let the anger wash over me, and with it came the power. I felt this odd sensation in my scalp. And my ears buzzed . . ."

Julian nods. "That's a bit like what it feels like for me, too. I just get out of its way, as you say. For me, it's more like lifting a gate that's holding water behind it. I let it go and the sensation floods through me."

I look at the urn resting on the rooftop. "So if I just think of something that makes me angry, I can unlock my Aristos."

He looks thoughtful. "It would be better if you didn't need the anger. That would be more useful should you be . . . on assignment."

I'm silent a moment. "On assignment to assassinate someone, you mean?"

Julian watches me carefully, then leans forward. "It won't be easy, Felicity. But it's important work."

I think of Rose, dragging the blade across that man's throat. Of the blood. I push down a wave of nausea. "Killing people?"

"It may be hard for you to see now, but the men we assassinate are marked for a good reason."

I fiddle with the edge of my sleeve and remain quiet.

"You've probably heard of the attempts on the Queen's life? So far there have been seven since she took the throne."

"Yes, I've heard rumors." The most recent attempt was just a few years ago by an insane man who shot at the Queen while she was riding in her carriage.

"The truth is, those seven attacks are only the ones that have made the newspapers. There have been three times as many planned, but those plots were stopped by the Morgana before they ever got far enough. And quite often, stopping such plots involves killing the men at the center of them."

Julian takes a seat on a stone bench at the edge of the garden, overlooking the countryside surrounding Greybourne. A pale stripe on the horizon heralds the coming sunrise. I take a seat beside him on the cold stone surface. "You've heard of the Fenians, right?" he continues. "The terrorists who caused that explosion in the Clerkenwell Prison years ago?"

I know about the Fenians, of course. Everyone does.

"Twelve people died in that attack," Julian says. "Including a seven-year-old girl."

Seven. Nate is seven.

"But what most people don't know is that there was a Morgana agent assigned to the man who placed that bomb. Someone, like you, who felt somewhat squeamish about the job he had to do."

"He was supposed to kill the conspirator?"

"Indeed."

"And because he didn't succeed, those people died? That little girl . . ."

"You see, there are consequences. The actions you don't take—those responsibilities you walk away from—can have repercussions you could never even dream of. Wouldn't want to dream of."

I stare at him.

"Do you remember the toast Hawksmoor made on your first night here? Marlowe's words? 'You must be proud, bold, pleasant, and resolute . . . And now and then stab, as occasion serves.' Over my years here, I've come to see the truth in that."

I tighten my jaw and look out at the rolling country-side, as the rising sun paints the surrounding pastures and hedgerows. A flock of birds lifts up from a distant meadow, taking to the sky with chattering song. This entire affair is confusing. Julian's words are so smooth, so convincing, but I must keep my head on straight. I need to know what I want, what I believe, and not because some handsome young man tells me it's so.

And yet, what he said makes an awful lot of sense.

Julian jumps up and brushes off his hands. "Enough of that. Let's try again with your Aristos."

I'm not sure I'm prepared for another attempt, but I know I'm not ready to leave the rooftop just yet. I'm enjoying Julian's company. I stand up and face him.

"Now, this time," he says, "try to find that feeling that accompanied your anger. That prickling sensation, the buzzing in your ears . . . the power. See if you can let that loose—without the anger—and lift the urn."

I look at him dubiously. This will never work. But Julian looks as hopeful as a puppy dog. I nod and place my hand on the urn.

"Okay, now just try to grasp that power," he says. "Let it off its leash. . . ."

I clear my mind and let go. After a minute, a weak stream of power calls to me. My skin begins to tingle . . .

And the urn shifts. Just a little. It's not a huge movement, but I do lift it a little higher than I did before. And this time, it's without a thread of anger.

I drop the weight and look up at Julian. He's watching me triumphantly.

"I did it," I whisper.

"Yes, Felicity, you most definitely did." My face splits into an enormous grin. The next thing I know, he's lifted me up into his arms and is spinning me around. "You did it!"

There's a flutter in my belly as he twirls me with strong arms. Our faces are close enough for me to see the shifting colors in his eyes, feel his warm breath on my face. Sparks skitter across my skin as I become aware of the length of his body against mine.

I remember myself and stiffen and he immediately puts me down. "Forgive me," he mumbles. And then he's all grins again. "But, Felicity, you did it."

I can't help but smile.

As we sit down again on the edge of the rooftop, I'm still breathing heavily with exhilaration. The sun is rising over the hills, birds are singing a symphony in the nearby woods, the lush smell of flowers from the gardens below surround us, the sky is ablaze with pink and lemon, dotted with vanilla clouds.

"We should be celebrating," Julian says.

Unbidden, a memory crashes into me, of that moment of tranquility with Kit by the riverfront, sneaking through the iron gate to enjoy our modest feast. I do my best to push it away so I can enjoy this triumphant moment.

Julian and I remain quiet for several minutes before he speaks again. "Listen, Felicity. I want to explain why I said what I did to Hawksmoor. Before the incident with the train and the gorge."

"When you told him I was useless?" I arch my eyebrow.

He grimaces. "Yes, that." He fidgets with his hands. "It's just—I'm worried about you. I think you have a lot of potential, I do. I think you could be an amazing asset to our team. But not if you get killed because Hawksmoor's pushed you out in the field before you're ready. I know there's a lot of pressure now to prepare for the Jubilee and select the final Candidate, but that's no reason to endanger people."

I nod and think back to that moment. The shame and my anger are softened a little.

"I've seen it before. It was four or five years ago. A Candidate went out on an exercise before he was ready, and . . ."

I swallow. He doesn't need to finish the story.

"You've been here that long?" I say, eager to change the subject. "No wonder you're so good." The moment the words tumble out of my mouth, I realize how they must sound. I flush and clear my throat. "That is to say . . . well, you discovered that you were Morgana at an early age, yes?"

He smiles. "There is a strong Morgana thread that runs through my family. They realized my gifts when I was five or six."

I think about Julian as a child. Growing up in that privileged world—one I can only imagine. "Do you have many brothers or sisters?"

He nods ruefully. "Three older sisters. Hence my exquisite curtsying form." He graces me with another deep curtsy, then stands up laughing, flashing me one of his bright smiles.

My heart lurches.

Julian cocks his head and examines my face. "I wonder why you formed such a block. By your age, most Morgana can't even *think* of hiding it."

I look down at my hands. "My father made sure, from a very young age, that we understood being Tainted was a very dangerous thing. And Nate's secret had to be hidden no matter what. For my father, it was more than the usual fear of the Tainted."

"More? Why?"

I don't feel ready to talk further about my past, but I glimpse Julian's eyes and see such genuine warmth and concern there.

"Because of my mother."

"What happened to your mother?" Julian asks gently.

"She trusted too easily. She saw the good in everyone she met. She didn't believe people—her own neighbors—would think poorly of her because she was Tainted, and she wasn't terribly careful to conceal her ability." My chest constricts, but I continue. "They turned on her, our own neighbors. They pulled her out into the street. They acted as judge, jury . . . and executioner. Right there, right outside our home, they stoned her to death. My father and I were out at the time, working in the market. There was nothing he could have done. . . ."

My voice cracks, but I take a deep breath and continue. "My brother was very young then, just a baby. My mother's gift was in the mental realm, just like Nate's."

Julian says nothing for a long time after I finish. He's gone pale and a thin white line circles his lips. He's angry. "That," he says deliberately, "should never have happened."

His voice is taut. "Felicity, I'm so sorry. Nothing I can say will lessen your pain. But . . . now I understand why your father was so adamant about keeping the secret."

Julian clenches his jaw. "Something must change. We aren't the enemy. Just because we're different . . ." He visibly struggles to control his emotions, then lifts his head. "You're going to get past your block. In fact, I think you have the potential to be one of the strongest Morgana agents yet."

I blush and look away, trying to wave away my guilt.

"I don't know why on earth you would say that," I reply. It's all I can manage.

"When Hawksmoor brought me here when I was ten, he said the people with the strongest blocks often have the potential for the most spectacular breakthroughs."

"Hawksmoor has been in charge that long?"

He laughs. "I think he's been in charge forever. The man is possibly immortal."

"Has he always been so . . . aloof? So full of secrets?"

"Always." Julian looks at me with an uncharacteristically serious gaze. "Be careful who you trust, Felicity. We are in a strange world here. You know those old maps, what is written beyond the borders of the known seas?"

"'Here be dragons'?" I offer.

"Exactly. Nowhere is that more true than here."

CHAPTER TWENTY-EIGHT

"'Who's the man that says that we're all islands shouting lies to each other across seas of misunderstanding?"

—Rudyard Kipling, *The Light That Failed*

After my success with Julian, I take to my training with new vigor. I'm determined to master my gift, if only to be able to properly defend myself the next time I encounter a Huntsman. Little by little, I improve, although I am still far behind the other Candidates. I am stronger and faster than a regular human, but still slow by Morgana standards. And there are elements I continue to struggle with: gymnastic climbing and combat. But I am on the right path.

My deportment tutoring with Isherwood continues, and for the most part I am advancing there, as well, though we are like cats in a bag, and she continues to regard me with great displeasure.

A late spring storm brews outside, rain lashing at the windows. Earlier, Hawksmoor, Isherwood, Neville, and the other Elders left the estate on "administrative business" in the village, and they won't be back until very late. I suspect they are planning the Royal Jubilee operation. My suspicions are confirmed when I see Julian walking around with a glower on his face, sulking. And though I, too, am curious about the Jubilee mission, I relish having free rein of the house.

"It's a dreadful night, Miss Cole," says Jane, as supper approaches. "If you'd like, I could have the cook put together a tray. You've been working ever so hard. You must be tired. . . ."

"No," I say quickly. "I'd like to go down."

I've been looking forward to dinner conversation. My pulse quickens a little as I wonder if I might be seated next to Julian again tonight. Last night we had such a lovely conversation about books, including a lively debate on which of Thomas Hardy's works is his best thus far: *The Mayor of Casterbridge* or *Far From The Madding Crowd*. . . .

I smile, and then a pang of guilt curls in my stomach. *Kit.*

As I make my way to the dining room, I firmly attempt to put the whole affair out of my head. Perhaps it's best if I don't sit near Julian.

The smells of roast beef and gravy and Yorkshire pudding make my mouth water as I enter the dining room. A quick glance at the table shows me the only available seat is across from Charlie, immediately beside Julian.

"Miss Cole, do join us," Julian calls out with a playful glimmer in his eye. "I think you could help us resolve a wager."

"I can try," I say, taking a seat.

"We're having a debate about philosophy," Julian says. "Who said the words: 'The only thing I know is that I know nothing'?"

"I say it was Aristotle," says Charlie, grinning enthusiastically. "But my man Blake here insists Socrates said it. He's blathering on about the 'Socratic Paradox' or some such."

I look between the two of them as they wait expectantly. "You're both wrong," I say. "Although you're right, Julian, it *is* called the Socratic Paradox. But it was Plato who wrote those words in the *Republic*, ostensibly quoting Socrates. But there's no record of Socrates ever having said the phrase. So it can only correctly be attributed to Plato."

Charlie's mouth drops open.

"Oh ho!" says Julian to Charlie, slapping the table with his palm. "Well, that sets us straight, doesn't it? I told you our girl would know the right of it!" He winks at me. "Well played, Felicity." Charlie scowls good-naturedly while I blush to the tips of my ears.

As I fidget with the napkin in my lap, a footman leans down at my side and whispers quietly, "Miss Cole? There is a gentleman from Oxford at the front gate who says he must speak with you. That he is an acquaintance of Neville's. He insists it's urgent."

Professor Garrick. "Of course," I say, standing abruptly, ignoring Julian's watchful gaze.

"I'll show him to the conservatory, miss."

No sooner have I entered the room than the door swings open and the professor hurries in. He's looking rather worse for the journey, his hair wild. Rainwater drips from his shoes onto the carpet.

"Professor! What are you doing here on such a night?"

His features are taut and he has a desperate look in his eyes. "There's something I've discovered. I didn't want to risk a letter, but I needed to speak with you immediately."

I take a seat in one of the armchairs. "It's all right, Professor. You're here now."

At that moment, Julian appears in the doorway. His glance swings between us with alarm. "Who is this, Felicity? How did he get here?"

I open my mouth to answer, but Julian doesn't give me the chance.

"Wait—did you give him instructions? *The passwords?*"

"I . . ."

Julian's jaw flexes. He turns sharply to the professor. "Were you followed? When you crossed the border was there anyone who could have seen you?"

"No. I mean, I don't *believe* so . . ."

"You don't believe so?" Julian turns to me. "Felicity, this is not good."

A wave of nausea rolls over me. "You don't think the Huntsmen can get inside now, do you?"

Julian rubs a hand through his hair. "I don't know. But I suppose we'll find out soon enough."

I turn to the professor. "Tell me. What did you find out?"

He flicks an uncertain glance at Julian. I'm worried, too—not just about Julian hearing this, but about the other eyes and ears in this place. "Go on, Professor."

"You know I mentioned a former colleague who was researching the Morgana? Well, I have been in communication with him. Today, I received his ledger of test subjects."

He shows me a page. "Look at the one five from the top."

Nico Alexei Cole.

My heart skips a beat. "My father was a test subject for Tainted research?"

He shakes his head briskly. "No, you misunderstand. My colleague wasn't doing testing that *created* the Tainted. He was doing testing to *cure* the Tainted. And your father was a subject for the preliminary formula."

I stare at him without comprehension. "But . . . how can that be?"

"Felicity, your father was Morgana, too." He pulls out another folder. "Here is his registration card. He recorded himself as being Tainted, and having fathered a daughter and a son who were also Tainted."

The world tilts. My father knew?

"Yes. I believe they were closing in on a cure until they abruptly abandoned their research. But my colleague says he's willing to speak with you. I can give you his contact information."

I glance at Julian. He watches me carefully, gauging my reaction to this news . . . and then, suddenly, there is an odd sound outside. His expression changes.

There is a sudden, deafening crash as one of the conservatory windows shatters. A crossbow bolt lodges into the chest of Professor Garrick. His eyes spring wide, and he immediately falls straight back. Dead.

CHAPTER TWENTY-NINE

"The night is darkening round me,
The wild winds coldly blow;
But a tyrant spell has bound me,
And I cannot, cannot go."
—Emily Brontë, "Spellbound"

Julian doesn't hesitate. He grabs me and we run. We have to get out of this room—lined with windows and undefendable. I glance back at the professor lying dead on the conservatory floor, but there's nothing I can do for him now.

The grand entrance hall is alive with movement and noise. Julian hollers instructions to the Candidates as the house staff pull weapons from a cupboard. And then Charlie appears at Julian's side.

"Go to the lookout in the attic," Julian orders. Charlie disappears up the curving staircase.

Although the Elders are not here, the Candidates and house staff have clearly drilled what to do in the case of an attack.

Huntsmen are at the doors, breaking them down. They will soon be climbing through.

I smell smoke. Julian grabs me, pushing me toward an ebony table on which rests a massive bouquet of lilies. "Quick. Get underneath and stay there."

"No."

I'm not going to hide. I'm going to stand and defend my friends myself. This is my fight. I brought the wolves to our door and I will beat them back again. Or die trying.

I know I don't have much to offer—I still can't reliably use my Aristos for much—but I am not going to cower.

Julian hesitates, then he nods. "In that case, you'll need this," he says, handing me a pistol and two knives. I tuck the pistol in the waistband of my skirts, one of the knives in my boot, and the other I hold loosely in my hand. I'm ready.

Doors splinter. Glass shatters. Huntsmen will crash in any minute.

"There are at least twenty-five of them!" hollers Charlie, flying down the staircase.

Twenty-five. They must have been planning this attack for some time. How could they have known? In the foyer, all the Candidates have now gathered. The initial shock seems to be giving way to something more organized. We number perhaps a dozen.

If we are all able to channel our gifts, we should be able to best them. My nerves thrum. There is no running away this time—not for them, and not for me. I'm back to back with the other Morgana Candidates: Charlie, Hugh, Rose, Julian, and all the others. I can taste it—the thrill of vengeance. This will be for Kit.

And then the Huntsmen break through. Three of them crash into the foyer from different directions. I have no time to think about it before the first one sprints straight for me, a man in a black bowler hat carrying a vicious six-inch knife. He comes at me and lunges. I level my pistol. He ducks under the bullet and keeps coming.

Ducks under *the bullet.*

It's then that my brain catches up with what I'm seeing: the Huntsmen aren't moving like regular people. They're far faster. Tearing through doors and windows, and up the walls. With inhuman strength. Superhuman speed.

The truth hits me.

The Huntsmen are Tainted, too.

CHAPTER THIRTY

"Imaginary evils soon become real ones by indulging our reflections on them."

—Jonathan Swift, *Miscellanies*

A black pit opens before me. We might have had a chance against regular men. But not against Tainted.

The man in the bowler hat is on me. Too quickly, he dispatches my weapons and begins dragging me from the fray. There is nobody to help—all the others are struggling to stay alive as Huntsmen flood into the hall. Knives flash, fists, limbs . . .

As Bowler Hat pulls me by one foot I kick and scream, fingernails breaking as I scrabble at the marble tile. Somehow, I have to channel Aristos. I reach out for it. I push past the terror, the confusion, the hopelessness . . . clearing my mind of everything and grasping for the feeling.

It's there, waiting for me. The now increasingly familiar sensation of a predator, straining at its leash. I just have to let it loose.

My ears begin to buzz and movement around me slows. That's it. I grasp harder. I have it.

A droplet of sweat from my captor floats slowly to the marble floor. Shattering glass sprinkles like confetti. I let the power infuse my body.

My assailant continues to drag me across the floor. He is strong and fast but he has one critical weakness: he assumes I can't channel Aristos.

I reach into my other boot for the knife and in a great lunge swing the blade in an arc that lands squarely in the hand wrapped around my ankle.

He bellows and loosens his grip for a second. It's all I need. In that instant, I wrench the blade free and flip myself onto my knees. As Bowler Hat turns, I drive the knife into his thigh. He stumbles. I come up and sweep his feet out from under him, flipping him onto his back, cracking his head on the marble tile.

I'm on my feet in an instant. I have to help the others. I sprint back to the melee in the foyer. It's pandemonium as the other Candidates struggle to keep the Huntsmen at bay. We are not winning.

I attack the first Huntsman I encounter, a wiry, swarthy man grappling with Hugh. From behind, I grab the Huntsman's shoulder, spin him, and issue a knockout punch before he has a chance to register I'm even there.

Aristos surges through me. I spin in time to see a Huntsman woman leveling a pistol at me. She sports a vicious scar over the bridge of her nose. It would seem she doesn't share Bowler Hat's goal of capturing me.

The bullet fires and I spiral beneath it. But as I come out of my spin she's upon me, pushing me down and drawing her blade, a whine of metal on metal. Her arm rises preparing to stab me in the chest.

I try to push away but she's impossibly strong.

And then her arm is wrenched backward and she's lifted off me. Charlie. I jump to my feet, grab a tall lamp from a table, and thrust it into her gut, winding her. Charlie delivers a crack to the back of her skull and she goes down.

"Felicity! You can channel—" he begins. But there's no time for pleasantries about what I can and cannot do.

Two more Huntsmen are there. One levels a crossbow. I hear the snap as the bolt is fired, knowing the next sound will be a singing whine and then a sickening thud as it slams into my chest. I dive out of the way, pulling Charlie down with me.

The bolt embeds in the stair railing. Charlie stands and immediately attacks a Huntsman bearing down on him. I wrench the bolt free, turn, and fly up the staircase, scooping up a discarded crossbow as I go. I need a better elevation.

I hear the sounds of pounding feet close at my heels, and then a voice I recognize. "Felicity!"

Julian fights off Huntsmen as we fly upward. When we reach the landing above the hallway, I plant my feet by the railing, pull the crossbow level, slam the bolt in, and scan the room.

Julian is by my side, picking off the Huntsmen with his own crossbow.

I hold steady to Aristos and breathe. Blood pounds in my ears. A Huntsman below raises an ax, about to strike down Rose as she fends off another attacker. I aim and fire. The arrow bolt strikes the man in the throat. His eyes go wide and he falls, dead.

I just killed a man. My vision goes fuzzy around the edges, and Aristos slips. The weight of the crossbow is suddenly too much and I drop it to the floor below.

As a wave of dizziness washes over me, I fall to my knees, trying desperately to grasp Aristos again. But I can't feel it anymore. I can barely think.

Julian will soon be overpowered by the Huntsmen racing up the stairs and scaling the wall to breach the banister. There are simply too many of them.

Despair gathers into a knot in my chest.

And then the front door—what's left of it—flies open and the Morgana Elders flood through.

Hawksmoor leaps into the fray, pistol drawn. Isherwood swings herself up onto the landing with us. The other Elders dive into the fight.

It's a matter of moments before the Huntsmen see the tide changing. They gather their troops and retreat, leaping out through smashed windows, flooding through the front door.

Charlie is on one side, Julian on the other. They lift me from my knees.

"Felicity, that was—incredible. Did you know you could do all of that?" asks Charlie, his eyes wide.

Hawksmoor cuts everyone off with a sharply raised hand. "Enough. We need to get moving. We're leaving Greybourne."

CHAPTER THIRTY-ONE

"Because I could not stop for Death—
He kindly stopped for me—
The Carriage held but just Ourselves—
And Immortality."

—Emily Dickinson,
"Because I could not stop for Death"

Hawksmoor barks orders at us all. The servants load the injured into the carriages and climb in. Everyone else—mostly all able-bodied Candidates—will be riding on horseback. Including me.

"Can you do it?" Charlie asks me with concern.

I nod, although I'm not sure I can—I've only had a few riding sessions. But what choice do I have? Besides, this is all my fault. I'll have to try.

We dash to the stables to saddle the horses. I'm terrified of hearing the sounds of the Huntsmen reappearing. I pray we can get out of here before they return with reinforcements.

The younger Candidates and most of the house staff are going north to catch a train headed to another estate in Yorkshire. The journey will take most of the night, but they will be far safer once they get there.

The Elders and senior Candidates, and a few servants who weren't injured in the fight, are headed to the London headquarters of the Morgana.

We fly across the darkened landscape. The storm has lessened a little. Now, instead of the earlier gale winds, it's merely a pounding rain. I grit my teeth, praying I can keep my seat and match the pace of the others. As it is, I can barely make them out.

While we ride, my mind clutches at one very specific question: How did the Morgana not know the Huntsmen were Tainted? In all our encounters, it never came to light. How is that possible?

But as I run through each encounter, it occurs to me . . . there was always something just off. On the train, we jumped off and into the gorge. In Oxford, the Huntsmen themselves aborted the attack by dropping over the edge of the bridge. Perhaps they were hiding the full truth from us until they were ready for an attack they were sure they couldn't lose.

We are aiming to catch the last London train but at our rest stop, I see Hawksmoor look at his pocket watch and I know we're not going to make it to the station in time. He alters direction slightly and we set off anew.

Almost an hour later, we're thundering across the terrain, and I can make out a faint rumbling—a new sound. I glance over my shoulder and see a train's lantern pointed toward our backs, steam rising up from it.

We're going to have to jump on while it's moving.

Not again.

"Listen," hollers Hawksmoor. "Half of those with Aristos will go first and help the others on. The other Aristos will take up the rear with me."

It's impossible. There are too many of us. But there's no time for argument.

We split into two groups—one aiming for the first cargo car, one for the rear. I'm in Hawksmoor's group. Rose, Hugh, and Charlie pull forward. They will be among the first to board. Before long, we are parallel to the track, the train thundering up behind and churning past.

We wait until the passenger cars slide by and the cargo cars pull alongside us. This is our chance. Hawksmoor makes the leap first, tearing open the cargo door to reveal a gaping hole. That's our target.

Among us, we help the servants and those Candidates not strong in Aristos. Only three of us have yet to board the train—Julian, Jane, and me.

"Come on, Jane, you can do it," Julian says. Terror whitens her face.

I tamp down my own fear. We can't leave her behind. I look over my shoulder to see how much more of the train remains. On the crest of a hill, a line of men on horseback appears, silhouetted by the moonlight. They are charging toward us. Huntsmen.

They won't catch the train, but if there are any stragglers . . .

I try to holler to the others, to warn them about the Huntsmen. But between the rain, the hoofbeats, and the thundering train, it's too loud.

I dig my heels into the flank of my horse to catch up. Forward, and on this train, is the only way.

"We'll help Jane aboard," shouts Julian. "Then I'll get you up, and I'll go last."

I nod grimly. Between us, we lift Jane up and toward the car, into the waiting arms of the others.

I try to grasp Aristos, but I'm too exhausted and too muddled.

Jane panics and glances back at Julian, scrabbling for his cloak. She hooks around it, halfway on board. "Jane, let go!" he shouts, but she can't hear him. The others are pulling her legs, but she won't release Julian's cloak. She's going to pull them both under.

Julian has no choice. I watch, helplessly, as he swiftly stands in his saddle. With Jane still clutching at his cloak, Julian leaps aboard. Both he and Jane tumble into the train car and Julian's horse gallops away.

I'm the last one. I don't dare turn, knowing the Huntsmen will soon be upon me. The train slips slightly ahead, gathering speed. I kick my horse's flank, but it's not quite fast enough. Pale, shocked faces grow farther away.

Terror rushes into my mind. I'm not going to make it.

CHAPTER THIRTY-TWO

"Quiet minds cannot be perplexed or frightened but go on in fortune or misfortune at their own private pace, like a clock during a thunderstorm."
—Robert Louis Stevenson, *The Strange Case of Dr. Jekyll and Mr. Hyde*

T he cargo cars slide out of reach as the train continues its acceleration. But there's still the caboose. There will be nobody to catch me there. I'll either make the jump or get sucked under.

More than ever, I need Aristos. I breathe in and out. Focus on the moment. Focus on calm.

And then the familiar feeling begins to call to me. The train, in my eyes, slows. Raindrops hang suspended in the air.

With one final burst from my horse, I stand up on his back and leap.

The cold, slick metal of the handrail slides under my palms. I squeeze with enough strength to bend iron and my feet come up under me. I gather myself in and stand, hugging the very back of the caboose. A tiny platform.

I've made it.

Some time later, I huddle with the others in the cargo car. We've fashioned seats from crates and boxes. I pray the train keeps going straight on to London, that the Huntsmen do not keep pace and board when we reach our next stop.

The car is quiet as we all contemplate recent events. I flick a glance at Hawksmoor. I know the attack was all my fault.

My head is thick with the aftermath of the siege, with the terror of our escape, with visions of Professor Garrick in the conservatory, dead, because of me.

But within all that, one thought struggles to the front of my mind: *my father was Tainted.*

He knew I was, too, even before I knew it myself. Why did he keep the secret from me? How deep did his deception go? How could I know so little about my family, about myself?

"When will we be able to return to Greybourne?" someone asks.

"We will have to stay in town until we can resecure the Academy, which may take several weeks. We will certainly stay on until the Royal Jubilee is over."

The Jubilee. It's only two weeks away.

Julian turns to Hawksmoor. "I don't understand. If the Huntsmen are Morgana, why are they hunting their own kind?" His leg bounces as he waits for Hawksmoor to explain.

Hunting their own kind. And we can no longer count on the advantage of our preternatural abilities. We are on level ground.

Terrifying as it is, knowing the Huntsmen are Tainted helps. I have a clearer understanding of my enemy and of my own abilities.

Hawksmoor plucks a speck of dirt from his trousers. "I do not have an answer for you," he says.

"Could that be the reason they kept secret that they are Morgana?" I ask. "To keep that advantage?"

The spymaster says nothing, inspecting his fingernails. The silence lengthens and pulls thin.

"Hawksmoor?"

He looks up at me. "They did not keep it a secret."

"Nobody knew . . . *Oh.*"

He maintains a blank expression.

"Why didn't you tell us?" I say, heat rising in my cheeks.

"He was afraid," says Julian, bitterly.

"Afraid of what?"

"Afraid of young, impressionable Candidates being lured away by the enemy."

"Is that true?" I ask. Hawksmoor remains silent. "You put us at risk. We didn't know the full strength of the enemy hunting us."

"I did," he says, "and for that, I apologize. I should have trusted you more."

I frown and look down at my hands.

"Maybe you can answer this, then: What do they want with Felicity?" Julian demands. "They were clearly there to attack all of us, but they seemed particularly focused on her." There's an edge to his voice. Something that almost sounds like protectiveness.

"I don't know what they want with Miss Cole. I wish I did. Truly."

"Is that *I don't know* the same as the fact that you didn't know the Huntsmen were Morgana?" Julian fires back.

Hawksmoor's face darkens. "I can see you are anxious, Mr. Blake. The issue with the Huntsmen is most definitely a predicament. Rest assured I will be taking a very close look at what went wrong here tonight. At the same time, we cannot let it deter us from our primary objective, which is to protect the Queen. The Golden Jubilee is nearly upon us, and that is what we must concentrate upon. The time has come for us to choose the next Candidate to promote to full agent status. If you are up to it, Mr. Blake, you can continue to work for the position. If you are too . . . *emotional*, however, about the potential danger to Miss Cole, then I require that you tell me so now."

Julian's face turns to stone. "You're right, sir. You can count on me. I still wish to be considered." Julian pointedly avoids meeting my gaze.

"When we get to London, we will accelerate the selection process," Hawksmoor announces. "We will begin additional training in the field, eliminating Candidates based on performance." He trains his gaze on me. "Miss Cole, this includes you."

My eyes go wide, but I quickly school my features. The only sounds are the creaks and rattles of the cargo and the rhythmic clacking of the train. I glance around. There are five of us, five Candidates: Rose, Julian, Hugh, Charlie, and me.

"As for the Jubilee," Hawksmoor says, "the Elders will continue making preparations. We will include the successful Candidate in our plans once he or she has been selected."

All at once, I know: *I want it.*

I want to become an agent. I want to win this competition, rise up, and be counted among the upper echelons, learning all their secrets.

Nobody says anything for several minutes, until Hugh clears his throat. "Have you considered the possibility that there's a mole inside the Academy, sir? It feels rather convenient that they happened to attack Greybourne when all the Elders were away, doesn't it?"

Hawksmoor's face is impassive. "We are considering all possibilities, Mr. Torrington." With that, the subject is closed, at least on the surface.

"What about the Huntsmen?" Charlie asks. "Will they be a threat at the Jubilee?"

"If the Huntsmen wanted to kill the Queen, there have been a thousand opportunities before now. I don't believe that's their game."

"But—"

"Neville is on the case," Hawksmoor says, his tone sharp as a cracked whip. "Once the Jubilee is over, we can all turn our attention to the Huntsmen again."

And that's the end of the conversation. But while Hawksmoor appears unconcerned, I have learned that nothing with him is ever as it seems. Even when he has the most unflappable exterior, there are always a hundred calculations going on beneath the surface.

Silence descends in the cargo car, and I become tangled in my own thoughts again.

When we get to London, it will be time to start training anew.

CHAPTER THIRTY-THREE

"Something of vengeance I had tasted for the first time; as aromatic wine it seemed, on swallowing, warm and racy: its after-flavor, metallic and corroding, gave me a sensation as if I had been poisoned."

—Charlotte Brontë, *Jane Eyre*

I awaken in a new bed in a smaller room—though still luxurious.

The memories from last night come flooding back tearing away the cobwebs of sleep. The smell of blood, the sounds of gunshots . . .

I think of trying to contact Nate, telling him the truth about our father, but what would I say?

I rise and dress quickly, then go downstairs. Or, I should say, go even farther downstairs. As it is, we are deep underground, somewhere beneath the British Museum. This bunker was built a few years ago when they started digging beneath London to build the underground railway. The

Queen commissioned a special side project—a top-secret London base for her enigmatic team of Morgana agents.

We are fully self-sufficient down here. Kitchens and laundry rooms, ventilated and climate-controlled bedrooms for all the agents, a war room, and a billiards room, of course. And a large gymnasium for training. Which is where I am now headed.

When I reach the gymnasium—an enormous, brick-lined space with a sprung wood floor and bright lamps hanging down—I find the other Candidates already there, paired off and sparring.

There are murmurs as I enter the gymnasium. I haven't made a decent showing during combat training since my first morning at Greybourne that first humiliating, painful day. But things are different now. I've figured out how to use Aristos. And everyone here knows it.

Isherwood turns her gaze on me, her expression blank. She's always thought I'm useless. Does she still believe that?

I lift my chin and meet her gaze.

Isherwood folds her arms, narrowing her eyes as she takes me in. After a long, agonizing silence, she nods. "Miss Cole, you will partner with Mr. Torrington," she says. I set my jaw and try not to flinch at the memory of being roundly beaten by Hugh on my first day.

His face twists in a grin. My feet, in soft leather boots, make no sound as I approach. As we face each other, I clear my mind and reach out for Aristos. It's there, waiting like a trained tiger.

We're just supposed to be sparring, going through training motions, but I can see from Hugh's expression that he means to do me more harm than that.

My skin tingles. I'm ready.

He comes at me, but I hold my ground as all movement slows around us. Still as stone. I let him think I'm paralyzed with fear. Because Hugh prefers using his arms—I know he focuses his strength training on his upper body—he will punch out. He'll probably go for a one-shot knockout. At the last possible moment, I drop down and sweep his legs out from under him. He crumples to the floor, and I'm on him like a predator.

I pin him down, impossibly fast. He is using his gift, too, but the truth becomes clear—mine is stronger. And suddenly, just like that, he's on the defensive.

I can feel all eyes on me now. Candidates have stopped their exercises to watch. It occurs to me—have I made a miscalculation showing this degree of skill? We are all adversaries now, even more than before.

My gaze meets Julian's. He stands with his arms crossed over his chest, watching, a smile curving the corners of his mouth. I flush and, for a moment, forget about Hugh.

And suddenly find myself airborne, thrown backward as he rallies. I pull my limbs in, midair, and land on my feet, stumbling only a little. He comes at me with all his might. I leap and hit a brick wall, then scramble to get away from it. He isn't stopping, and he has murder in his eyes. I can hear Isherwood shouting to him, calling him off, but either he doesn't hear, or doesn't care.

It doesn't matter now whether it would be wiser to conceal the full strength of my gift. The second Hugh approaches, I leap straight up. There's a lantern overhead and I cling to it. Hugh churns under me like a freight train, and the moment he passes, I drop down, knocking him to the ground. One blow to the back of the neck and he is unconscious.

The gymnasium is silent.

I leave Hugh there and walk away. Without thinking, I flick a glance at Julian. His expression has turned more serious. His eyes have a glimmer of something I can't quite identify—could it be sadness?

Isherwood claps her hands, calling for attention. "That's enough sparring for now," she says briskly. "You're all dismissed."

As the others begin gathering their things, I quickly slip away.

Safely back in my room, I open my mind. It has been too long since I've talked to Nate.

Felicity?

I exhale and my shoulders relax. It's so good to hear his small voice.

I'm here, Nate. Are you well?

Oh yes! We're having treacle pudding tonight for tea . . .

I smile and listen as he describes the seaside picnic they went on two days ago, and the wooden toy sailboat he built—all by himself—last week. Then I tell him my news, that we've relocated to London—while skirting around the events that led us here—and that I'm continuing my training. *I knew you could do it,* he says. *I bet you're the best one there.*

I didn't plan on telling him about the competition, yet somehow it comes out.

Maybe you're going to be the one! he says, his sweet voice full of excitement.

Perhaps, I say, humoring him. I pause, thinking. *That doesn't mean I'm not coming to get you soon.*

He's quiet a moment. *Won't you miss it?* he asks.

The Academy? No. Not at all.

But even as I say it, I'm not sure it's the truth. Once I leave, I'm certain I'll never see these people again. A dull ache forms in my chest as I think of Julian. And then an immediate twist of guilt. *Kit.*

No, it would be better to leave, and never see them again.

I consider telling Nate about our father. The words are almost out of my mouth. But I hesitate. He chatters on for a while, telling me about the cook and the nanny and an escapade that involved chasing runaway chickens. His voice is filled with giggles. *Oh, you should have seen Nanny, Felicity . . .*

Later that evening, I have Jane bring me dinner in my room. After I finish, I slip out and climb through the old chimney sweep hatch that leads to the rooftop. Not all old buildings have one, but I knew exactly where to look. Many of my old Whitechapel friends were chimney sweeps, after all.

The manicured parks and pretty townhouses of the fancy neighborhoods of London spread out before me. Farther to the east, dirty smoke rises in pillars—the factories, the slums. What was once my home. Is it still? The silver ribbon of the Thames cuts through the darkness of London.

I take a deep breath and recall my training session from earlier today. I am getting better. I only hope I will be ready the next time I encounter the Huntsmen—wherever they are out there.

CHAPTER THIRTY-FOUR

"Hell is a city much like London—
A populous and smoky city."
—Percy Bysshe Shelley, "Peter Bell the Third"

I arrive at the music hall, nestled in the shadowy streets of Bluegate Fields in East London, just north of the docks. The hall is alive with raucous music and laughter and the sound of coin changing hands. Officially, this may be a music hall, but everyone knows it for what it is: a gambling den.

And tonight is a test.

Hawksmoor has told us that all five Candidates will be present on this mission, but after tonight, based on our performance, the field will be narrowed to three.

"A key quality for an agent is to blend in. To be covert—no matter what the environment," he said. And then he gave us our mission, which made me shudder. "This is a *team* operation," Hawksmoor said. "Do not get caught. Work as a group. Do not leave anyone behind."

We all came our separate ways to the music hall. I walked here through some of the worst neighborhoods I know, carrying a carpet bag and jingling with bracelets and brass coins.

I am disguised as a fortune-teller.

The truth is, I would never go anywhere near this place, even when I was living in Whitechapel. Everyone knows the Bluegate is a gathering place for the worst of the criminal underworld.

When I arrive, I scan the room and quickly locate Rose. She is looking at me with a disapproving twist to her mouth. She campaigned fiercely to get me off the team, and removed as a Candidate. "She has no experience," she complained to Hawksmoor. "She'll fail the group."

Truthfully, I can't help but agree with her. What chance do I really have? There's no way I would be selected.

That doesn't mean I'm giving up, though.

"Don't spoil your disguise," Rose hisses to me as I pause directly behind her near the gambling tables. Rose is dressed in woolen trousers and a cap, disguised as a boy. "Do not ruin this for me." She doesn't need to say anything. I'm already worried about my disguise, and a hundred other things besides.

Charlie and Hugh are stationed by the piano. Julian is by the roulette wheel. I will take up a position in an upper gallery, above the stage. Rose is going to be stationed at the card table where she'll play faro. From our varied positions, we are on the lookout for our mark, a notorious gangster named Rupert Crutchley.

"Are you sure you playing at the table is a good idea?" I ask Rose in a low voice.

"Of course. I can blend in anywhere. I'm the top student in intelligence."

"But these places—they have very firm rules. One misstep—"

"Please," Rose sniffs. "This rabble? I doubt that."

I try to explain, but she cuts me off. "I don't think you should worry about me, Felicity. I think you should worry about *yourself*."

I look at her dubiously and we go our separate ways.

Everyone has moved to their assigned positions. We are fanning out, searching for our target. Hawksmoor told us there would be an operative here to report back on our performance.

He also briefed us on a backup escape plan. "Should things go amiss, there is a door that lets out onto an outside stairwell on the top floor in the attics. An operative will be placed there to protect the exit. My goal is not to get you killed."

Somehow, I find this less than reassuring.

At the hall, I take a seat at a small table by the gallery railing. It's a perfect spot. I can view all the people gathered below—men, mostly. Criminals, almost all. I'll need to keep my wits about me if I want to make it out of here alive. I scan the crowd, looking for our target. The quicker we find him, the quicker we can be finished with this business.

A man approaches my table. "You can tell me my fortune?" he slurs.

I dig my nails into my palms but keep my face composed. "Of course, sir."

I run my fingers over his upturned palm, close my eyes, and start making up a story. "You have fallen on hard times recently. But you will soon meet a stranger . . ."

And then, an unexpected feeling of sadness infuses me. I crack one eye open and look at the man. "Did you say something?"

He looks at me blankly. He hasn't said a word.

I frown, but continue on. "There is a trip in your future . . ." I say, wondering where this idea is coming from. "You need to go north, but you are wondering whether to bring your family . . ." He looks startled.

At that moment, a loud cheer rises up from below, and movement catches my eye. A man in a distinctive green cloak has entered the hall and is receiving a rowdy welcome.

That's our target: Rupert Crutchley.

I locate Julian, who looks up at me, and I incline my head to the front door. He glances in the same direction, then gives a curt nod. I brusquely wrap up the drunkard's fortune and leave him at the table. Gathering my skirts, I wind my way down the stairs.

Rose has spotted our target, too. She moves to the gambling table where Crutchley is settling himself. I sidle up near the same table and identify a suitable victim nearby, a dim-looking man with a bulbous red nose. "Care to have your fortune told, sir? No charge . . ."

As I hover nearby, doing an impromptu palm reading, I hear snatches of Crutchley's conversation with his entourage.

". . . and what about Jones? Is he in, too?"

"If he can drag his sorry arse out of the Tianjin House."

"Unlikely." They laugh.

Tianjin House? Why does that name sound familiar?

"Maybe we should go down there and haul 'im out. It's not far from 'ere."

My thoughts are tumbling, trying to remember why the name is important. But I glimpse Julian approaching and return to my performance. I need to stay focused on the job.

As planned, Rose takes this moment to cause a loud distraction. She's not only playing the role of a boy, but a boy who can't hold his drink. She takes a slug of whiskey and stumbles back, knocking into a few people. She does it well—not too hard, nothing to cause a fight, of course. Just enough to draw attention.

Providing the perfect opportunity for Julian to lift a slim black book from within the folds of Crutchley's cloak.

Julian's theft is smooth and perfectly executed, and lightning fast—all thanks to Aristos. My mouth crooks into a smile. He would have made an excellent cutpurse had he grown up in Whitechapel.

At that precise moment, Charlie walks across the gambling hall floor, passing Julian. The moment Julian turns away from the lift, he slips the book to Charlie. The handoff is seamless.

Charlie keeps moving without breaking his stride, and disappears up the stairs. In a back room, Hugh will be waiting. Together they'll make copies of the names within the notebook, and then Hugh will bring the book back down, and we'll have to slip it back into Crutchley's cloak.

Rose continues gambling and I continue pretending to read fortunes while we wait. Julian chats to strangers near the bar. I dare a glance at Crutchley and hope the trickle of sweat dripping down my back doesn't show. *Quickly, boys.*

At last, I see Hugh at the top of the stairs, and Charlie strolling around the upper gallery. They both look relaxed. They've been successful in their task.

Then, I move to Julian. "Care to 'ave your fortune read, sir?" I ask.

"Why not?"

I blather on bits of nonsense, keeping an eye on Hugh, who is making his way down the stairs and through the crowd. The band fires up a jolly tune and the smells of cigar smoke and sour ale fill my nose.

When Hugh draws close, I flicker a glance at Julian. He winks. And then hollers at me. "What do you mean, woman?" People around us startle. "Why, that's the worst fortune-telling I've ever heard—" He gives me a shove. I see an apology flicker in his eyes. Heads snap in our direction. Black eyes glitter with voyeuristic interest, sniffing a potential brawl.

At that moment, Hugh slides the book back in place. Flawless.

I turn and slide away. Julian takes a swill of his drink, grumbling about charlatan palm readers.

I exhale. We did it.

When I'm a little farther away, I glance back, just at the moment Rose loses a hand. Her face pinches, the same way I've seen when she's displeased and feeling haughty.

Just stay right there, Rose, I say under my breath. *Not yet.* But she moves her chair back from the table, just a little, and I know what she's about to do.

No.

I pick up my skirts and lunge toward her. She must be stopped from leaving the table. But it's too late. I can't reach her in time. She leans across and scoops up her coins.

We are undone.

I watch the men's expressions change. Crutchley grabs her. "Where do you think you're going, *boy?*"

"I'm taking my winnings and leaving," Rose says imperiously. "Unhand me."

This isn't gambling protocol. In the middle of a game, the low person at the table does not simply walk away. Rose may know the rules to navigate the tearooms in Kensington and the drawing rooms in Chelsea, but she clearly doesn't know the rules here.

Crutchley grabs her, his hand catching her cap. As it comes loose, her hair tumbles down.

Hair that is not only feminine, but glossy, curled, and clearly belonging to someone of a much higher class.

"What's this?" he demands. "*Ah*. Thought you could run with the big boys, did you, girlie? Well, let me show you what it's like down here in the gutter. . . ."

A blade flashes between Crutchley's fingers. He stabs it down on the table, straight into Rose's hand.

CHAPTER THIRTY-FIVE

"Though a good deal is too strange to be believed,
nothing is too strange to have happened."
—Thomas Hardy, personal notebooks

In an instant, I reach the table, grabbing Aristos as hard as
I can. Gambling cards and chips fly through the air, hovering unnaturally as everything slows around me.

Lifting up my skirts, I leap onto the table and skim
across cash and cards and drinking glasses. I cartwheel over
it all and, in one smooth movement, pull the knife from
Rose's hand. She's a rag doll in my arms, having passed out
when the blade entered her flesh.

Instantly, I fling her over my shoulder and leap over
tables and chairs toward the exit, ignoring the howls of protest as I dodge the thugs who lunge to restrain me.

I hand Rose off to Hugh, and he darts from the Bluegate
Fields into the street. I turn to locate Julian and Charlie.
I'm not about to leave them behind. Not in this world—my

world. The men in here won't be kind to liars and pretenders. They'll show no mercy.

My friends, however, are nowhere to be seen. They must have bolted through the back door. As I turn to do the same, a pair of angry thugs blocks my way. "Get 'er," one of them growls.

I'm now facing a slew of irate members of the criminal underworld. Abruptly, I turn to the staircase. If I can just make it to the secret exit on the top floor—Hawksmoor's fail-safe.

Somehow, I outpace my pursuers. In the corridor, I find Julian.

"In here!" he hollers to me, flinging open a small door and the filthy curtain that covers it. Charlie's already inside, but he's rooted to the spot, gawping at something just out of my sight. Julian and I come to a sudden halt.

Hawksmoor's agent is there. But he's dead, stabbed in the back. And the doorway that's meant to be our exit is completely bricked up.

We're trapped.

"How will we ever get out now?" Charlie demands, panic setting in.

A single oil lamp flickers, throwing shadows along the wall. I slow my breathing, thinking through our situation. There must be a way.

Julian searches the room, flinging aside boxes and old curtains, hunting for another route. But Charlie's frozen where he stands. I place my hands on his shoulders. "Charlie, breathe. We can do this together."

It's a matter of seconds before the thugs will be upon us. Charlie, eyes wide, is making nonsensical sounds. My gaze sweeps the space, searching for a solution.

Then it hits me. I've got a plan to get us out of here.

I grasp the oil lamp and throw it down in the doorway. It catches on the filthy curtain and flames spring up.

"What did you do that for?" Charlie screeches. But I ignore him. I've created a distraction that should buy us a few moments.

Wasting no time, I go straight to the tiny old hatch meant for the chimney sweep. It was boarded up, which is why Julian didn't notice it.

Smoke billows up and flames lick at the walls. Julian and I quickly peel away the boards and then all three of us are clambering out of the hatch onto the rooftop of the ramshackle old building.

Shouting rings out above the crackling of the flames. A cool breeze ruffles my hair. It's too far a drop down to the streets. We'll have to find somewhere lower.

I run ahead, scrambling across the rooftop. Julian's right behind me.

Charlie has snapped out of his panic by now, and we leap across the rickety rooftops, the slums of London below our feet. As we leap across a gap, it suddenly hits me, the thing I needed to remember.

Tianjin House is just around the corner—that's the opium den where Sig says his former colleague, the expert on the Huntsmen, now spends all his time. I wonder . . .

"Felicity, keep up!" hollers Julian.

Under the night sky and the smog of the city, we make our tripping escape across the rooftops. Tianjin House will have to wait. My stomach tightens. We'll have to answer to Hawksmoor about our botched operation first.

All five of us stand before Hawksmoor. We are in the war room—charts and maps line the walls behind the spymaster and his enormous desk.

"Miss Pritchard, you failed to be covert," he says to Rose. "You failed to consider the rules of the location you were infiltrating. Perhaps worse, you considered yourself above others. Superior." He fixes her with a piercing look. "As Morgana, we have certain abilities. But we are not better than others. We are not *above* others. Never forget that. Miss Pritchard, you are out."

She is stone for a moment. Silent. Then her face grows eggplant purple. "That's ridiculous!" she blusters. "I'm the most qualified." She glares at me. "You're going to get rid of *her*, too, right? She doesn't deserve a place here."

Hawksmoor ignores Rose's sputtering. With difficulty, she's escorted from the room by an agent. Once her protests have faded, Hawksmoor turns back to us. Specifically, to Charlie. "Mr. Spooner, you fell to pieces at the most inopportune time. The bricked-up exit? That was a test."

Julian utters a strangled sound. "You—planned that? You did that to us on purpose?"

A man walks into the room. It's the agent from last night—the one who had a knife sticking out of his back. The one I saw dead with my own eyes. He's certainly not dead now.

"This is Agent Nelson. You'll see he is just fine."

Charlie gapes. Julian's mouth is a hard line.

"Mr. Spooner," Hawksmoor continues, "an agent needs to be quick on his feet, ready to formulate a new plan at a moment's notice. Out in the field, things will rarely work out the way you've planned, and you need to be able to adapt. I'm sorry to say, you're out."

I bite my lip and glance at Charlie. Unlike Rose, he maintains a dignified demeanor. Lifting his chin, he utters a simple, "Thank you for the opportunity, Mr. Hawksmoor. It's been an honor," before leaving, but he flicks a glance at Julian and then at me before he passes through the doorway. "Good luck, you two." I can't be sure that there's not something more in his words.

Hawksmoor leans back in his chair. "Mr. Blake, Miss Cole, and Mr. Torrington . . . it's just the three of you remaining."

I look, bewildered, at Julian and Hugh. How is it possible that I'm still a competitor? But now that I am so close, I can practically taste victory.

"Your next test begins tomorrow," says Hawskmoor. "I suggest you prepare. And that you wear your finest."

Tomorrow? Our finest? He dismisses us without another word.

But just before I pass through the door, Hawksmoor clears his throat. "Oh, and Felicity? You will require a proper hat."

CHAPTER THIRTY-SIX

"We are all in the gutter, but some of us are looking at the stars."

—Oscar Wilde, *Lady Windermere's Fan*

As I make my way back to my rooms, questions tumble in my mind.

Of all the matters churning through my head, one eclipses the rest: I need to get to Tianjin House. But the prospect of sneaking out into the night, back to the East End, fills me with dread. If only I didn't have to go alone.

I am lost in reflections, working out my plan, as I round the corner and smash into someone coming from the other direction. A tall, very solid someone. I bounce back, and would surely fall, if not for a strong set of arms that grabs me firmly. I find myself looking up into Julian's face.

His scent envelops me: soap and pine needles. The warmth of his hands penetrates the fabric of my dress.

"Those are some rather deep thoughts, Felicity. I suspect a penny would be poor payment for them," he says, flashing me a charming grin that makes my knees feel loose.

"My apologies, Mr. Blake . . ." I begin. But then an idea occurs to me. I hesitate. "Actually, may I speak with you about a difficult matter?"

"Certainly," he says casually. "How can I be of assistance?"

There's a sudden unpleasant flutter in my stomach—like leathery wings flapping in a deep cavern—and I feel a familiar stab of guilt. It's not that I want to forget about Kit, but . . . I wonder if I will ever be free of my past. I do my best to ignore the sensation; I'm simply asking Julian for help. Besides, we're friends. And Julian has always been quick to help me.

I glance down the length of the corridor. It's deserted for now, but that could change in an instant. "It's a rather sensitive matter. Is there a chance we could go somewhere more private?"

Julian begins to smile. And then he straightens, as though he's just remembered something, his easy manner replaced by one that's much more formal.

"I'm sorry, Miss Cole, I have an appointment that has entirely slipped my mind."

"An appointment? At this hour?"

He nods. "Perhaps another time."

He walks away and turns the corner, and I'm left alone in the empty hallway, blinking. What on earth was that? He was clearly lying.

My cheeks flush. I think back to all the times Julian has been kind. Attentive, even. Was he just playing a role?

Of course that's all he was doing. He's a spy. He's Hawksmoor's protégé. It's part of the job.

Everyone was right about Julian after all. It was ridiculous for me to think we were friends. Or . . . even, perhaps, something more.

It's better this way. I don't need the distraction.

I stride off, determined, toward my rooms.

The next morning, less than two weeks before the Golden Jubilee, I step into the foyer of the underground headquarters where everyone is already gathered. The satin gloves I wear, my shoes, the elaborate hat atop my head, it's all the very finest—the most exquisite clothing I have ever worn. The idea of attending an event where everyone will be dressed this way—well, that terrifies me more than anything else.

Today, our field test is taking place at the Royal Ascot, the premier horse racing event that is, arguably, the highlight of the social season. I place a hand on my stomach to quell the butterflies.

As I stand waiting for the carriage, I try to recall everything I've learned in Isherwood's deportment lessons, but my mind is strangely blank. I am a fraud.

I flick a glance at the other Candidates waiting beside me, Hugh and Julian, and try to read the thoughts beneath their neutral expressions. Am I the only one feeling apprehensive about our mission? Surely not. Today's operation is an assassination.

Beneath our finery we are all dressed in gear—underclothes designed by Sig to protect against stab wounds, yet provide enough flexibility for movement, and custom-made harnesses for our weapons and tools. I have lined my gown with the instruments I may need: a poison vial in my bodice, knives at my hip and within the folds of my skirts, and a garrote within my hair ornaments.

"The most difficult part of an agent's job is to kill someone in cold blood," Hawksmoor said as he briefed us over breakfast. "Today's test will determine whether you are able."

Kill. My stomach had curdled at the idea and I'd pushed my breakfast plate away. Still, Rose had been able to do it on the train. She assassinated someone and barely batted an eyelash. Would I ever be capable of such a thing?

Hawksmoor had sipped his tea and showed us a photograph. "This is your target; he will be at the Ascot. He is a criminal of the nastiest sort—the kind that hides behind his privileged life and believes himself above the law. We have intelligence that indicates he is deeply involved in a plot to kidnap the Queen's youngest child. Among the three of you, you'll need to come up with a plan to find him and assassinate him—all covert, of course."

"And the person who does the killing will be the victor?" Hugh had asked.

Hawksmoor lifted a small silver spoon and cracked the top of his soft-boiled egg in a perfect circle. "There's more to becoming a successful agent than simply being a knife. Life as a Morgana is about loyalty, resourcefulness, and cleverness. The agent who makes the poorest showing will be eliminated." Hawksmoor removed the top of his egg and replaced the spoon on a saucer. "It's also important to know your team. Know everyone's strengths, and use them to best advantage."

When we arrive at the Ascot, I try to still my nerves as I exit the carriage. I place a gloved hand on Julian's offered arm, just as we've practiced so many times before. All around me are the sounds of the crowds and the ceremonial parade band, the smells of freshly cut grass and horse manure. Ladies and gentlemen in the most elaborate, brightly colored fashions promenade upon lush lawns, carrying parasols and tiny cups of champagne or Pimm's.

I expect to see much raising of eyebrows from the footmen standing outside the carriages, but their faces don't so much as flicker. I glance at Julian, wondering if we are succeeding in our deception, and his face is as serene and handsome as ever. He shows not an iota of concern. The fluttering in my stomach eases, just a little.

I'm happy Julian isn't looking directly at me; I'm not quite sure what to say to him. After his abrupt coldness last night, it's clear to me this will be a business relationship, nothing more. And that's exactly how I'm going to treat it.

We take our position near the track, and the races begin.

The earth rumbles as the horses fly around the track. A thrill goes down my spine; the exhilaration is contagious. There's riotous color everywhere I look: the banners, the gorgeous dresses and suits, the parasols, the hats.

Hugh is elsewhere, locating our target in the man's private viewing box. I'm fiddling with my parasol beside Julian when a young man walks by us, very finely dressed in a gray morning suit. He has stylishly coiffed hair and an aristocratic cut to his jaw. A very handsome young man indeed.

Julian stiffens. He attempts to turn away, but he is a moment too late.

"Good God, Blake—is that you?" says the man, stopping abruptly. Two friends, other young men equally finely dressed, also pause.

"Hello, Cavendish," says Julian. There's a distinct tension in his voice. Barely restrained contempt.

"What the devil are you doing here?" inquires Cavendish. There's an amused, condescending curl to his lip. "I haven't seen you since you were kicked out of Eton."

There's a brief snort from the man standing off Cavendish's left shoulder.

Julian bristles. "I wasn't kicked out, as you well know. I . . . withdrew."

He withdrew from Eton to attend Greybourne? But of course that had to have been kept a secret. Julian would essentially have dropped out of Society, which would have meant a great fall, no doubt, in the eyes of his circle.

The young man waves a hand dismissively. "Yes, yes. That's right. But seriously, old boy, what have you been doing with yourself?" His accent is excessively plummy and posh, like it was specifically designed to be irritating. "It can't have been anything of significance or I would have heard about it." He chortles, like he's made a great joke. I give Julian a gentle tug. We should move away.

"Actually, I—"

"Well, now just wait a moment," Cavendish says, now fixing his gaze upon me. "And who is *this*?" He lifts my hand to kiss it. "Miss, may I introduce myself, since Blake here is clearly too classless to do so?"

Julian's nostrils flare slightly. Haltingly, he makes the introductions. And then quickly adds that we are expected elsewhere.

Cavendish laughs. "Oh, I'm sure you are, Blake. It must be a great opportunity for you to be here, after dropping off into oblivion." He winks. "Hoping to find a seat at the big table again, eh?"

Julian is dangerously silent.

"Don't blame you a bit," Cavendish continues, "though I'm not sure what scraps you're going to find at this stage. Not many positions for a washed-up dropout—"

Julian moves quickly. Like a viper. "Listen, you little prig," he says in a low voice an inch from Cavendish's aristocratic nose. "I am involved in affairs you could never even fathom."

Cavendish looks confused for a moment, then scoffs. "Oh please, Blake."

Julian attempts to gather himself and I try desperately to catch his eye. *Not worth it, Julian.*

"Is that all you've got to say?" Cavendish says, his pompous face a mixture of pity and disdain. *"Affairs you could never even fathom?"* he mocks, laughing outright.

Julian's nostrils flare. "I'm a spy, you maggot," he hisses. "And an assassin."

Cavendish's laughter abruptly cuts off. Julian wraps my hand around his arm and we stalk away.

Halfway across the lawn, I spot Hugh, hovering near the entrance to the private boxes. He has removed his top hat and holds it in his left hand—his signal to us. He's located our target. He intercepts a plump middle-aged woman and draws her away. This is the target's wife. Hugh will be keeping her out of the way while Julian goes inside the private viewing box to do the job. She and Hugh disappear out of sight.

Julian releases my arm and begins to stroll toward the private boxes; I backtrack and go around the other way, on alert for any sign that he is being watched or followed. My job is to be a lookout. I fiddle with my parasol. It is how I am meant to signal the others when the time comes.

But as Julian approaches the box, he is suddenly surrounded by Peelers, uniformed policemen. I can't hear what they're saying, but in a moment it becomes clear they are detaining him. A few feet away, Cavendish stands speaking earnestly with one of the policemen and nodding with great satisfaction.

The bloody bastard ratted us out.

A black police coach pulls up and Julian has no choice but to let the Peelers load him in and take him away. I stare helplessly, twisting my parasol. Hugh is nowhere in sight. We'll have to abort the mission. We've failed. Not only Hawksmoor's test, but we've enabled our target to go free and continue his terrible plans.

Unless . . . there's still one possibility.

A true spy will always find a way.

CHAPTER THIRTY-SEVEN

"What we think, or what we know; or what we believe, is in the end, of little consequence.
The only thing of consequence is what we *do*."
—John Ruskin, *The Crown of Wild Olive*

I stand on the lawn of the Ascot, clenching my hands and trying to decide my next move. Hugh is nowhere in sight, distracting the target's wife. Time is running out. The target won't stay in the private box forever. A small voice says to me: *you could do it.*

And more than that. You *have* to do it.

What were those words of Christopher Marlowe's? *You must be proud, bold, pleasant, resolute . . . and now and then stab, as occasion serves.* I tighten my fists and cling to the words like a raft.

I watch and wait, praying for Hugh to return. I could signal him, and he could do the kill. But why wait for him? I'm just as capable; I know I am. But if I'm going to finish the mission, it has to be now. The window of opportunity is closing and the team is depending on me.

A great cheer rises up from the track. The horses are coming down the home stretch. A footman strolls by carrying a tray of drinks, and I casually take a cup of Pimm's. Checking to make sure I'm not being observed, I slip to the rear of the building where the private boxes are housed, preparing myself for my task.

I am Tainted. I am an assassin. I have been living and training with the Morgana for months now. It's time.

I slide the vial of poison from the bodice of my dress, uncap it, and pour the powder carefully into the Pimm's. When it's dissolved, I open the door to the private box. Catfooted, I slip inside. The door snicks shut as I surreptitiously lock it behind me.

A man dressed in a fine gray suit and top hat idly stands watching the races below through a pair of field glasses. He turns his head and sees me standing there. "And who might you be?"

"Oh, I must have taken a wrong turn. I was meant to be meeting someone else, except . . . he doesn't appear to be here." I pout. "Would you like this? It's quite refreshing but . . . I've already had two." I hold out the cup. He gives it a glance and then waves it away.

I swallow. I'll need a new strategy . . . I run through my options—gun, garrote, knife, poison, snap his neck— I've practiced them all. *The knife, yes.* I begin to slide the blade out of my sleeve, and then hesitate, and it slides back again.

I could have killed him seven times by now, seven different ways. But I simply don't have it in me.

At the sound of footfalls, my attention is pulled back to the target. He's moved closer and his eyes have gone black.

"Imagine my surprise when you just walked right in here, Miss Cole." His voice is even, quiet. Dangerous.

I go stiff. How does he know my name?

"What's wrong? You look suddenly concerned." He smiles wolfishly.

I take a step backward. This is a trap.

"I must tell you, you're prettier than they described. Not that it matters. You'll earn me a tidy sum either way. Warwick will be most pleased."

His cold gaze bores into me. The rasp of his hands as he rubs them together sends a chill down my spine.

Behind my back, the blade slips again into my hand. I take another step back, keeping my gaze tethered to the mark, and curse silently. Why didn't I kill him when I had the chance? Has my hesitation cost me my life?

Breathing out, I let go and feel the pulse of my power, letting Aristos burn bright all around me.

The man comes at me, then. Fast. Tainted fast.

Huntsman, then.

I know what I must do. As he lunges at me, I drop down, sweeping low into a perfect, courtly curtsy (thank you, Agatha Isherwood), and immediately propel myself forward, sliding straight underneath his legs and out the other side. Before he can turn, I'm on my feet, my arms around his neck before I drag the knife across his throat.

Blood is everywhere.

He doesn't make a sound as he goes limp.

It is done.

Several hours later, I am back at headquarters. Julian, Hugh, and I stand before Hawksmoor in the war room as we did the night before, but we are a very different group. Julian has been released from police custody, courtesy of Hawksmoor's quiet intervention, but his shirt and trousers are stained with dirt and he has a defeated slouch to his shoulders.

Hugh has learned of everything that's happened, and looks triumphant, though he keeps shooting me wary glances. I am nothing like he expected.

As for me, I can barely begin to understand what has just occurred.

"I assume you've made your decision, sir?" asks Julian, trying to gather his dignity for the edict that is surely about to come.

"A secret agent does not receive accolades for his work," Hawksmoor begins. "He does not receive awards. There is no glory. Those in his life will have no idea what he actually engages in. His Aunt Mildred—unless she, too, happens to be a Morgana agent, and perhaps not even then—will not be *proud* of him."

Julian's throat bobs as he attempts to swallow. He remains silent.

"The moment you start looking for glory, Mr. Blake, that is the moment you are no longer suitable as a Morgana agent."

I bite the inside of my cheek.

"Mr. Blake, you're out of the running," Hawksmoor says flatly. "You may go."

Julian walks out silently.

Later that afternoon, alone in my room, Jane brings me a light meal, then draws me a bath. "It's just down to you and Mr. Torrington now, Miss Cole," she says after I emerge from the water that was far less soothing than I'd hoped. I do not reply, staring at my reflection as she brushes my hair. Though I wear a warm robe, I feel chilled.

"Mrs. Isherwood said to tell you the final test will be tomorrow morning. Your time this evening is your own."

My eyes snap to hers in the mirror. She watches me with concern, but says nothing more.

A plan forms in my head. Tonight is my final chance.

CHAPTER THIRTY-EIGHT

"In a moment I knew what had happened. I had slept, and my fire had gone out, and the bitterness of death had come over my soul."

—H. G. Wells, *The Time Machine*

A thick fog curls around my ankles as I approach Tianjin House. My skin is cold and clammy despite the wool coat and cap I snuck out of the headquarters' cloak room. I've disguised myself as a young man, all the better to blend in. Wandering this part of town alone as a woman was out of the question. Opium dens are the sort of place I took care to avoid even when I lived in Whitechapel.

Gaslight lanterns try in vain to drive back the gloom. While black coaches clatter past ramshackle, sooty buildings, I make my way on foot. I move swiftly over slick cobblestones, moonlight glimmering in the puddles between the cracks.

I have only been away from Whitechapel for a few months, but already I have grown used to the comforts and safety of my new life. Still, I have nothing to fear. I have skills now. And, besides, I have little choice if I want to find this cure.

I secreted away from headquarters when everyone else went down for dinner. I'm sure nobody will notice my absence. And if I can get the answers I need about the Huntsmen, it will be worth it.

Inside Tianjin House, the air is warm and damp and dark. The powerful scent of incense and opium twines through the smoky interior. Patrons lounge in red-cushioned alcoves, smoking their water pipes and drinking tea. They are from all strata of society, yet their features share a glazed, faraway look, their eyes glassy.

I examine each face as I pass. The sooner I find Dexter, the sooner I can be on my way. I am risking everything to find him.

Sig's old daguerreotype of his former colleague gave me the particulars of my target's appearance. I'm hoping Mr. Dexter hasn't changed much since the image was taken.

I avoid eye contact as much as possible, though most here are in too much of a stupor anyway. One or two follow my movements, and I speed my search.

As the minutes tick by, I chew the inside of my cheek. Perhaps Dexter is not here tonight, or no longer frequents this place. Perhaps he's dead.

I keep moving, even as I grow more anxious. It's not just about the danger. Hawksmoor discovering this betrayal weighs heavily on my mind.

And then I spot Dexter. He looks thinner and more timeworn than in the daguerreotype, but it's him, I'm certain. He lounges on a chaise tucked partially behind a silk curtain. His skin has a gray cast to it, and bruise-like shadows make his eyes look sunken.

I slide onto a cushion in the booth next to his.

"Mr. Dexter?"

He continues to stare ahead blankly.

"Mr. Dexter, sir, if I may have a moment of your time—" I begin, then curse under my breath, and correct my language. *Damned deportment training.*

"Oy. You dead, mister?"

Dexter is barely conscious. I close the curtain a little, hiding him from view, then grasp a pitcher from a nearby table and throw the cold contents in his face. He barely flinches. But he does, at least, focus on me.

"You gonna finish that?" I ask, eyes going to his pipe.

He shrugs and makes no objection as I reach for the mouthpiece and pretend to smoke. His rheumy eyes fasten on my face but still he says nothing.

"All out of bob, you see," I natter, by way of explanation. "Not a penny to my name." I exhale and sit back. He nods with sympathy. Money troubles are something he can understand, I'm sure. "Although . . . I heard a rumor yesterday," I continue, choosing my words carefully. "Somethin' about a job opportunity with a particular group of people. Delivery work. That's somethin' I can do, I reckon."

"Sure you could," he slurs and drops his gaze. I hardly expect him to be lucid under the opium's influence, but I'm hoping his defenses will be lowered enough that I can get a little information out of him.

I lower my voice and lean in close. The smell of him—unwashed, covered in his own filth—makes me gag. "The people doin' the hiring are called the Huntsmen, they say. That's the word on the street. Know anything about that lot?"

His head goes up. "Huntsmen? Best stay away." His voice is gruff, gravelly, like he hasn't spoken in a year.

I pause, nodding. "Maybe you're right."

I reach for the pipe and pretend to smoke again.

After a moment, I clear my throat. "But . . . let's say I do want to see about this job. Lend a hand, maybe, and help meself, too. Any idea how I might find them?"

Dexter's brow furrows. He shakes his head.

I glance around. A tall, slender woman in a glossy black gown stands on the other side of the room, watching me through narrowed eyes. When I first arrived, I noted her closely monitoring the patrons of the opium den, pacing slowly through the room. She must be the mistress of Tianjin, the woman in charge. She motions to a man standing beside her.

I don't have long. Time for my next gamble. I produce a drawing I made of the pattern on the Huntsman's pin. The actual pin is still with Sig in his lab. "I saw this on one of the toff's cloaks once," I say. "It's strange. Any idea what it means?" I scan his face for a reaction.

Dexter looks at me clearly for the first time, glances at the paper I've pressed before him, then laughs, a weak, wheezy sound.

He reaches for the pipe, mumbling. "Pleasure, a most mighty lure to evil."

I frown, but the statement tickles my memory.

Plato. He's quoting Plato?

"You know it?" he says, seeing the recognition in my eyes. "How about this one, then? *Until philosophers are kings . . . cities will never have rest from their evils.*"

More Plato. He's clearly lost his grasp on reality. His eyes roll back and he falls onto the chaise. His breathing slows. He's asleep. Or possibly on his way to death. Either way, I'll get nothing more from him.

My time is up. The guard starts to cross the room. I pull my cloak about me and slip out of the alcove and quickly away. I'm out the back door before the man can reach me.

The moment I feel the cool, foggy night air in the alley behind Tianjin House, I know I've made a mistake.

Five men stand beside a black carriage, arms folded, waiting.

Warwick is among them.

CHAPTER THIRTY-NINE

"How cheerfully he seems to grin,
How neatly spreads his claws,
And welcomes little fishes in,
With gently smiling jaws!"
                    —Lewis Carroll, "The Crocodile"

I reach for Aristos, but it's too late. Two more Huntsmen are on either side of the doorway, and they grab me, and the others are upon me before I can blink.

They hustle me out to the street and stuff me into the coach. The side of my face presses into the velvet of the seat cover as I struggle. Warwick slides in like a serpent, settling himself on the bench opposite me.

"An interesting spot to visit, Miss Cole," he says. "I know you come from the streets, but I truly thought you'd left all that behind."

Another Huntsman—a woman—slips in beside me. And then another on my other side. I recognize him from the train. I hazard a glance at the woman—glossy black hair, red lips, angular cheekbones, eyes dead and cold, like a spider's.

I focus on my breathing. I must stay calm.

Warwick shouts to the driver and the horses leap forward. The carriage bumps over potholes as we race through the streets. A second carriage, just ahead of us, carries the other Huntsmen.

The woman, the Black Spider, quickly binds my wrists in front of me. I fix Warwick with the most hateful glare I can muster. "You're despicable. You're hunting your own kind. Why?"

He shrugs, unruffled. "I have reasons."

"What reason can you possibly have for trying to stop the Morgana?"

He leans close to my face, his hot breath assaulting my cheek as his nostrils flare. "I'm not trying to *stop* the Morgana, you foolish girl. I *am* Morgana. The way Morgana are *meant* to be."

"What are you talking about?"

His rage recedes as quickly as it flared and his expression melts into placid amusement. "Out in the open."

I snap my mouth shut. The carriage continues rolling ever forward through the night, and soon, we've left the city behind. I catch glimpses of shadowy countryside, but no other clues to our destination. There's no point in demanding where he's taking me. He won't answer.

Finally, Warwick breaks the silence. "Now, before we get much farther, there's something I must do." He withdraws a black leather case. Inside rests a glass syringe to which he attaches a long, steel needle.

"What's that?" I demand, my eyes going wide as I strain against the Huntsmen on either side who labor to hold me still.

This cannot be the end. I can't leave Nate alone. I won't leave him to fend for himself.

I grasp as hard as I can to Aristos, but it's no use. They are too strong. My arms are pinned in front of me, bound at the wrists. The woman grips my arms and roughly pushes my left sleeve up above my elbow.

Light glints off the cruel tip of the needle. A sharp pain burns through my arm as Warwick plunges the needle into my flesh.

But instead of pushing the plunger down, as I expect, Warwick draws it back and the small glass tube fills with my blood—deep red. Horrified fascination unfurls within me, and I stop struggling as I watch my blood curling into the vial.

Warwick removes the needle and the Huntsman on my left presses a stinging cloth against my arm. Warwick gazes at the vial of my blood with something approaching . . . reverence. I suddenly feel ill. He tucks the vial into its black leather case and snaps the clasps shut.

"Your father would be very proud of how cooperative you're being, Miss Cole."

"You know nothing of my father."

"On the contrary. In fact, I knew him quite well."

Dread prickles up my spine. "What are you talking about? My father would never have worked with someone like you. He was an honorable man. He was helping search for a cure."

"I'm so sorry to disappoint you, my dear, but your father was assisting us. And it wasn't a cure we were looking for. Although—to be fair—that might have been what *he* thought at the time. But nonetheless, the advances we made with the use of your father's blood—it was the closest we've ever come."

"Come to what?"

Warwick smiles, but doesn't answer.

A horrible thought occurs to me. "Did—did you kill him?"

"Of course not. His death was most inconvenient." Warwick's mouth pinches with irritation. "We were so close to perfecting the formula, and then . . ." He pats the black leather case and smiles wolfishly. "But now, thanks to you, we have a new hope. You should be flattered, Miss Cole. Your blood is the missing key we need."

"What on earth are you talking about?"

He lifts a lock of my hair and my skin crawls as his hand traces down the side of my face. "Such interesting coloring.

So different than the usual English rose. Dark hair, lovely skin, green eyes. Your family is from Greece, is it not?"

"It is. What of it?"

He shrugs again. "Well, if you haven't figured it out yet, far be it from me to spoil the surprise."

I can't make sense of what he's saying, but I have the feeling the truth is just within reach—if only I could remember. If I could grasp onto the missing piece of the puzzle. . . .

The carriage gives a lurch and there's a loud thump, and then the driver calls out. We're tossed into the air as the carriage careens off the road and comes to an abrupt halt.

"What's happened?" Warwick hollers as we struggle to right ourselves. Before I can even contemplate escape, the three Huntsmen grab at me. Warwick turns to my captors. "She's not to move an inch." He leaps from the carriage to investigate, leaving me pinned between his associates.

I wonder if we've suffered a broken axle. I crane my neck to see out the window. Another carriage has stopped just ahead. We are much farther into the countryside than I'd realized. Forest surrounds the country lane, mist creeping between the trees, obscuring shadows and muffling sound.

Perhaps this is my chance. I consider how long Warwick might be gone and how I might break free.

"Don't even think of it," says the woman, her icy voice slicing through the hush.

Both Huntsmen are peering out the left carriage window, straining to see what's caused our delay. I catch a flicker of movement to the right. A figure darts along the edge of the woods, a few feet away. I recognize the gait, the silhouette of broad shoulders.

Julian Blake.

CHAPTER FORTY

"All such things touch secret strings
For heavy hearts to hear."
           —Dante Gabriel Rossetti, "Even So"

Glancing at my captors, I bite my tongue to keep from crying out. They haven't seen Julian yet. Surprise will be our only advantage.

I still myself and let Aristos flow through me. Time slows before my eyes; the Black Spider turns her head and her hair moves with unnatural slowness. I'm ready.

Julian stops moving, partially tucked behind a tree. His dark hair is damp and wild. How did he find me?

From the shadows, his eyes meet mine. He puts a finger to his mouth, motioning for me to stay quiet. His glance flicks to the front of the carriage, where Warwick must be speaking with the driver.

We wait. I keep my eyes down, staring at my hands. There's a flicker in my peripheral vision. Julian is moving quickly toward the carriage. I twist and bring my arms up toward the the Black Spider and catch her right under the chin; her head snaps back.

The door to the carriage flies open and Julian reaches in to grab the Huntsman on my right and fling him out of the carriage. I scramble out. The woman is out cold, slumped on the seat.

Julian and the man struggle on the ground while I slice through my binds on a sharp edge of the carriage door. In a moment, Julian gains the upper hand, delivering a knock-out punch. The Huntsman goes still.

A shot cracks out, barely missing Julian as he ducks. Warwick is charging toward us, pistol drawn. Julian grabs my hand and together we run for the trees. I expect to feel a bullet ripping through my spine at any second.

There, just past the tree line, a horse is tethered to a branch, the breath from its nostrils misting the air. Julian leaps into the saddle and pulls me up behind him in one swift movement. He spurs the horse forward and my hair whips in the wind as we gallop away.

We fly through the woods, weaving madly between trees and rocks and leaping across small brooks. My hands are frozen, clenched around Julian's waist.

"We have to keep going," Julian says over the thundering of his horse's hooves. "Just a little farther."

Several minutes later, we reach a small glade. Julian slows the horse to a walk and leads us to a spot tucked away from any visible paths.

After we dismount, he retrieves some water from a brook. I drink while he attends to the horse. The water is gloriously cool and clean. It drips down my chin and I wipe it away with my hand.

"We can rest here. But only briefly," he says. "Are you hurt?" Concern furrows his brow. Concern and . . . something else. Fear?

"Not really, although they took . . . some of my blood."

Julian goes very still. "They what?"

I tell him about the syringe.

"Let me see your arm." He examines the spot where the syringe pierced me. "Does it hurt?"

"Not anymore."

His jaw flexes. "Why would they do such a thing?"

I shake my head, and explain what Warwick said about my father, but Julian can make no more sense of it than I can.

Shuddering, I move to pull my cloak around me, but remember I left it behind in Warwick's carriage. Cold seeps into my bones. My clothes are torn; my boy's disguise is now filthy and ripped at the shoulder from my struggle with the Huntsmen.

"You're shivering," Julian says. He removes his cloak and puts it around my shoulders. It's heavy and warm and smells like him.

I take another long sip of water and then watch him carefully. "How did you know to come find me?"

"I followed you from headquarters. I saw you in the opium den and was about to approach when you slipped out the back. Next thing I knew, you were being shoved into Warwick's carriage. I couldn't get to you in time."

I blink at him. "You followed me?"

He nods briskly, then turns to busy himself with the horse's saddle. His ears look a little pink, but I can't be sure in this light.

"You're still shivering," Julian says. He hesitates, rubbing the side of his face. "I'd rather not build a fire. It would announce our location, and if there's a chance they're still following . . ."

"I know. I'll be fine."

"Here." He moves closer and puts his arm around me. It's incredibly inappropriate, but I don't care. I'm not about to let etiquette get in the way of a little warmth. Not when I've just been snatched from the clutches of my enemy.

I lean into his side. He smells like leather and soap, and faintly of sweat. Through the cloak, his body is like a furnace.

Julian followed me. He came to rescue me.

"Why did you follow me?" I ask softly. He says nothing for a while.

"I was . . . worried about you."

"Worried?"

"After Ascot. I thought maybe it had been rather difficult for you."

"But the other night. You were so . . . distant."

"Perhaps. But that doesn't mean I'm not concerned for your welfare. That I don't"— he hesitates—"care for you."

My heartbeat quickens. Did I hear him correctly?

"I'm glad all they did was take a little of your blood, Felicity. That they didn't hurt you worse than this." He pulls me tighter.

And then his face is in front of mine. We are so close. . . .

His mouth is warm and soft. Chills spread all over my body. The world tilts beneath me as I try to make sense of it, but I can hardly think. And then . . . I stop trying. He kisses me more deeply and my head floods with starlight. I melt into his arms . . .

Then, just as abruptly, he pulls away.

"I'm sorry, Felicity. That was incredibly inappropriate."

"No, I—" I begin.

He looks down. "Can you forgive me? I don't know what came over me. My deepest apologies—"

"No, I'm not upset. I just want to know why." I swallow. "And then . . . why you stopped."

He is quiet a long time and refuses to meet my gaze. My pulse hammers in my ears.

"I'm sorry," he finally repeats. "We . . . should, er, get moving."

I bite my lip, my eyes suddenly hot. We both climb back on the horse and make our way back to headquarters, speaking no more of it.

"They stole your . . . *blood?*" Isherwood says, alarmed.

Julian and I stand before the panel of Morgana Elders. "Why would they do that?" Julian demands.

Isherwood shakes her head. "I have no idea."

Hawksmoor has been quiet throughout the interview. He'd been waiting for us when we returned, and then summoned us before a committee of the Elders. We had no choice but to tell them the unadulterated truth.

"I still don't understand," says Isherwood, her frosty glare boring into me. "What were you doing at Tianjin House in the first place, Miss Cole?"

I swallow. "I had hoped to learn more about my father. I recently discovered he was Tainted, too," I say, parsing my words carefully. I glance at Sig, seated beside Isherwood. "You mentioned Mr. Dexter before. I thought he might have some answers." I mention nothing about the real reason I went to the opium den, the Huntsmen pin, nor the cryptic answers I received from Dexter.

Isherwood's mouth purses. "Did you find the information you were seeking, Miss Cole?"

I shake my head. "It was a wasted exercise."

"In the carriage," Hawksmoor begins, "what were Warwick's exact words as he extracted your blood?"

As I speak, I strive to keep my voice even and strong. I know I'm in trouble.

Warwick's taunts make no more sense to the Elders than they did to me.

"He said something about perfecting a formula?" Sig asks. "Could they be developing some kind of . . . weapon? To use against other Morgana?"

"But why would the Huntsmen want to develop a weapon like that?" I ask. "They're Tainted themselves."

"Yes, but if they want power, they'll have to defeat the Tainted who aren't on their side, won't they?" says Julian.

I nod. The Elders murmur over and debate the idea, but reach no firm conclusions.

Hawksmoor, however, cuts with surgical precision to the one fact I was hoping he'd ignore. "And so you went to the opium den alone, Miss Cole. Is that correct?"

I lick my lips. "Yes, sir."

"You told no one of your plans?"

"I didn't wish to involve anyone else. . . ."

He closes his eyes and lowers his head for a moment. When he pulls his gaze back to mine, his face has been washed of all emotion. "It's not because of your disobedience," he begins. "Nor is it a case of you putting yourself in harm's way. It's your steadfast refusal to become a member of this team. In spite of the months you have spent training, you still do not consider yourself one of us. And, I'm afraid to say, that is why I am eliminating you as a Candidate."

CHAPTER FORTY-ONE

"After all, the true seeing is within."
—George Eliot, *Middlemarch*

That night, I lie awake thinking, twisting restlessly in the bedsheets.

In the morning over breakfast I'm told I'll be helping to prepare for the Royal Jubilee operation. I am to assist Sig with the secret weapons, which will be hidden inside the garments of the agents who will be acting as a patrol. The mood at headquarters is reaching a frenzy now that we are only a few days away. Preparations for the Jubilee are the only thing anyone is talking about. But there is no mistake: I am not going to be anywhere close to the action. I am auxiliary now. From among all of us, Hugh Torrington has been elevated to the role of full Morgana agent.

As for Julian, I see him very little over the next few days. He has been assigned an entirely separate set of tasks. And when I do see him at meals, it's incredibly awkward. He'll barely meet my gaze.

One evening, I'm sitting with Neville in the parlor. Candlelight flickers on the richly papered walls. The unspoken events of the past few days clot the air with an almost palpable thickness.

"You're quiet tonight, Miss Cole. Deep in thought?"

"I suppose so."

"And how are you adjusting to your new responsibilities?"

I have been working with Sig.

"Everything coming along well?"

I shrug. "As far as I can tell. I'm not privy to all the plans."

"And that bothers you?"

I'm surprised to realize that it does.

"You were enjoying the challenge," he says, watching me intently. It's not a question.

I look down at my hands. "It was . . . so different from anything I had experienced. All this was so different. So new. At first, I hated it. All I wanted was my old life back. But then . . ."

"You began to feel attached."

A dry lump lodges in my throat. I haven't spoken with anyone about this. Not even Nate. After a bit, I nod. "I started to feel like I was part of something bigger. Something more important than just myself."

"And then you began to control your abilities."

I look up at Neville, eyes bright. "It felt amazing. Exhilarating."

"And you wanted to win."

"Not just for the sake of winning. But a part of me had started to believe in what we're doing."

"And now?"

"Now . . . I don't know. I'm not sure what lies ahead."

I stop short of telling him how tempted I am to run away.

And I keep to myself one more piece of information: I am no closer to answers about how one becomes Tainted, and I have not yet found a cure. How can I take care of Nate when we'll be forever hunted? It will be no kind of life.

In the days that follow, I try to stay focused.

I spend a great deal of time in the headquarters' library, poring over books about the Morgana, trying to formulate my next steps. I keep recalling Rufus Dexter quoting Plato: *Until philosophers are kings . . . cities will never have rest from their evils.* I wish I could recall why those words are so important.

When Sig doesn't need me in his laboratory and I can no longer stand to read and research, I go to the gymnasium to train. Although I've destroyed any prospect of fieldwork, I find I enjoy the movement and the exercise. And the chance to further hone my use of Aristos.

Until I am able to find a cure and a way out of this world, I'll need to protect myself.

At last, it's the day before the Royal Jubilee ceremony. Tonight, there will be a grand banquet at Buckingham Palace, and tomorrow will be the parade and ceremony in

Westminster Abbey. At the banquet, every British aristocrat will be in attendance, not to mention the representatives of all the royal families from abroad. The city is teeming with the excitement of hosting so many important foreign visitors; the streets feel like a festival. There is music in every square, and the delicious smells of food as the people of London prepare to celebrate in their own ways. The city feels lighter, lifted from the dreariness of daily life, even if this holiday atmosphere will only last a short time.

The mood at Morgana headquarters is somewhat different. We are not celebrating so much as preparing for every disaster that could befall the Queen and her entourage. Neville works night and day, monitoring the intelligence provided by his network of spies. Isherwood drills the agents mercilessly. And Hawksmoor watches it all with a sharp eye and the intensity of a man performing relentless mental calculations.

As I'm helping Sig with the finishing touches on the agents' concealed knives, there is a knock at the laboratory door. Unexpectedly, for the second time in a week, I'm hauled before the council of Elders.

"Miss Cole," says Hawksmoor. "One of our seasoned agents has unaccountably fallen ill, which means we will be shorthanded at the banquet tonight." The other Elders stare at me, watching my reaction carefully. "The members of the council have decided, after much deliberation, that you will fill in. It is not our first choice, but we have few alternatives.

We are prepared to elevate you to agent status . . . but only for this event."

I go very still. Am I hearing this correctly?

"We will only do this if we can count on you," he says, and then pauses. "Can we?"

Full Morgana agent. It feels like a string has been plucked inside me; it vibrates a deep hum. I've been given another chance.

"Yes, you can count on me."

Hawksmoor steeples his fingertips and I can see doubt flicker in his eyes, but he says nothing. I am dismissed, but am to report to the war room for a briefing in thirty minutes.

Jane helps me prepare, dressing me in my gear and fastening my outfit with all the tools I'll need. She clucks excitedly. "It's ever so lucky they decided to give you a second chance, isn't it?" Her fingers move excitedly as she brushes out my hair.

A hummingbird flutters at my throat. "I must confess, Jane . . . I hadn't realized how much I wanted this."

"Of course you wanted it!" she exclaims. "Why wouldn't you?"

I open my mouth, then close it again. How can I explain it to her?

I straighten my spine. No matter. As Hawksmoor said, this is just a one-time mission. Then I'll be able to concentrate on finding a way back to Nate again.

Once with the other agents, Hawksmoor walks us through the plans, using maps and charts, assigning duties to us all. We are then dismissed to warm up in the gymnasium before we're given a light, nourishing meal.

It is then that I learn that it will be impossible for me to keep my word to Hawksmoor.

CHAPTER FORTY-TWO

"There is nothing more deceptive than an obvious fact."

—Sir Arthur Conan Doyle, *The Adventures of Sherlock Holmes*

In the gymnasium, warming up with the others, I realize I am a weapon short. A knife holster attached to my left leg is empty. I excuse myself and hurry down to Sig's laboratory to find the blade I need.

The room is empty. Perhaps Sig is in conference with the Elders, making final preparations. The entire space is disorganized and dusty and smells of vinegar and chemicals. I wonder how I'm ever going to find what I need. This close to the coal furnace, the air is warm and dry. Papers litter every empty space, covering bits of equipment, which are strewn haphazardly throughout the room, the result of the frenzied preparations of the last few days.

I begin my hunt. And that's when I see it. A stack of envelopes shifts, and I notice that one of the letters is addressed to . . . me.

The blue inked handwriting is proper and formal, but not a hand I recognize. It's impossible for me to resist picking up the envelope—Dr. Alistair Middlesex. I know no one of that name.

I stare at the letter, then flip it over. The envelope's flap is somewhat ragged. Just slightly rippled, a tiny tear. It has already been opened and resealed.

Were the Elders going to give it to me? Doubtful. And though I found this letter in Sig's laboratory, I have difficulty believing he is the one behind this subterfuge.

Hawksmoor is my next thought. If the spymaster has read my letter, I'm certainly going to, too. I carefully unseal the flap.

> *My dear Miss Felicity Cole,*
>
> *Your name was put forth to me by a colleague who has fallen into, shall we say, difficult times. However, you managed to rouse him sufficiently long enough to explain your predicament, and it appears you made quite an impression.*

I pause. He must be talking about Rufus Dexter.

Suffice it to say, I do recall working with your father, and was very sorry indeed to learn of his passing. There is a great deal you need to know, but I fear it is too convoluted a tale to put to paper. I would be pleased to speak with you in person and to discuss my research toward a cure for your . . . affliction, but I am afraid I will only be in London for one more day. Circumstances have grown more dangerous, and I will be going abroad, indefinitely.

Should you wish to speak, you can find me before the morning of the 21st of June at 38 Berkeley Square.

I remain yours humbly,
Dr. Alistair Middlesex

I glance at the clock ticking away in the corner of the laboratory. The Jubilee banquet will begin at Buckingham Palace in four hours. But if I don't go see Dr. Middlesex tonight, I'll forfeit my only chance.

Can I be across town and back in time? Then something else occurs to me. What if he's able to cure me . . . tonight? It would change everything.

A vision flashes in my head. Me as one of the Morgana agents, defending Queen and Country, taking action for the betterment of the world—yet doing unspeakable things. Exhilarating things.

The image changes. Me and Nate, like old times, running away, finding a seaside town or a small city where I can work in a cotton factory or sell my flowers in the local market. Not an easy life, but a simple one. Safe.

I carefully replace the letter in the stack on Sig's desk, then go to my room and retrieve my traveling cloak and gather every last penny I possess. The doctor may not require payment for his cure, but I don't wish to leave it to chance. Briefly, I consider speaking to Julian, telling him where I'm going. But I think better of it. What would I even say?

I creep along the corridor to the back exit. My gloved hand is on the doorknob when I hear a sound behind me.

I swivel. Agatha Isherwood stands in the corridor, hovering like a specter.

"Where are you going?" she demands, folding her arms over her chest.

I hesitate. "I have an errand I must complete."

"You are aware that we begin dressing and preparing for the Jubilee within the hour."

"I'll be back in time," I assure her.

She runs her tongue over her teeth. "I don't believe you will be."

I say nothing, trying to gauge what her next move will be.

"The team is counting on you to do your part," she says simply.

I can't suppress the short laugh that comes out. "I don't know why it would bother you if I wasn't there—you've always said I'm useless."

"Not anymore."

I stare at her, unable to conceal my shock. I have no response for her unexpected words. But I refuse to let this change anything. Turning on my heel, I start to walk away.

"Felicity, you miss your old life. That has been clear from the start. But that life, and that girl, the one who first arrived on our doorstep with wide eyes . . . that girl is gone."

I stop. Her words cut straight to the quick. Perhaps it wasn't Hawksmoor who opened the letter, after all.

"The sooner you accept that, the sooner you'll be at peace with who you are. What you truly can be."

"I cannot accept it," I say, my voice scarcely more than a whisper.

"Then you will forever be a wandering soul."

I turn to face her, raising my chin. "Are you going to stop me?"

She presses her lips together, but I can tell from her expression that she won't.

I swallow, ignoring the lump forming in my chest. "I'm leaving then." I hesitate. "And I will be at the Jubilee in time."

"We'll see."

I step into the street outside where it is pouring. Buckets of rain sluice down the streets and across the sidewalks. In the carriage, I give the driver directions, and we pull away from the house. The drum of the horse's hooves is a soothing distraction.

CHAPTER FORTY-THREE

"Witchcraft has not a pedigree,
'Tis early as our breath,
And mourners meet it going out
The moment of our death."

—Emily Dickinson, "Witchcraft has not a
pedigree"

I tell the driver to stop the carriage just down the street from the doctor's address in Mayfair. I'm not sure why— I'm afraid the doctor will refuse to see me, perhaps, or that he will be in too much of a hurry to leave.

In spite of the rain, I climb from the carriage and approach on foot. The elegant townhouses make a graceful curve, bordered by manicured hedges and black iron gates. My insides twist as I consider the possibility of finally receiving answers. The possibility of a cure.

Then I notice a carriage parked in front of number 38, and I walk closer, frowning.

And register what's odd. There's no driver.

I step toward the door. It's slightly ajar.

Something is definitely not right. I should leave, return to headquarters. But what if the doctor is in trouble? And . . . what about the cure?

A window on an upper floor glows and I can make out shadows moving within. Somebody is in there. Two other windows on that level are dark. The far one will be my destination.

After glancing over my shoulder, I slip around the side of the house. The rain has dwindled to a drizzle. Using a trellis for footholds, I climb swiftly to the second-story window and pry it open. Aristos flows through me as I crawl into the darkened room. Once inside, I pause, listening. I hear nothing, but I know people are here, so why is there no sound?

A canopy bed looms before me. An odd scent of geraniums hovers in the air. I creep through the hushed darkness, my feet sinking into plush carpeting as I scan for clues in the richly furnished bedroom. There's a large family portrait—the doctor and his family, no doubt. Dr. Middlesex is a distinguished-looking man with a trim, dark beard. Out in the corridor, my heart thrums as I approach the lit room. A wedge of watery light slices into the corridor.

As I reach the doorway, I peer inside; a man standing in the center of the room drags a six-inch blade across the doctor's throat.

CHAPTER FORTY-FOUR

"It was but for one minute that I saw him, but the hair stood upon my head like quills. Sir, if that was my master, why had he a mask upon his face?"

—Robert Louis Stevenson, *The Strange Case of Dr. Jekyll and Mr. Hyde*

Blood gushes from the slash, pouring over the doctor's traveling cloak and onto the silk carpet. The doctor is a stranger to me—but he looks exactly like the figure in the portrait.

In contrast, the man who just slit the doctor's throat is anything but a stranger. And this is the fact that causes me to freeze in horror, even more than the blood streaming from the doctor's neck:

Humphrey Neville. The Intelligence Master. My ally. My friend.

The room narrows, the walls closing in. I grasp onto a thought: *I need to get out of here.*

I turn, but my way is blocked by the Huntsman woman from the carriage—the Black Spider. I'm trapped.

She silently backs me into the room, a hint of a smile curling her lip. I'm doing frantic calculations, trying to plot an escape but also trying to make sense of what I've just witnessed.

"Miss Cole," says Neville evenly, "I hadn't pegged you to be so . . . punctual. To the end, always surprising."

His use of the phrase "to the end" turns my blood cold. I swivel to face him. "What are you doing, Neville?" I choke out, positioning myself so I have a view of both Neville and the Black Widow. So I can see their hands. "How could you?" My eyes wildly swing back to the dead body on the floor.

"The doctor?" Annoyance spasms over his face. "It's unfortunate you happened to choose this method of entry. Things would have been much easier for you had you simply arrived in a carriage and knocked on the front door."

Neville sounds exactly the same as he always has. The effect is chilling.

I flick my eyes around the room, looking for another means of escape. There is nothing. The window is too far away, and tightly closed. There's a small table, a few vases scattered about, and a chaise longue with silk cushions. An elegant room for a horrific conversation.

"He could have helped us," I say, voice ragged. "He might have had the cure."

"Cure?" Neville laughs, an eerie sound, given the sight of blood covering his gloved hands. "Miss Cole, there is no cure. He would have told you that." Neville inclines his head toward the dead doctor. "Haven't you figured it out yet? My dear, there is no cure, because being Morgana is simply who we are. It's not something that can be changed."

"What—what do you mean?"

His eyes flash. He's enjoying this. "I mean that *until philosophers are kings . . . cities will never have rest from their evils.*"

Plato again. Like Dexter quoted in Tianjin House.

"The truth is, we have a unique history," Neville says. "Our ancestors escaped the disaster."

"What disaster?"

"You've heard the stories. The great flood. Surely an educated girl like you has read the classics?"

Plato. The flood. The legends . . .

It all clicks into place. My eyes lock on his. "Are you talking about . . . Atlantis?"

"There was only one part Plato got wrong in his account. Not everyone from Atlantis perished. Before the city disappeared below the water, some escaped—our ancestors, yours and mine. Some called us demigods, but that's not accurate."

"How is that possible?" I say, my voice small. "It can't be."

"You know it's the truth. You can feel it in your bones."

"The Morgana—" I begin.

"The *Morgana*," he cuts in, "is the ancient name for the descendants of Atlantis. Morgana means 'from the sea.' Perhaps this looks familiar?" He removes his cloak pin and I stare at it. It's the same as the one that fell from the Huntsmen on the bridge in Oxford. "This is the symbol of Atlantis, an ancient mark full of power."

My balance feels suddenly off and my vision is growing fuzzy on the edges.

"And now, Miss Cole, you have a choice before you—the choice I intended to present you with here, tonight, away from Hawksmoor's poisonous influence. You can join me or you can perish with the others who refuse to see the truth, those who stand in our way."

I can barely form words. "Join you—"

"What we can do, it will soon be clear to everyone."

The Black Spider takes a step closer to me. Her voice sends icy needles down my spine. "For generations the Morgana have been forced to hide away, secretly, doing covert work, hiding our abilities. But we should be out in the open. Taking positions of power. Not scurrying around in dark corners."

I look between her and Neville. "You can't just take over."

"Of course I can't. That would be absurd. I'd need to have a plan formed over many years and meticulously scrutinized, wouldn't I?"

I stare at him. "You already have one."

He glances at the grandfather clock in the corner of the room. "It won't be long now."

"The Jubilee?"

He smiles at me, perversely pleased. "The beautiful thing is that people are absurdly predictable, including their fascination with elaborate celebrations. The pomp. The circumstance. Too bad today's celebration will forever be marked as a day of tragedy."

"Are you going to kill them? All those innocent people?"

His face darkens. "Who says they are innocents?"

"You don't have to do this, Neville."

He looks at me with pity. "Such naïveté. It's almost sweet."

"How are you going to do it?"

He smiles again. "It's really quite brilliant, actually. If I do say so myself." But he says nothing more. Of course he doesn't. He's not stupid, not about to tell me all his secrets just because I've asked.

Who did he mean when he mentioned the *others*, standing in his way?

Hawksmoor. It must be. And the other Elders, too. Maybe even the other agents and Candidates. I have no idea how far Neville's madness extends. I glance at the Black Spider. Fear grips me as I wonder, for the first time: where are the rest of the Huntsmen?

A desperate urge takes hold. I have to get back to headquarters. All those months of careful planning for the

Jubilee, all of the agents' work . . . it's all compromised now. It was little more than playing into Neville's plans right from the beginning.

Neville takes a step closer to me. "One last chance to change your mind. It's such a shame. It would be nice to have such a powerful Morgana on our side."

I glance between him and Black Spider. "What on earth are you going on about?"

He gazes at his fingernails, unhurried. "Your family is from Greece. Direct descendants. Which means you have the full expression of gifts. Mental and physical gifts."

I smile with satisfaction. At last, something he is wrong about. "No, I don't. I only have physical abilities, Aristos. My brother is a Sophos."

He looks at me with something that resembles pity. I have the feeling I have walked into a snare.

His next words ribbon out slowly, deliberately. "What brother?"

A warning tugs at the back of my mind, but I have no idea what would make him say this. He knows about my family, I'm sure he does. "You know full well *what brother*. His name is Nate."

Neville sighs and plucks a bit of lint from his jacket. "Felicity, I'm afraid . . . your brother has been nothing more than a trick of the mind, something you've imagined. The Sophos ability—it's within you."

"That's ridiculous."

"Is it? Think hard, Felicity. You did have a brother—once. But he was just a baby. He died when your mother did. Cut down by a mob that feared people like us."

I open my mouth to protest. But I hesitate.

"Of course, Hawksmoor knew your mind had created an imaginary brother to cope. He used his own Sophos ability to manipulate you into joining the Academy. But make no mistake, Felicity. Nate is dead."

Neville is lying. I reach out to prove him wrong. I reach for my brother . . .

But Nate is not there. I try again, shutting out Neville's words. *You have no brother.*

At once, my carefully constructed imaginings fall away, and I know it's the truth. I can feel my brother slipping away, feel the connection to the cottage on the sea dissolving, becoming unreal, sliding through my fingers. Everything unspools inside me.

I remember then: the market square when my father and I returned home that day, years ago. Not just the bloodied body of my mother, but also the tiny, broken body of a baby at her feet. . . .

I gasp. A sharp, shooting pain goes through my chest. I have no brother.

CHAPTER FORTY-FIVE

"Parting is all we know of heaven,
And all we need of hell."
—Emily Dickinson, "My life closed twice before
its close"

I feel weak, like a stiff breeze could blow me away. Disintegrate me like a pillar of sand. I forget what I have to fight for. My brother is gone.

I will never speak to Nate again. Never see him again . . . How is that possible?

My vision clears slightly and I become aware of my surroundings again, standing in the doctor's parlor between Neville and the Black Spider, the two people I'll now have to fight if I want to live.

But I have no strength, no will. And then, the Black Spider comes at me with terrifying speed.

A crystalline thought cracks through: I'm not ready to die. I focus on the reasons why I must stay alive. I grasp for

Aristos . . . but there's nothing there. *The shock of the truth about Nate*, I think dully.

The Black Spider slams into me, smashing me to the ground. A blade in her hand glints in the gaslight. The next heartbeat will be my last.

A gossamer thread of Aristos floats into my mind. I grab for it. Time slows—the high-pitched buzzing of a housefly in the corner of the room becomes a low rumbling roar.

Her knife arcs downward like it's moving through molasses, and I roll away just in time. The blade slashes my sleeve. The fog in my mind clears and I grab more firmly onto the power. My feet kick the Black Spider backward. I spring to standing but she quickly recovers and she, too, is up again in no time.

I grapple for one of the vases and smash it into her face. As it explodes into shards, she collapses back. She might be unconscious for only a few seconds, but that's the best chance I'm going to get. Without hesitation, I lunge for the door and fly toward the staircase. Neville's footsteps are right behind me. Halfway down the curving stairs, he grabs my cloak. It rips away, but I keep going.

An enormous chandelier hangs from the foyer ceiling. I vault over the smooth banister and grab one of the elaborate arms. The chandelier swings wildly and gives a lurch as it loosens from its fixture in the plaster ceiling. I release my grip and drop down, landing in a shower of crystal fragments. My feet slip on the marble, but I catch my balance in time to see Neville surging down the staircase, the blade he used to kill the doctor clutched tightly in his hand.

I lunge for the front door, grasp the brass doorknob . . .

"You're not going anywhere," Neville snarls.

Then, something unusual happens. I hear a thought in my head—no, more of an idea. A feeling of warmth toward Neville. *He's not so bad after all. He's certainly not a monster. Why would I have ever thought that?*

I find myself wondering why I've been fighting in the first place. Frowning, I look down at my hand on the doorknob. *I don't have anywhere to go—why would I be leaving?*

I turn back to face Neville as he strolls across the foyer. *Humphrey Neville is my friend. He has always looked out for me. He'll know what to do.* I take a step toward him.

Then, there's a great crack and shudder from above, and the remains of the chandelier come crashing to the floor. Neville barely jumps back in time to avoid being crushed.

I blink, staring at Neville.

Evil. Trickster. He was wielding Sophos on me.

Clutching Aristos as firmly as I can, I fling open the front door and throw myself through it. Legs and lungs burning, I run with every ounce of strength I possess. I know I'm moving impossibly fast to anyone who happens to be watching from their glazed windows, but masking my powers is the least of my concerns.

I hazard a glance over my shoulder. Neville shouldn't be able to catch me on foot—he doesn't possess Aristos, as far as I know. Although it's suddenly apparent to me that I know so little. The drizzle has turned to fog. Mayfair's darkened streets are empty, save for two carriages and an omnibus rumbling along the cobblestone. Neville is thankfully nowhere to be seen. I race through the shadowy streets, my feet splashing through puddles, gaining speed with every step.

I keep running, and don't stop.

CHAPTER FORTY-SIX

"She left the web, she left the loom,
She made three paces thro' the room,
She saw the water-lily bloom,
She saw the helmet and the plume,
She look'd down to Camelot.
Out flew the web and floated wide;
The mirror crack'd from side to side;
'The curse is come upon me,' cried
The Lady of Shalott."
—Alfred, Lord Tennyson, "The Lady of Shalott"

I'm huddled in the darkness, an empty shell. The partially complete skeleton of Tower Bridge rises up above me, steel girders and cables groaning in the winds. It rained off and on as I ran here from Mayfair, though I barely noticed the weather. My only aim has been to get as far away from Dr. Middlesex's house—and Humphrey Neville—as possible.

It is twilight. Under heavy clouds, the wine-dark Thames flows its perpetual path, deep and swift. A faint whiff of fish and salt and rust rises from a nearby barge. I need to decide what to do next, but I can hardly think.

Nate is dead. Actually, it's worse than that. He was never alive—not really. Not the seven-year-old boy I knew. He was nothing more than a product of my imagination, a figment of my twisted brain.

I can't even begin to dissect what Neville said about the origins of the Morgana. *Atlantis?* It's absurd. It doesn't feel real. But the loss of Nate is entirely real, sharp and cold as a razor.

The chill of the rain and the wind from the river seeps into my bones, but I don't care. I want to climb the scaffolding of this bridge and scream into the night. All of that effort searching for a cure, all my hopes and plan to save my brother. My stupid, naive plan . . . it was all pointless.

There is nothing keeping me here. No cure. Nothing for me to search for. I can leave London, run from this nightmare. On the river, barges and steamboats glide under the partially constructed bridge, heading out to sea. I could stow away, wake up somewhere different, start anew. There's no reason to stay.

But that isn't quite true.

There's everyone attending the Royal Jubilee. The royalty, the nobility, the leaders from across Europe. Everyone who isn't Morgana. They will soon be dead, too.

And the other Morgana. Charlie, Isherwood, Hawksmoor . . . and Julian. Everyone from the Academy.

They are in grave danger. If they aren't already dead. My stomach twists as I think of Julian. I picture his face. His incredible, heart-crushing smile that I will never see again.

I don't know how Neville plans to execute his plan. But I do know one thing: I am the only person who knows he has one. And I may be the only person who can stop him.

But what am I meant to do? I'm just a flower girl from the streets, an immigrant's daughter from the slums. For a long time, I stare up at the skeleton bridge and the sky above it, a velveteen curtain, embroidered with sequins.

I know what I must do. The truth is, I'm not simply a flower girl from the streets. Not any longer. I've become so much more.

CHAPTER FORTY-SEVEN

"You must suffer me to go my own dark way."
—Robert Louis Stevenson, *The Strange Case of
Dr. Jekyll and Mr. Hyde*

I have to save Julian and Hawksmoor and all the others.
But even though I've made the decision, I have no idea
how to put thought into action. The odds are impossible.
Me against the entire Huntsman organization. I'll likely
fail, but it won't be because I did not try.

As I make my way back to the street, the rain starts up
again, shifting from heavy drops to sheets. My clothes are
soaked and I shiver on the side of the road. Raising my
hand, I wave down a passing carriage for hire.

As the driver pulls on the reins and steers to the side
of the road, an urge to run away comes over me again. It
would be so much easier to flee.

The driver stares at me as I hesitate, twisting in the rain,
suddenly unsure what to do. The horse paws the cobbles,
mist puffing from his nostrils.

"Come on, love. Get inside. You'll catch your death," the driver says. I look into his kindly face. Deep smile lines crease the skin around his eyes.

I climb inside the carriage. He bends down and glances inside. "Where are we off to?"

I'm sorely tempted to tell him to take me as far away from here as he can, but through the small window I glimpse his hands as they hold the reins—workmen's hands, rough from a lifetime of labor. If I don't stop what the Huntsmen have planned, what will become of those who've lived lives of plain, honest, hard work?

"To the British Museum."

❧

Just outside the museum sits a newsstand, a small door cut into its side. When no one is watching, I slip inside and travel down a long, dark, narrow staircase that leads deep underneath the street to headquarters.

I stop suddenly when I reach the door at the end of the passage. It's slightly ajar, the lock and the handle smashed.

The Huntsmen are already here.

CHAPTER FORTY-EIGHT

"'Do you know where the wicked go after death?'
'They go to hell,' was my ready and orthodox
answer."

—Charlotte Brontë, *Jane Eyre*

I creep across the threshold and into the secret tunnels. Water drips from a pipe up ahead. The echoes down here are strange, bouncing off walls that twist and turn. I must find the others somehow. If they're here . . . and if the Huntsmen haven't yet killed them.

I hear the faint scrape of footfalls. Someone is just around the next bend, coming toward me. A patrol, perhaps? I've nowhere to hide. A tall, muscled Huntsman turns the corner, unhurried. My only advantage: I already have hold of Aristos before he knows he needs his own ability.

I have no weapon—only my bare hands. They will have to be enough. Before he has a chance to react, I've leapt at him, using the tunnel's wall as a springboard. Thank goodness for all those hours Isherwood forced me to train.

I kick out, catching the Huntsman in the chest. He goes down slowly, to my Aristos eyes. As he falls, I reach out and snatch the long knife from his belt.

As I leap over him, I can tell he's channeled his own Aristos, because instead of crashing flat on his back, he back-somersaults and rolls straight up to his feet. Murder flashes in his eyes.

But I'm already there, kneeling with his knife pointing up, and in a second, I've thrust the blade up under his ribs. It's hard for me to imagine anything more horrifying than the feeling of biting into a man's soft underbelly with a cold knife. Possibly worse is the sound—a squelching slice.

We are now face-to-face, and his shock gives way to a slack dullness as I thrust deeper and the tip of the knife penetrates his heart. He collapses. It's over.

As I stand over his body, panting, I feel a spasm of triumph and relief. It makes me want to rip my own skin off. What kind of person feels such a thing?

But there's no going back now. Not now that I've killed one of them. The temptation to turn and escape—I push that down inside me. A black pit opens as I wonder how many more times I'll have to do this before I reach the others. If I even have it in me.

Then, a man's voice enters my head. *Felicity? Good lord. You're here.*

I recognize the voice immediately, though I've never heard it inside my head before. Hawksmoor.

So. It's true. Everything Neville told me is true. Hawksmoor can get inside my head. He knew the truth about Nate, and it's how he tricked me all along.

My insides burn with the betrayal, but it doesn't matter. Right now I need to push all that aside and focus on staying alive.

Where are you? I try to say. But it's too unfamiliar a task. I was able to talk to Nate because—I know now—I was imagining it. But *truly* using Sophos abilities? That I do not know how to do.

Nate.

Despair threatens to rise up, but I quash it as best I can.

I can feel you trying to communicate, Felicity. Don't waste your energy. You're going to need it.

He's right. I turn to the task of plundering weapons from the Huntsman I just killed and listening to Hawksmoor as he details the situation.

There are eleven Huntsmen. They have locked us inside the cargo hold. They tell us they'll soon begin pulling us out, one by one, to execute us.

Hawksmoor doesn't say who is locked there with him. He doesn't say whether anyone has been killed yet, and I have no way of asking. I think of Julian and an icy hand grips my stomach.

Me against eleven. I glance at the dead sentry. Ten. I squeeze my eyes shut at the thought of killing again. But I have no choice. It's me, or them.

Somehow, I will have to divide the Huntsmen so I can take them on one or two at a time.

Hawksmoor gives me further instructions: *Warwick is here. Eight of them are guarding us, and two are out in the tunnels. Take those two out first.*

He seems to have a lot more confidence in my skills than I do. I tuck myself into an alcove and piece together a plan.

CHAPTER FORTY-NINE

"Terror made me cruel . . ."

—Emily Brontë, *Wuthering Heights*

It doesn't take me long to set up the contraption that will serve as my trip alarm. I have to be careful—if it falls before I'm ready, I won't have time to hide. With steady fingers I work, ears pricked for unexpected arrivals.

I've gathered sconces from the corridors and now attach them up so they are balanced, held in place by a cord suspending them from the ceiling. I remember seeing a haberdasher do this once in Whitechapel—stringing together a collection of jars so they stayed together, making it impossible for thieves to pilfer one without toppling the lot.

Then I position the string over a gas lamp fixed to the wall. I estimate how long it will take for the string to burn through. I dash away and tuck myself into a crevice and begin silently counting in my head.

A loud crash echoes through the tunnels as my con- traption falls. I smile with triumph. At least something has gone right.

Within moments, I hear footsteps approaching. I'll intercept them as they pass by, or at least I hope to.

There is no shouting. They are not so artless. The foot- steps slow and become hard to distinguish. If only I knew more. Will it just be one guard, as Hawksmoor said, or will they have sent out more? Are they armed? But I'm not a mind reader.

Except . . . maybe I am.

I reach out with my thoughts, probing the void, grop- ing in the darkness, searching for something that feels . . . human. Then it's like I bump into something with my mind. It feels alive. It somehow seems as though it has warmth.

The connection comes in fragments like kaleidoscope shards, splintered and distorted, but I can still get a general sense—one man and one woman. Is it the Black Spider? I can't tell.

I can, however, distinguish that the man is far stronger and faster than the woman, but also more apprehensive. She is . . . angrier. And better trained, with a tighter grip on her fear. She's carrying a knife; the man has a gun.

They are ready to kill. Just like the sentry was. And unless I want to die today, I'm going to have to eliminate them first.

I'll need to disarm the man first. But I'll only have time to ambush one of them.

I need Aristos now. But, to my horror, when I reach for it, it's not there. Instinctively, I let go of my hold on Sophos. And there, waiting for me, is Aristos. I try to reach back for Sophos, but now it has disappeared.

Holding both abilities proves impossible, like trying to hold on to sand. The tighter I grip, the more it crumbles in my fingers.

I'm out of time. The Huntsmen arrive.

I grasp for Aristos and lunge like a viper from my hiding spot just as the male Huntsman steps before me. In one swift movement, I've wrapped my arms around him and dragged the knife across his throat. His gun fires, but it goes off into the tunnels, harming no one.

The woman rushes me—a blonde, not the Black Spider after all. Her knife is out, and I have a single heartbeat in which to retrieve the Huntsman's gun. And though I am able to grasp the metal, it costs me dearly—the woman leaps on top of me.

I roll away, just before she plunges her blade into my heart, but not before she manages to graze my shoulder. I'm up, scaling the wall, using a shelf as a foothold, gripping tightly to Aristos. Pushing back with my feet, I spring back and land a second before she does. I aim and fire the pistol. Right into her chest.

Before her body even hits the ground, I'm sprinting away. The struggle was anything but discreet; other Huntsmen will be coming. But at least now I'm armed.

I double back toward the cargo hold, releasing Aristos and gripping onto Sophos, feeling out in the darkness for the other eight opponents. Pausing, I take stock.

For the next group, I'll need to use a different strategy. They aren't stupid. And I'd prefer to not use the gun again—it will draw too much attention.

The ceiling is crossed with rafters—all the better for an ambush.

I swiftly pull myself up, hiding in the shadows of the ceiling. And wait. Someone will come along to investigate.

Once I'm hidden, I let Aristos go and grasp Sophos. I feel for the nearby Huntsmen. It's not long before I bump up against that same feeling of humanity. This time, there's only one person, a man.

I'm ready. And I'm confident after my last two encounters. As I wait for my mark to pass beneath me, my mind spools forward to the next Huntsman and my next plan.

It's due to this brief distraction that I move a second too early. My landing is slightly off, giving the Huntsman a fraction of a second's warning.

Suddenly I'm on my back, pinned, and he's looming above me. His eyes are fire.

The flash of a blade arcs overhead.

CHAPTER FIFTY

"An animal may be ferocious and cunning enough, but it takes a real man to tell a lie."
—H. G. Wells, *The Island of Doctor Moreau*

I grab on to Aristos as hard as I can. Time slows even further; a drop of sweat from the Huntsman hovers over me. My knee thrusts up to meet his groin. He grunts and his knife misses its mark. Still, he recovers almost instantly, taking another slash at my chest.

But, unfortunately for him, he's loosened his grip. My arm comes up and blocks his hand. With a surge of strength, I flip him off me. He regains his feet quickly as I struggle to my knees, and comes at me again. But I shift to the side just in time. He loses balance, just slightly. And before he can stumble forward, I move behind him, catch his head, and wrench. His neck snaps and he drops instantly.

I fall to my knees, trembling, catching my breath.

I won't make that mistake again.

Over the next thirty minutes, I systematically take down two more Huntsmen without incident. I hold my focus tight, switching from Sophos and Aristos to locate, then eliminate, each opponent.

Felicity. Hawksmoor's voice penetrates my focus. *I can tell you're doing an excellent job out there—*

I wait for the "but" that's sure to come.

They're getting agitated as their numbers dwindle. They're preparing to begin their executions. If you could get here more quickly . . .

I whittle their group down by two more. I know the Huntsmen have discovered some of the bodies from the shouts that echo through the tunnels and the panic seeping into the ether. I put a knife into the chest of the next Huntsman; they're down to three.

There is a single guard watching us now, Felicity. The other two, including Warwick, are out hunting for you.

It's time. I turn toward the center of the labyrinth and head for the cargo hold.

There's a cell inside headquarters, designed to hold prisoners who might need interrogation. I'm sure Hawksmoor never imagined being imprisoned there himself. The question is how am I going to get close enough to the guard without him detecting me?

The iron-barred prison sits in the center of a cavernous room with a guard mezzanine all the way around the perimeter. Multiple tunnels feed into the mezzanine. I approach slowly, knowing the guard is on the lower level, pacing outside the prison cell, though he can't yet see me. As I grow closer the faint smell of geraniums reaches me. Where have I smelled that before? The scent triggers something in my memory but it flits away.

I lower down to my stomach and slither forward. There, in the cell, are five of the Morgana: Hawksmoor, Charlie, Isherwood, Julian. And Jane. Why would they take Jane? I frown. There has to be a reason.

My friends don't look good. Hawksmoor, particularly, has been badly beaten. But Isherwood looks worse—she's lying down on the floor, and appears to be unconscious. They are restrained in iron shackles. They do nothing to signal they are aware of my arrival. Nothing, except the barest flicker of an eyebrow, from Hawksmoor.

Where is everyone else? I wonder. Are they dead? I try once more to send a thought to Hawksmoor.

The rest of the Morgana . . . ? I'm not sure it worked. But then Hawksmoor's voice comes back to me. *Some of them made it out before we were ambushed. And some were already at the Jubilee banquet. Of course, I can't be certain which agents are on our side. Some of our ranks may have been working for Neville all along.*

I don't know what to say. I can only think about my next steps. Moving along the mezzanine, I get as close to the spot over the guard as I dare. I will have one chance and I need to use it to its best effect. I consider using the pistol. But Warwick would hear and come for me right away. I'm not sure I'd be able to release the others from the prison cell before he gets here.

No, I need to take this one down silently if I can.

I wish I were better with knife throwing. I need to be down there. Hand to hand. I carefully withdraw the knife and grip it tightly. If I can jump down behind him, I can cut into his neck before he has a chance to react. It will be the quickest and quietest method.

I drop down. At the last second, just before I land on the ground, he moves away easily, spinning to face me.

A smile spreads across his face.

Did you think I didn't know you were there? A new voice slices through my thoughts—the voice of the man in front of me.

He has Sophos, too. My blood turns to ice as I realize I've walked into a trap.

He levels his pistol and fires.

CHAPTER FIFTY-ONE

"The tyrant grinds down his slaves and they don't turn against him; they crush those beneath them."

—Emily Brontë, *Wuthering Heights*

The Huntsman doesn't fire at me. He shoots straight through the bars at the Morgana standing closest: Charlie.

I scream as Charlie's chest blooms dark red. He falls back, and Julian catches him.

"Warwick has changed his mind," the Huntsman says to me. "He wants you alive, after all, Miss Cole. Lucky for you. Not so lucky for them. I will shoot them all if you don't comply."

I gingerly place my knife on the ground before he can harm anyone else.

"Felicity! Behind you," Julian calls out, still cradling Charlie's head.

I spin just as the second Huntsman arrives—the Black Spider. She must have been waiting just outside the cargo hold.

"Come nicely," she says, holding out a pair of handcuffs.

I set my jaw against the frustration. I'm so close. A part of me wonders where Warwick is, how long it will be before he arrives, whether he really would honor his word to keep me alive?

"Do I really need to explain the situation again?" asks the Huntsman. He raises his pistol toward the prison cell again.

I shut Sophos down—it can't help me now. The Huntsman fires in Julian's direction.

Julian twists to duck under the bullet, but with my time-slowed vision I can see it's not going to be fast enough. Panic grips my belly. Then a blur comes from his left, knocking him out of the bullet's path. He collapses on the ground, safe from the shot. Jane sprawls unharmed beside him.

Jane. She pulled him down. Of course she did. I can't believe it hasn't occurred to me before now—she may not have made the cut as a Morgana agent, but she still has abilities.

"Lucky," mutters the Huntsman.

His momentary distraction gives me the opportunity I need. I lunge, knocking his gun away. We grapple and I try to remember every single thing I've learned in combat training. In my peripheral vision, I'm aware of the Black Spider raising her weapon.

I spin the Huntsman between me and Black Spider, who fires her pistol at that instant. The shot hits the Huntsman in the chest and he drops.

An angry scream rips from Black Widow's throat. She lunges at me, but I whirl away and back handspring right over her, coming down behind her. I'm moving faster than I ever have before.

"Felicity, you can do this. *Take them.*" I am vaguely aware of Julian's ragged, desperate voice coming from behind the bars.

Before the Black Spider can so much as turn, I've wrapped her head firmly in my hands—wrench and . . . *snap!*—she crumples to the ground.

I struggle to a stand. Warwick will be here any second.

I race to the bars. *Where are the keys?*

They must still be on the Huntsman guard, the one with Sophos. I push him over, ignoring his cold, vacant eyes, and find them tucked in his waistcoat. I fumble with the ring as blood pounds in my ears. My hand is shaking as I slide the iron key into the lock and turn. It releases with a clunk.

Everyone is still shackled. Isherwood is still unconscious, Charlie is bleeding rapidly, though Jane appears to have stanched it somewhat. Hawksmoor looks gray.

I reach Julian first, and quickly release him. With the clink of the metal, I exhale.

I'm not alone in this anymore.

"You did it," he cries. His eyes are overly bright. He presses his mouth to mine. For a moment, I'm lost in the kiss. Soft, warm, my knees are wobbling. Time doesn't simply slow; it stands completely still.

And just as suddenly, he pulls away, eyes wide. Sparks still skittering across my skin, I glance at everyone else. Jane stares at us, mouth gaping, while the hint of a smile twitches Hawksmoor's mouth.

But it passes quickly as he sways and goes even more pale.

I busy myself with releasing Hawksmoor next. We have to get out of here as quickly as possible. As I work the shackles, I can still feel the warmth of Julian's mouth on mine. My head spins. . . .

Then there's a faint scraping sound behind me. I turn to see Warwick standing frozen in the doorway. Our eyes lock.

He's mine.

Warwick doesn't hesitate. He spins and breaks for the corridor, fast as a whip. I give chase, Julian right behind me. Warwick might be a coward, but he's impossibly quick. And he seems to know exactly where he's going. Within a minute, I do, too.

He darts through the headquarters exit, out to street level. I barely register the coaches and omnibuses clattering along Montague Street as we tear faster than any humans should. A few blocks away from the museum, he dashes into Russell Square—a leafy, elegant garden area lined with pathways, in which a coach and driver sit waiting.

I sprint toward the coach, keeping pace, but I'm not gaining. Julian's breathing is labored right behind me. I know Julian is stronger and faster than me, but his injuries must be slowing him down. As I race after Warwick, Kit flashes in my mind. This is the man who murdered Kit. My stomach burns with the memory of that day; the gunshot blisters my brain again. He's not going to get away from me this time.

Warwick pulls ahead, bounding into the coach. The driver cracks his whip and the horses leap forward. But even as my feet devour the distance, I know I'll never reach them in time. I swivel around, looking for an empty hackney cab to hail or commandeer. But the square is empty and quiet.

Shouting rings in my ears; I don't know where it's coming from.

And then fingers close around my arm. "Felicity, *stop*," Julian says, panting. "We won't catch him."

"No, I can find a way—"

He grasps my shoulders firmly and gazes directly into my eyes. "You have to stop. We'll get Warwick another day. Or perhaps we won't. Right now, we have to return to the others. The Jubilee . . .There's more at stake. Neville will be carrying out his plan, whatever it is. . . ."

I hesitate. The desire for revenge flows hot and bitter through my veins, vengeance for Kit's murder. "No. You don't need me."

"We do need you," Julian says. "And . . . you need us. You are an essential part of this team, Felicity. We do this together or not at all."

And I know it's the truth. I squeeze my eyes shut, then take one last glance at Warwick's coach as it quickly grows smaller, vanishing into the fog.

My eyes dart to Julian's and I nod once, grimly. Together we go back the way we came.

We return to the headquarters. I quickly share what I've learned of Neville's plans, though it's little more than what they already knew.

"We have to get there now," says Hawksmoor, though he's slumped against a wall and looking ashen. Charlie's gunshot, I now see, was to the shoulder. He'll live, but he appears to have lost a lot of blood.

"With all due respect, sir," Julian says, shaking his head, "I don't think you're going anywhere. You can't even stand."

Hawksmoor closes his eyes against the truth. "It will have to be you two."

"Actually, Jane is coming with us, too," I say firmly.

Everyone looks at Jane. "I . . . beg your pardon, miss?"

"She's the only other one of us not injured," I say, "and she has her own set of skills."

Jane opens her mouth, shocked, but she doesn't protest.

Julian clears his throat. "Felicity is right. Jane—are you willing?"

"I am, sir," she says, voice wavering only a little.

Hawksmoor is quiet, eyes slightly narrowed as he regards us. Then he gives one brisk nod. "So be it."

Jane positively puffs out her chest. I flash her a grin and we prepare to depart.

As Julian and I quickly piece together our strategy, I risk a glance at Hawksmoor.

Without looking at me, he casually says, "It would be best, I think, if you direct your murderous thoughts toward our opponents, Miss Cole. Although I know, of course, why you are upset."

I press my mouth into a tight line. Now is not the time, I know, but I can't contain my anger. "You lied." I brace myself for some twisted perversion of the truth—he'd never lied outright; he'd simply not corrected me of my assumptions. . . .

He doesn't reply at first, then nods. "Indeed."

I blink. "You tricked me into joining the Academy."

"I did. I had my reasons."

"I'm going to do everything I can to stop Neville tonight. But after that—your manipulation failed. After tonight, I'll be leaving the Academy."

Julian makes a sound of protest, but Hawksmoor shushes him. "Miss Cole is free to do as she wishes. Now, let's get on with what must be done."

Several minutes later, my stomach roils as the three of us race to Buckingham Palace. The palace will be teeming with Huntsmen, I'm sure. Neville will be poised to release his device or poison, designed to kill everyone—or, at least, all those who stand in his way.

I only hope I can stay alive long enough to stop him.

CHAPTER FIFTY-TWO

"I walk, not seeing where I tread
And keep my heart with fear,
Sir, have an eye, on where you tread,
And keep your heart with fear,
For something lingers here."
—Robert Louis Stevenson, "LXX," *New Poems*

The three of us arrive at the palace, but stick to the shadows where we can observe the main entrance and the guests arriving there in ornate carriages.

"Be careful," Hawksmoor warned before we left him. "Neville will be lurking somewhere. He would never miss the opportunity to oversee his project and admire the results."

The rain has stopped, and the palace is festooned with gold banners and swaths of purple velvet, the windows alight with shimmering crystal and candles. Music from a chamber orchestra floats from the doors that have been flung open for the celebration. Someone announces the arrival of the Crown Prince of Austria as the Turkish ambassador's retinue makes its way up the carpeted stairs adorned in swirls of jewels and silk and a cavalcade of Indian royalty appears in gilded, glittering carriages.

I force myself to stop gaping at the spectacle and refocus on our task. All these people—they're all doomed unless Julian, Jane, and I discover and thwart Neville's plan. I note the nearest clutch of Queen's Guards, standing watchfully in their smart red uniforms and tall black bearskin hats.

"Should we warn them?" Jane asks, watching the guards anxiously. "They could help—"

"We would never be taken seriously," says Julian, shaking his head.

"It would only land us in shackles. Or worse," I add. "No, we have no choice but to find the threat ourselves and quietly eliminate it."

"It's the only way," Julian agrees.

There are too many guards immediately stationed around the palace. We'll never get in that way. We move farther away, eyeing the guests as they arrive.

A line of ornate carriages promenades slowly toward the palace for the banquet, pulled by gleaming horses adorned with ribbons and bells. The street is lined with smiling, waving crowds, the air pulsing with their cheers.

An idea germinates in my head.

Jane bites her lip. "How are we going to get in?"

"The way everyone else is, of course," I say with a faint smile. "In a carriage."

They both turn to stare at me.

"Well, maybe not in a carriage, exactly. More like *underneath* a carriage."

"What did you say?" comes Jane's shocked response.

Julian turns back to watch the parade another moment, considering my idea. "It might work," he says slowly. "And at this point, it's all we have."

Jane is quiet a moment, then says, "I could create a distraction. You can use that moment to slip underneath."

I frown. "But then you won't be able to come into the palace with us."

"You won't need me in there. I don't have the training you two have—I might be more of a hindrance than a help. But I can help get you in."

We wait for the right carriage, one with enough ornamentation at the bottom edge to conceal us.

"That's the one," says Julian, nodding as it creeps down the line. We quickly, surreptitiously patch together a plan.

Jane runs out and falls in front of a horse. The creature stops abruptly, halting the parade, and a gasp rises up from the crowd. One of the horse guards utters a barked command and worried chatter circulates through the onlookers. I don't see any of this ruckus—I only hear it. Julian and I are moving fast, using Aristos, slipping underneath our target carriage.

We hold onto the underframework of the carriage, barely breathing, expecting a call to be raised that someone has seen us.

Nothing happens. Through the scrollwork, I see Jane as someone is helping her up. She's unharmed. A satisfied smile on her face tells me she knows we're on our way.

Once inside the inner courtyard, we wait until everyone dismounts from the carriage, and once the coast is clear, we slip out and slink into the shadows.

We duck through a doorway and head down a narrow staircase. Our first task will be to find some kind of disguise. Uniforms, ideally. As we pass through a heavy doorway, my eye catches on something stamped in the iron of the doorframe.

We move through the door, and I see the stamp in the iron—GUILDFORD & CO—the ironworks factory my father once worked for. I suppress a wave of nausea. How I wish he were here to help me now.

"You all right, Felicity?" Julian asks, seeing me hesitate.

"Yes. Fine. Let's go."

He doesn't move, still watching me with concern.

"Where do we start?" I ask.

"The kitchens," says Julian. "If he were going to use some kind of poison, he'd introduce it there."

Julian and I make our way, without being noticed, down to the kitchens. We hide in the larder. The next person who enters will end up regretting it—although he'll never know what hit him.

In truth, it turns out to be a maid, and we take her down swiftly. I briskly swap my clothes with hers. Her black frock and white pinafore are a little large, but I tuck them as best I can.

Now all we need is a man's uniform. There are so many staff buzzing about here, surely one or two won't be missed. In my maid's uniform, I go out into the corridor to wait for a footman or a valet to pass by. Someone about Julian's size. After a few moments, I spot an excellent target.

"Beggin' your pardon, sir," I say. "Could you help me lift something? It won't take but a moment."

The footman looks annoyed, but follows me into the larder, where Julian and I make quick work of him.

We stuff both unconscious bodies behind a large wall of crates, so they won't be seen by the next person who comes in here for onions or butter. Julian slips a sleeping draught past their lips. They'll be out for hours.

"What next?" I whisper.

"You look around the kitchens, and I'll go up to the dining hall and try to locate the Morgana agents posted there."

A frown creases my forehead. "How do we know Neville hasn't turned those agents, also? Can we be sure they're on our side?"

"Good point."

We stand in silence a moment, weighing our next steps.

"Right," Julian says. "Trust no one. Only ourselves."

"Only ourselves," I echo.

"There are agents around, and likely Huntsmen, too. Be careful. We'll meet back here in fifteen minutes."

"What am I looking for?" I ask.

"I have no idea. Anything out of keeping."

Julian disappears up the stairs and I head toward the kitchens. The clatter of dishes and the smells of roasting meats and browning pastry fill the air.

Anything out of keeping. What on earth would that be? A bomb? A vial of poison? As I move about the kitchens, pretending I'm exactly where I'm supposed to be, I do my best to avoid eye contact with the other staff. Mostly, it's not a problem. Everyone is bustling about, stirring things on stovetops, preparing platters of food, polishing silverware. I pass by a cook whose eyes lift and clap on mine. "Oy, come here," she says. "Bring this tray up to the dining room. I've got no idea where James has gone, and the last thing I want is a girl above stairs . . . but it can't be helped. Get on now."

I start to object, but there's nothing I can say. I grab the tray and carry it up the staircase.

As I approach the banquet hall, the air ringing with the sounds of tinkling silverware and music from the chamber orchestra, I feel a fizz of excitement. Of course a maid isn't meant to be inside the dining hall, so instead I hover near the open doorway, surveying the scene.

A long table fills the enormous hall. People are dressed in their absolute finest. Never have I seen so much silk, velvet, diamonds . . . all in one place. The guests are gathering, mingling, and taking their places.

As I scan the faces, I catch more than one surreptitious look. A lady absently adjusts her gloves, but I'm certain she's using the opportunity to take stock of the gentleman to her left. The gentleman stands stiffly. Too stiffly? Is he hiding something? Across the room, another lady delicately opens her fan. She brings it close to her face and coquettishly gazes over the edge. Do her eyes betray an intensity that doesn't belong? Who is she watching?

Anxiety crouches in my stomach. Time is running out. I imagine all these people—all the lords and ladies and foreign royalty and dignitaries—dropping dead.

But I can glean no clues from this bewildering scene. I scan the room more closely—the ceilings, the corners—for anything amiss. An explosive, a weapon of some sort. But there's nothing I can detect.

The butler spots me, looking scandalized. "I was told to bring this tray up," I say quickly. He nods briskly and takes it from me, moving swiftly back into the melee.

Before I turn to go, I spot Julian inside. He walks smoothly, as though he's exactly where he's supposed to be. He goes to the sideboard, smoothly grasps a decanter of sherry and begins topping up glasses. As he moves through the guests, he quickly and subtly takes stock of each person.

The other servants are so busy with their own tasks, they take no notice of him.

I feel the tingle of being watched. My gaze lands on a lady on the other side of the ballroom. Her eyes quickly flit away from mine and she melts into the crowd.

Am I attracting attention because I don't belong in this room? Or is it something else? Either way, I need to go, quickly, and continue the hunt in the servants' quarters. Julian will have to handle this room.

On the narrow stairwell back downstairs, I turn on the landing and bump into a man on his way up.

"Beggin' your pardon, sir," I say quickly to the man, who appears to be a valet. But as I move to pass him, I glance into his eyes. My blood chills.

Huntsman. I'm certain.

I tuck my head down and hurry down the remaining steps. Behind me, I hear him continue to go another few steps up the staircase, but then the sound stops.

Before he reaches the top.

My heart thunders. I exit the stairwell and take a sharp left, hurrying away. Desperately, I try to recall what I've been taught about evading pursuit. What did Isherwood say? *Change your outward appearance, if at all possible.*

In the corridor, I spot a hooded cloak hanging on a hook. I throw on the cloak and pull up the hood, stuffing my hair under it. Moving quickly, toward the kitchens, I slouch and change my walk. It's not much, but it might buy me an extra few moments.

Isherwood's voice rings in my head. *If you believe you're being followed, it's best to stick to crowded places where it is far easier to lose yourself in the bustle.*

I had planned to go to the servants' quarters and storage rooms to search for evidence of Neville's plot, but that will have to wait. I take a sharp turn into the kitchens and dive into the tangled mass of servants and house staff, bubbling pots and clouds of steam.

When I reach the far side, close to the pantry, I hazard a glance over my shoulder. The Huntsman is at the entrance of the kitchens, scanning the room. I duck out of view behind a tall shelf of pots and pans, my chest in a tight knot. I pull the hood a little lower and after another few moments peer out. Frustration spasms over the Huntsman's face as he turns and leaves the room.

In the kitchens, I squeeze my way past cooks and scullery maids, avoiding eye contact. The clatter of dishes and pans vibrates in my ears. I pass a kettle of soup bubbling on a stove, fragrant with curry spices and nutmeg. Mulligatawny—my father's favorite, not that we were able to have it very often. More thoughts of my father push to the surface, and I curse my inability to focus. Of all the times to become distracted . . .

Unless . . . my mind is trying to tell me something.

Like a beam of light, a thought suddenly strikes me. My father died in a poisoning incident of sorts—a gas leak at the factory. . . .

And how does gas travel?

It rises. Which means . . . we need to look down. *The basement.*

I move to the kitchen doorway that leads down to the basement. I'm willing to bet it's down there. The poison is deep underneath Buckingham Palace.

As I open the doorway, the faint smell of geraniums reaches my nose. It triggers a memory. I have smelled that particular scent before. I recall from the deep recesses of my memory that some poisonous gases have pleasant smells, like flowers or freshly mown grass. It was something I learned months ago during my spy training at Greybourne.

The hairs on the back of my neck lift as certainty grips my belly. I stare down the dark staircase leading beneath the palace.

It wouldn't be smart for me to go down there alone. Where is Julian? He's late for our rendezvous. Time is running out. I grasp my Sophos ability and attempt to reach out to him that way. *Julian. Where are you?* But I get nothing. Of course I don't. Julian doesn't possess Sophos.

It's a risk, but I have no choice—I have to go on my own. When nobody is watching, I slip through the basement doorway and race down a long staircase that carries me two levels down. Willing my footsteps silent, I creep along a narrow corridor. The tunnel continues a long way, and there's nothing to see but a cold, dark corridor. My hopes begin to dwindle the longer I walk.

Just as I begin to despair that I've followed the wrong suspicion, I reach an ironwork door—a gate, more than anything. I grab the cold, rough metal with my hands and pull. It holds fast. Peering through the bars to a platform beyond, I can just make out the precipitous drop down to an underground canal. Gas lanterns on the cavern walls illuminate the strange canal. It's beautiful, in a way; I never would have dreamed this is what lies beneath Buckingham Palace.

The water of the canal runs swiftly, and it looks deep. Where it leads, I don't know. And there, at the back wall of the platform, right beside a large hearth, is a device made of brass and clockwork, containing glass vials filled with pale yellowish fluid.

And it's ticking.

My blood goes cold. That's it.

I stare at the vials. They must contain some kind of poison. Something toxic to humans. Neville wouldn't put anything in there that would kill Morgana, too.

Would he?

From where I stand, I can tell the fumes are perfectly positioned to go up the chimney, and I wouldn't be surprised if it connects to a hearth in the dining hall above. Once the clock winds down, the gas will rise and kill everyone there.

I know I should go back to find Julian . . . but what if there's not enough time? I can't read the face from here.

There has to be a way through this gate. I stand back to look more closely at it. It's iron. Forged. By a blacksmith.

A blacksmith.

A memory of Kit in his blacksmith's apron swims into my mind. Forged iron has a weakness, but I can't recall what it is. And then the memory crystallizes. Kit and I sneaked away to our riverside picnic.

The hinges. They come apart.

I pull on the metal, ripping my fingernails, ignoring the pain. I concentrate on getting through to the device on the other side.

The components soon draw apart—first the top one and then the lower one. I'm through. Now off its hinges, the door clangs open and I knock it aside so it leans on the wall running alongside.

I carefully approach the device and stop. What am I to do with it? Smash it? No, surely not. I wonder if I can deactivate it somehow, turn off the timer . . .

Then someone clears his throat and a figure materializes from the shadows: Neville.

CHAPTER FIFTY-THREE

"The wretch, concentred all in self,
Living, shall forfeit fair renown,
And, doubly dying, shall go down
To the vile dust, from whence he sprung,
Unwept, unhonored, and unsung."
—Sir Walter Scott, "The Lay of the Last Minstrel"

"I see I underestimated you, Felicity Cole," he says flatly. Without further conversation, he points a pistol straight at me, and fires.

But I have already grasped Aristos. Everything slows down. The drips in the cavern slacken to a deep rhythm. The bullet comes at me and I bend back beneath it. What would have been a killing shot slices through the air and into the stone.

I rebound fast, bringing my leg up to kick the gun out of Neville's hand. I barely register his frustrated expression. Again, he has underestimated me.

A look of determination settles on his features.

I need to walk to the edge. Over the railing and into the deep canal below.

I shake my head and the fog lifts, briefly. Was that my thought about the canal?

The mist descends again. *Of course it was me. Everything will be all right once I get to the edge. Once I go into the water.*

With halting steps, I walk to the edge, still unsure. The thought doesn't make sense, somehow. But I keep moving. As I approach the edge, the sound of water hums in my ears pleasantly. *I must get closer.* I glimpse Neville's face. His lip is curled in a satisfied smile.

But . . . if Neville is pleased . . .

Enemy, I think. I glance at the swiftly moving water far below. *No.* This is wrong.

I struggle to maintain control of my own mind. *He's influencing me with Sophos.* It's the only clear thought I can manage. Then I remember one important thing: he isn't the only one with that ability.

I may be less experienced and my skill may not be as strong, but I am Morgana. I drop Aristos and grasp Sophos, holding fast as I envision a shield, a wall, a block.

The urge to walk off the ledge weakens. I fortify my mental shield. *You can't control me.* Neville's eyes widen slightly and I know he's heard me. Can I do it again?

Stop, I think, pushing the thought forward. *You don't need to do this.*

But I'm reaching for too much. He may be hearing me, but my words mean nothing to him. And the bomb continues to tick.

There's only one advantage I have over Neville. I can fight. But if I let Sophos go, he'll be able to control my mind again.

I will have to fight without Aristos. I learned enough through my training at the Academy, I hope.

Holding fast to Sophos and the mental shield I have created, I marshal all my regular strength. Without warning, I lunge forward and clobber Neville straight in the jaw, a good old-fashioned right cross. He's concentrating so hard on trying to sway my thoughts, his physical reflexes are delayed and he barely defends himself.

His head snaps back, and down he goes.

No longer shackled by Neville, my thoughts fly free. It's like coming up for air, my head bursting above water. I take a step toward him, looking for the pistol that skittered away. I need to finish the job.

But I don't immediately see the weapon, and I have something much more urgent to deal with: *the device.*

I dash toward it and crouch down in front of the tangle of tubes, wires, and clockwork. If only Sig were here. I can see absolutely no way of deactivating the mechanism, short of smashing it. But who knows what that might trigger?

The clock on the device appears to be moving backward. It's counting down. And there are only six minutes remaining. I have to get this bomb out of here.

Then, there's a sound behind me.

I pivot as Neville struggles to his feet, grinning. Blood smears his teeth. "You're wasting your time. There's no way to stop it," he says. "Every non-Morgana in this building will be dead in five minutes. In fact, everyone within a mile will be."

"Neville, this is madness. Turn off the bomb."

"There's only one way of deactivating that device," he says flatly.

"And you're not going to tell me what it is."

He laughs but says nothing more. Tendrils of foreign thoughts creep into my mind. Thoughts of the canal. Thoughts of water. Thoughts of drowning.

No! I am not going to let him in.

Somehow, I use Sophos to press his influence away. But physically, he's well out of reach now, the device between us. And he's too clever to be caught off guard again. He doesn't need to attack me—he just has to keep me at bay until the device detonates.

I'll have to channel *both* Sophos and Aristos. But I'm not certain that's even possible.

Terror shoots through me at the idea. What will I become if I do that?

The ticking of Neville's device pounds loudly in my ears. It's time for me to let go. It's time for me to stop doubting that I can be anything more than a lowly girl from Whitechapel. Everything I've been clinging to is so very real, but it's also holding me back. Whitechapel. Selling flowers. My father. Kit. Squabbles with Beatrice. Spending tuppence on a warm mutton pie . . .

All those things are part of me, but I can be more. I can choose to be whatever I want.

And right now, I choose to be powerful.

I let it all go—all the doubt and the uncertainty. It falls away, dissolves. The action is easier than I imagined. And with that lightening, I know I can grasp both Aristos and Sophos now.

Power surges through me.

Everything slows.

The canal water stops moving.

I throw myself into the air, hurling over the top of Neville, and then somersaulting toward the pistol that rests on the ground behind him. I pull it up just as he is turning to face me. Flip around, aim, and fire.

Bright red blossoms on his forehead, right between his eyes. He falls back like a stone, right over the railing, toppling into the waters of the canal far below.

I have no time to think about it; no time to celebrate my triumph. Every non-Morgana in this building will be dead in five minutes.

I have to get this bomb out of here before it detonates.

Without hesitation, I grab it and run.

CHAPTER FIFTY-FOUR

"'When you have eliminated all which is impossible, then whatever remains, however improbable, must be the truth.'"
—Sir Arthur Conan Doyle, *The Case-Book of Sherlock Holmes*

Cradling the device, I head straight up the cellar stairs, through the kitchen, and out the door. If I can only get it onto the streets, far away from Buckingham Palace, away from the building and all the people within . . .

The moment I pass the tall black iron gates, I realize my mistake.

The streets of London are filled with people—revelers celebrating the Royal Jubilee. They're everywhere. Laughing, dancing, drinking. Filling the parks, thronging into the streets. And all within reach of Neville's poisonous gas. Even if I've managed to save those within the palace, I've doomed everyone else.

So foolish. I should have stayed underground, beside the canal—

The canal, the water . . . Neville said there was only one way to stop the device.

At once, I know what I must do. Neville wasn't trying to make me drown myself again—in spite of his efforts to guard his mind, I was reading his thoughts about how to deactivate the bomb.

As I take a step off the street to go back inside the palace, a shot flies past my ear. The Queen's Guards are there in front of the gates, leveling their rifles. They're shooting at me. I glance down at the package I carry. It looks exactly like a bomb. It *is* a bomb.

I want to scream. They don't understand.

More shots. I hold fast to Aristos and dodge them. My heart thundering, I sprint down Birdcage Walk, the tree-lined path that leads straight to the Thames. *I must get to the river.*

The clock on the device reads three minutes. With my enhanced speed, I might be able to make it. Then, a hot fire poker slices into my arm. I fall, barely stopping the bomb from smashing on the ground.

In an instant, I'm back on my feet, gritting my teeth against the pain. Scarlet blood flows freely from my shoulder. If I get shot again I won't make it. I have to keep moving. I have to run.

Then, a black horse comes flying around the corner. *Julian*. He scoops me into the saddle.

I'm gasping for breath. "Must get the bomb to water—"

He nods grimly and we fly down the path to the river, dodging people, trees, and carriages. I glance at the clock mechanism, counting down. One minute to go.

"Clear the way!" Julian hollers.

We're close, but there are still so many people around. We fly past the Parliament buildings, hurtling across the intersection, weaving among carriages and crowds.

Julian steers his horse straight onto Westminster Bridge. With no time to think, I dismount, ignoring the pain in my shoulder, and race to the railing and toss the bomb straight into the swirling river below.

I breathe out, relieved, as the device hits the water.

But . . . it doesn't sink. How is that possible? And then I understand: the gas in the bottles is keeping the bomb afloat—it will go off anyway. Everyone on this bridge, on the banks, within a mile, will be poisoned. . . .

I clamber onto the railing and dive straight in, grabbing the bomb on the way and pushing it below the surface of the Thames. Part way down, it explodes, vials shattering, rocking my body abruptly backward.

The world goes fuzzy around the edges. I lose track of which way is up. It's almost black down here, underwater. And my skirts . . . so heavy. My boots . . . I can hardly kick my feet in them.

And everything is so cold. . . . I'm so tired.

I take a breath of cold water, feeling dark, liquid peace close around my heart as I stop struggling . . .

A firm hand closes around my arm and yanks me roughly. I have a vague awareness of being towed to the surface.

My head breaks the water, and strong arms haul me to the shore. I cough and sputter and take a giant breath of sweet air before flopping onto the bank, trying to catch my breath. Julian is soaked beside me, doing the same.

People have gathered, attracted by the spectacle. Carriages have stopped in the middle of Westminster Bridge to see what the commotion could be.

But people are behaving normally. Whispering to one another, exchanging glances, pointing at us. Nobody is writhing from poisoning. *We did it.*

I turn to Julian. "You saved me. I—I don't know what to say."

"You saved everyone else, Felicity. The least I could do was jump in to haul you ashore." He flashes me a grin, between gasps. My stomach flutters, and it has nothing to do with the water I swallowed. "Of course, had I given you another minute, you'd probably would have saved yourself." He shrugs. "But . . . we're a team."

I nod. A team. The word sounds warm, safe, wonderful. And exactly right.

CHAPTER FIFTY-FIVE

"My sun sets to rise again."
—Robert Browning, "At the Mermaid"

Inside Westminster Abbey, under gothic arches that soar to the heavens, a hushed anticipation hangs in the air. The galleries are swathed in red silk; every seat is filled with royalty, nobility, and other honored guests, dressed in their finest. The smells of candles and roses fill the air.

I drink it all in. Stone walls and stained glass windows muffle the sounds of trumpets and drums outside. The cheers of crowds grow louder and closer, announcing the imminent arrival of the Queen herself, in her open landau drawn by eight cream-colored horses.

Growing up in the slums, I never dreamed I would be here one day. Whitechapel is just down the river from where I sit now, but it is a world apart. All the great kings and queens are buried beneath the Abbey, and many other great men: Sir Isaac Newton and Charles Darwin. My stomach flutters. I hope I don't do anything to embarrass myself.

I glance at Julian beside me. Seated on his other side are Hawskmoor, Isherwood, and Sig. Charlie, Hugh, Rose, and the other Morgana are to my left. Together we occupy a small upper gallery—a discreet position of honor. Jane did her best to disguise our black eyes and bandaged gunshot wounds, and we are all dressed in our finest.

There was a moment I thought I'd never see these people again.

I smooth the skirt of my gown—a gorgeous pale blue silk—then rest my gloved hands in my lap. It surprises me how comfortable I've grown in such elegant, rich clothes. But, then again, nothing in life is quite turning out as I'd expected.

I gaze around the Abbey, struggling to keep the awe from my face.

"Shall I pinch you?" Julian leans over and whispers.

"Cheeky," I whisper back reproachfully. "But, yes. I think somebody must. In truth, I can hardly believe I'm here. I feel like the Metropolitan Police are going to haul me away any second. . . ."

"The fact is, this is all because of you."

Surprised, I turn to face him.

"It's true. We're all here because of your quick thinking."

"The boy is quite right," says Hawksmoor, inclining his head to me.

I try to prevent the smile that's creeping onto my lips. I know, of course, that the general public will never know what happened. With a little luck, history will never record any of the events of last night, and all the royals and aristocrats here today will continue in blissful ignorance of how close they came to losing not only their positions of power, but their lives. Only the Queen knows; Hawksmoor debriefed her early this morning.

The choir begins singing a hymn. Ethereal voices float through the air. A lump forms in my throat as I think of Nate. He would have loved to be here. But, no. That doesn't make any sense.

That fateful day in the market feels like another lifetime ago, one I can never go back to. I bite my lip, lost for a moment. Then Julian squeezes my hand.

I think of the legendary people buried beneath the stones of this abbey. Death is not always a bad thing. Just like the Great Fire of London that swept through so many years ago. It killed thousands, but it rid the city of the plague, and ensured a future for those who survived. For a rebirth to happen, there needs to be disaster and loss.

I once thought I could only be happy if I had my old life back. But I have a new destiny now. I lift my chin. It's time to let the past go.

At that moment, the doors to the abbey swing wide open and pipers announce the Queen's arrival. Beefeaters stand to attention on the steps beside the grand doorway, guarding her entrance. There is riotous color everywhere; gold and jewels sparkle in the bright sunlight.

I shift in my plush velvet seat as Queen Victoria begins her procession down the main nave, trailed by attendants. Once she comes to a halt at the front, standing before the Archbishop of Canterbury, she glances up at our tiny gallery. My heart feels like it might thump straight through my rib cage.

The Queen nods subtly to us. Her eyes go briefly to mine, locking with my gaze for a second. A hint of a smile flickers across her face. I am frozen, caught in the moment.

It's more than enough thanks.

CHAPTER FIFTY-SIX

"'I'll teach you how to jump on the wind's back, and then away we go.'"

—J. M. Barrie, *Peter and Wendy*

I descend the stairs at Greybourne Academy. It feels good to be back in the Oxfordshire countryside, among the farms and the hedgerows. Just a few days ago, Hawksmoor and Sig finalized the security border. We are protected again.

For now.

My thoughts turn briefly to Warwick. He's still out there, somewhere. Likely regrouping, and possibly planning another attack. But we'll be ready. I, for one, will relish the opportunity, when it comes.

The smell of freshly baked bread reaches me as I walk past the stairwell that leads to the kitchens. Outside the training rooms, the air sings with the ring of practice steel. As I cross the marble floor outside the training gymnasium, I spot Julian. He nods, a serious, businesslike gesture, but there is playfulness in his eyes.

"Good morning, Miss Cole," he says.

"Mr. Blake," I say, nodding in return.

He falls into step beside me as I stride down the corridor toward the foyer. His hand brushes mine, lingering just a little longer than necessary.

"Now, you know that's not fair," he says, eyebrow raised.

"What's not fair?"

"We're sparring tonight during training. And now you're trying to distract me. But I know your tricks, Miss Cole, and it's not going to work."

"Mr. Blake, you have only *begun* to discover my tricks."

He guffaws. "Fine. I'll see you later. Try not to scare the greenie, all right?" He heads off, winking at me just before he leaves.

After another minute, I arrive at the foyer, just as Hawksmoor walks through the door, a new recruit in tow. "Miss Cole," he says, "I'd like to introduce you to our newest Candidate. Oliver, this is Miss Felicity Cole. She will tell you everything you need to know."

Oliver is clearly a street urchin. Taking in his ragged clothes and pointed, filthy face, I feel a pang of sympathy—and knowing—flash through me. Did I look like that? His eyes are wide white circles within a grimy face, taking everything in with barely contained terror.

"Right. I'll leave you in her very capable hands. Oh, and, Oliver? If you become half the agent Felicity Cole is, you'll be doing just fine." With that, Hawksmoor strides away.

Fighting to keep a smile from my face, I stand before the new recruit, hands on my hips. I know he thinks his life is over. The truth, of course, is that it's just beginning.

"Welcome, Oliver. Welcome to Greybourne Academy. Let me start with a simple yet most critical lesson you'll learn here." I bend down to him and take his shoulders in my hands. "You must be proud, bold, pleasant, resolute . . . and now and then stab, as occasion serves."

I stride ahead, leading Oliver to his new quarters. We pass through a long gallery, where a portrait of our founding father hangs. Oliver looks up at it. "On the train, Hawksmoor told me this was all started by the playwright, that one who was supposed to have been killed, but who didn't actually die when everyone thought he did? Kit Marlowe?"

"Christopher, actually. Although I believe some of his friends—Shakespeare included—called him Kit."

The words die in my mouth. My body goes numb.

No.

My mind spools back to everything I know. Everything about my old life and that fateful day in the market. And I realize, after all I've been through, that it's possible I don't know anything at all.

ACKNOWLEDGMENTS:

Writing *Game of Secrets* was an incredible adventure, to be sure, and there are several people I need to thank, people without whose support this book would never be sitting in your hands.

Thank you to Sandy Lu, my agent extraordinaire, for all your tireless work and steadfast support.

Thank you to Alison Weiss for being a spectacular editor (and for loving this story as much as I do), and the entire team at Sky Pony Press, for being wonderfully supportive and lovely.

Thank you to my fellow Sky Pony authors, who have been there with encouragement and friendship throughout this publishing journey.

Thank you to my fellow debut YA authors (both the 2017 Debuts and the Electric Eighteens) for all your camaraderie and advice.

Thank you to the lovely, supportive SCBWI group for critique and cheerleading: Jennifer Honeybourn, Leslie Wibberley, Ruth Olson Bigler, and Bonnie Jacoby.

Thank you to the whole wonderful SiWC community, and especially Kathy Chung, kc dyer, Laura Bradbury, and Tyner Gilles. I credit the annual SiWC conference with not only kickstarting my writing career but continuing to provide inspiration and motivation year after year. I particularly want to give a huge virtual hug to my good friend Eileen Cook for so much advice, critique, and guidance every step of the way.

I am indebted to Karma Brown, my rockstar critique partner and writing bestie. And thank you to Annabel Fitzsimmons and Rebecca Stanisic for writerly companionship, especially our dreamy, delicious writing retreats.

Thank you to my mom and dad for . . . everything. And to my sisters Deb and Vivi for being my best friends forever.

And finally, thank you to my husband, Ken, for being wonderful in a thousand ways, and to my boys, Griffin and Holden, for being my biggest fans. I love you always.